# SKIN AND BONES

## MABLE MCCOY

## LILIANA HART

*To Scott-*
*I love growing old with you.*

*And to Lincoln-*
*Because you'll always be the first grandbaby.*

# ALSO BY LILIANA HART

**JJ Graves Mystery Series**

Dirty Little Secrets

A Dirty Shame

Dirty Rotten Scoundrel

Down and Dirty

Dirty Deeds

Dirty Laundry

Dirty Money

A Dirty Job

Dirty Devil

Playing Dirty

Dirty Martini

Dirty Dozen

Dirty Minds

Dirty Weekend

Dirty Looks

Dirty Liars

Dirty Valentine

**Addison Holmes Mystery Series**

Whiskey Rebellion

Whiskey Sour

Whiskey For Breakfast

Whiskey, You're The Devil

Whiskey on the Rocks

Whiskey Tango Foxtrot

**Laurel Valley**

Tribulation Pass

Redemption Road

Midnight Clear

Forgiveness River

Atonement Trail

If you don't like the road you're walking, start paving another
one.

DOLLY PARTON

# CHAPTER
# ONE

I had no plans to become a widow at the tender age of twenty-four.

I also had no plans to own a tea shop on a sleepy South Carolina island, but I've discovered life doesn't give two figs about my plans. Life on Grimm Island taught me that lesson. Here, the oak trees drip with Spanish moss and secrets hang just as heavy in the humid air.

The Perfect Steep—my tea shop and little kingdom of mismatched chairs and vintage tea pots—sat on the corner of Harbor and Lighthouse. From the outside, it was Grimm Island gentility personified—soft blue paint with crisp white trim, black shutters, and a sweeping wraparound porch where two rocking chairs waited patiently as if ready for Southern hospitality itself.

Inside was a different story entirely. Inside was pure me.

My name is Mabel McCoy, and I'd done a good job of pretending to be gentility personified since my husband died ten years ago. But I'd noticed lately there were times when I was starting to feel a bit frayed around the edges, and I wondered how long it would be before people started to notice.

My tea shop was what I affectionately called organized chaos with a tea obsession, a phrase that would have made Patrick smile if he'd lived to see it. Shiplap walls that should have been pristine white were instead painted a pale yellow on one wall, mint green on another, and a soft lavender on the third—the result of my inability to choose just one color and my stubborn refusal to start over once I'd begun. The heart pine floors creaked like they were telling secrets, especially in the three spots by the register that I'd learned to hop over during busy hours.

Ceiling fans with blades shaped like giant leaves spun lazily overhead, stirring the air that always smelled of whatever tea blend I was experimenting with that day. Today it was something with bergamot and cinnamon that made the whole place smell like Christmas morning, even in the middle of May.

I glanced at the hideous cherub clock on the wall—a wedding gift from Patrick's grandmother that I couldn't bring myself to take down despite its beady-eyed stare. Five thirty. The afternoon crowd had thinned out, and I had about thirty minutes before the Silver Sleuths would arrive for their monthly book club meeting.

I caught a glimpse of myself in the mirror and smoothed back a stray blond curl. At least the island's humidity was good for something—my vintage waves actually seemed to like it. I reapplied my red lipstick, the one bit of glamour I never skipped, and hummed along with Frank Sinatra as he sang "I Get a Kick Out of You" through the speakers.

I'd just finished boxing up a special tea blend to deliver to Mrs. Pembroke when the bell above the door jingled. Deputy Mark Reynolds strolled in, his uniform crisp despite the late hour, that easy smile crinkling the corners of his eyes.

"Just in time," I said. "It's almost closing time."

"My timing's always been impeccable," he replied, removing his hat. His rust-colored hair had gone silver at the temples since I'd known him, but his pale blue eyes still held that same kindness they had since I'd been a kid. "Got any of that cinnamon tea left? Been a day."

"For you? Always." I turned to prepare his usual as he settled onto his regular stool at the counter. "Rough shift?"

Reynolds sighed, running a hand through his hair. "Milton left us a mess to clean up. This new sheriff's asking a lot of questions and digging through files none of us even knew existed."

"And that's a problem?" I asked, sliding his to-go tea across the counter.

"Can't say I blame him," he said. "But it's just stirring up the past. Sheriff Milton did a lot of damage and people are hurting. He even went through the case files from when those three girls went missing. That might have been before you were born. But those girls' families still live on the island. No need to dredge it all up and put them through that again. Some things are better left buried, if you ask me."

He took a sip of tea and closed his eyes in appreciation. "Perfect as always, Mabel. Don't know what I'd do without my evening fix."

I smiled. Reactions like his to my teas were my favorite part of the job. It might seem boring by most people's standards, but I didn't need much. I considered myself a simple, easygoing woman.

"So how's the new sheriff working out?" I asked, wiping down the counter.

"Beckett?" Reynolds shrugged. "By the book. Bit of an outsider, but seems decent enough. Time will tell if he sticks around." He glanced at his watch. "Guess my break is over. You closing up for your book club tonight?"

"How did you know about that?" I asked, though I wasn't really surprised. Nothing stayed secret on Grimm Island for long.

He tapped the side of his nose and said, "Hey, I'm a cop. I know things." He finished his tea and slid a five-dollar bill across the counter.

"On the house," I told him.

He put the five in the tip jar anyway and gave me a wink. "See you tomorrow."

As the door chimed behind him, I went to clear china cups from a corner table, wiping it down and giving my last customer a side-eye because he'd been sitting there for three hours and kept filling up his teacup with whatever was in the thermos he'd brought from home. I was getting ready to shoo him along when he hurriedly shoved his things in his bag and hurried out the door.

"Rude," I said, cleaning up his mess. "Almost time, Chowder," I said to my French bulldog, who was sprawled across the window seat, his wrinkled face looking particularly judgmental today. "The Silver Sleuths will be here soon."

Chowder snorted and rolled onto his back, his stubby legs in the air.

"I'll take that as excitement. Just try not to con Walt out of all his treats this time. You know what the vet said about your cholesterol."

I wiped down the large round table by the front window—the Silver Sleuths' preferred spot for their meetings. They liked to see and be seen, a requirement for five seniors who considered people-watching a competitive sport. I'd arranged six chairs around it, knowing that somehow they'd rope me into joining, despite my protests.

I gave my sea-green dress a final smoothing. It was vintage, with those puffed sleeves I loved, and paired perfectly with the pearl pendant Patrick had given me on our first anniversary.

Frank's crooning faded, and Ella and Louis came on, deciding whether or not they could be friends as they debated the correct pronunciation of the word tomato. Chowder gave a soft woof and rolled to his side so he could look at passersby out the window.

"I agree," I told him. "I could never fall in love with someone who says tamahto. A bit too pretentious for my taste."

Chowder woofed again in agreement. There were some moments when Chowder and I were in perfect accord.

I'd just finished arranging a fresh bouquet of flowers in the center of the table when the bell above the door chimed again.

"Do I smell lemon scones?" Deidre Whitmore called as she bustled in, fifteen minutes early as usual. Her silver hair was secured in a haphazard bun with what appeared to be a pencil, wayward curls flying in all directions. She carried an enormous tote bag, and I knew it was filled with books and enough butterscotch candies to survive an apocalypse.

"Fresh out of the oven," I confirmed, smiling despite myself. Ms. Whitmore had been Grimm Island's librarian for most of my life—a woman who had seemed positively ancient when I'd been a kid—only to finally retire a few years ago. Somehow, she looked exactly the same as she had twenty years earlier. I still couldn't quite shake the feeling that I should whisper in her presence. I also had trouble remembering to call her Deidre instead of Ms. Whitmore.

"Wonderful! I brought some of my lavender shortbread to share," she said, extracting a tin from her bag. "The recipe's from 1897. Found it in the historical society archives."

I smiled and took the tin from her. "You know you don't have to bring food, Ms. Whitmore. This is a tea shop. I'm happy to provide all the refreshments."

"Call me Deidre, dear," she reminded me for what had to be the hundredth time. Her bright red culottes were a blur as she made her way to the prepared table. She untied her red-and-white striped sweater from around her shoulders and put it on the back of her preferred chair to save her spot. "And nonsense. It's a book club, and book clubs have potlucks."

The bell jingled again, and Walt Garrison marched in with military precision, followed closely by Dottie Simmons and Hank Hardeman.

"Five forty-two," Walt announced, consulting his ancient waterproof watch. He wore pressed navy slacks with sharp creases, a matching windbreaker, and the thick-soled shoes his orthopedist insisted he wear for fallen arches. "Right on schedule."

"We're early, Walt," Dottie corrected, adjusting her green cat-eye glasses. "The meeting doesn't start until six."

"Early is on time, on time is late," Walt replied with the air of someone who had been saying the same thing for at least seventy years.

"And late is unacceptable," Hank finished with a sigh. "We know, Walt. We've known since 1972."

Hank had spent a good part of his career as a federal judge and had finally retired a few years ago at his wife's urging. He was a no-nonsense sort of man, but he'd taken to wearing shorts since his retirement, showing off knobby knees and the black dress socks he wore pulled up to the middle of his shins.

"Where's Bea?" I asked, noting the missing member of their quintet.

"Picking up Mr. Whiskers from the groomer," Dottie explained. "That cat gets more salon appointments than I do." She patted her freshly cut bob that had been dyed the jet black of her youth.

"Tea will be ready in a minute," I said. "I've got Earl Grey for Walt, oolong for Deidre—"

"And chamomile for me," Dottie finished. "You're a dear to remember."

"It's not exactly difficult," I said. "You've ordered the same thing for the past three years."

"Consistency is the foundation of character," Hank declared.

I retreated to the counter to prepare their tea. This monthly ritual had become so familiar I could probably do it in my sleep. First Thursday of every month, the Silver Sleuths Murder Society would descend upon my shop for their book club meeting, which inevitably dissolved into island gossip and wild speculation about whatever mystery novel they'd selected.

The bell jingled again, and Bea Livingston swept in like a tropical storm. Today she wore a flowing caftan in a peacock print so bright it had its own weather system, paired with earrings the size of small chandeliers. Her red hair sizzled with electricity.

"Sorry I'm late," she announced, though she was actually ten minutes early. "Mr. Whiskers was uncooperative." She held up her hands to display several small scratches. "Battle wounds."

"I have some antiseptic cream," I offered.

"Don't bother. I've survived three husbands and more hurricanes than I can count," she said with a dismissive wave that sent her bangles jangling. "A few cat scratches are nothing."

She settled into her usual chair and immediately leaned forward. "Now, before we start, has anyone seen our mysterious sheriff today?"

I rolled my eyes. The whole island was fascinated by the new sheriff. Maybe because he'd been brought in because of a scandal. Maybe because he wasn't a local. Or maybe because none of the gossips could get any personal information out of him. But the Silver Sleuths' sheriff watch made the CIA look like a bunch of amateurs.

"Not since yesterday," Walt reported. "He was at the pharmacy picking up a prescription."

"Did you see what for?" Deidre asked, leaning in so eagerly she nearly knocked over her teacup.

"Couldn't tell," Walt said, clearly disappointed by this gap in his intelligence gathering. "Brown paper bag, folded at the top. Very discreet."

"Blood pressure medication, most likely," Hank declared with authority. "Law enforcement has the highest rate of hypertension of any profession."

"Could be pain medication," Dottie countered, tapping her fingers thoughtfully on the table. "Did you notice how he rolls his neck? I bet it's arthritis. Unless he's addicted to pain pills. That's a whole other problem."

"Maybe it's something more…personal," Bea whispered, raising her eyebrows.

All I could do was shake my head. The poor sheriff would have an interminable disease by the time they got through with him. "Or it could just be allergy medicine," I offered. "I've seen him sneeze every time he walks past the magnolias on Harbor Street."

"Interesting that you've noticed his sneezing habits, Mabel," Bea said, her smile spreading like warm butter.

I felt my cheeks flush. "We live on a four-thousand-acre island. Everyone knows everything."

"Clearly not everything," Walt said, rubbing his chin thoughtfully. "Otherwise we'd know what was in that prescription."

"You all do realize that stalking the sheriff is probably illegal, right?"

"It's not stalking," Deidre protested. "It's community awareness. You should just ask Jerry, Hank. Don't you two play golf together?"

Hank grunted. "Jerry holds confidences better than a Catholic priest. He's a pharmacist with scruples."

"Imagine that," I murmured.

"He'll be here any minute." Dottie said with a meaningful glance at the clock. "It's almost closing time."

She wasn't wrong. For the past three weeks, ever since Sheriff Dashiell Beckett had been appointed to replace our disgraced former sheriff, he'd developed a habit of stopping by The Perfect Steep just before closing time for his evening tea. Black, strong, no sugar, splash of milk. It was the most predictable thing about him.

"He's very consistent," I said, trying to sound casual. "Professional habit, I guess."

"Or he likes the view," Bea suggested with an exaggerated wink in my direction.

I pursed my lips. "He likes the tea, Bea. That's all."

"Mmhmm," all five seniors hummed in unison, with identical expressions of disbelief.

"So what's the book this month?" I asked, desperate to change the subject.

"*The Graves of Walter County,*" Deidre said, producing a worn paperback from her bag. "About a series of cold cases in a small Texas town in the 1960s."

"How many victims?" I asked, despite myself. These murder mysteries were admittedly a guilty pleasure.

"Seven," Dottie replied eagerly. "All buried in the woods behind the killer's house. But he didn't bury them deep enough and when heavy rains came one spring one of the bodies was washed into the creek and floated all the way downtown. Victim was a girl that had gone missing from the college in the next town."

"The killer strangled all his victims with his belt," Walt said. "Had a real unusual belt buckle that left an impression in the tissue."

"The author's research was impressive," Hank added, reaching for a scone. "Though I found myself quite irritated by his abbreviations of words. He kept using the word anal for analysis, as if that's some kind of shorthand those of us who deal in crime use on a daily basis. I can tell you I've never uttered the word anal in my courtroom."

I stifled a laugh, entertained by the absurdity of the conversation.

"Pass the clotted cream," Walt said, unfazed. "I enjoyed the book. It reminded me of a case in Annapolis back in '82."

The bell above the door jingled, and I didn't have to look up to know who it was. A hush fell over the Silver Sleuths as Sheriff Beckett entered, right on schedule.

He was still in uniform, dark pants and a short-sleeved button-down that fit well across his broad shoulders and hugged his biceps. His dark hair was slightly tousled by the wind. A thin scar ran along his right jawline, barely noticeable unless you were looking for it because of the stubble he'd let grow.

"Evening, ladies. Gentlemen," he nodded.

"Sheriff," Walt replied.

"Good evening, Mrs. McCoy," Sheriff Beckett said, turning to me with a polite nod. "Hope I'm not interrupting."

I smiled at the formal address. After ten years as a widow, "Mrs. McCoy" felt like a well-worn sweater—comfortable, familiar, and something I had no desire to take off.

"Not at all, Sheriff," I replied. "Just in time for your usual?"

"Please," he said with a small smile that didn't quite reach his eyes.

Sheriff Beckett smiled with his mouth, but his eyes always remained watchful, alert. It was slightly unnerving and, if I was being honest with myself, slightly fascinating.

"Book club night?" he asked, glancing at the table where the Silver Sleuths had spread out their books and notes like battle plans.

"First Thursday of every month," Deidre confirmed, straightening her glasses with a librarian's precision. "We're discussing *The Graves of Walter County*." She held up the book.

"True crime?" he asked, raising an eyebrow. "I saw a TV special on that case. It was fascinating."

"We only read true crime," Dottie explained with a dismissive wave. "Fiction is too..." She paused, nose wrinkling like she'd smelled something unpleasant. "Unrealistic."

The corner of Sheriff Beckett's mouth quirked up. "How so?"

"Too many coincidences," Hank declared. "And the detectives—"

he jabbed a finger toward Beckett, "—are too incompetent, so the amateur sleuth ends up solving the case. It's ridiculous."

"Unlike real detectives, who welcome civilian input," Beckett said dryly, his eyes crinkling at the corners despite his deadpan delivery.

Walt leaned forward, elbows on the table, entering what I'd come to think of as his intelligence-briefing posture. "Depends on the detective," he countered. "And the civilian. Some of us have relevant expertise."

"Is that so?" Beckett asked, accepting the to-go cup I handed him, his fingers briefly brushing mine.

Deidre sat up straighter, fairly bursting with pride. "Walt was career military. He spent thirty years in Navy intelligence," she said, patting Walt's arm. "Worked for the Department of Defense before he retired. Appointed by the president."

"Really?" Beckett asked.

Walt nodded. "If I told you about it I'd have to kill you. Top secret security clearance."

"And of course Dottie was a pathologist with the Charleston medical examiner's office," Deidre continued.

"It's true," Dottie said, cleaning her glasses. "I've had my hands in a lot of bodies."

Deidre's eyes widened comically, but she continued as if that were a perfectly normal thing to say. "Hank was a federal judge."

"They called me The Hammer because I liked to put the final nail in a criminal's coffin as I sentenced them," Hank added.

Dottie rolled her eyes. "I've known you for forty-five years, and I've never heard anyone call you The Hammer." She patted his hand to soften the blow. "But you were tough on those criminals."

"I spent almost fifty years as a librarian," Deidre said. "But my true love is research. I can get lost for days in research. And then there's Bea..." Deidre paused, looking like she was unsure what to say. "Bea—"

"Had access to more secrets than the CIA," Bea said with a theatrical flourish of her bangle-laden wrist. "Society columnist. You'd be amazed what people will tell you at charity galas after two gin and tonics. I've got the dirt on every player in town if they've been here long enough. Of course, I've got the dirt on anyone who thinks they're anyone in the whole state. The South loves old money and family secrets."

Beckett looked thoughtful as he sipped his tea, his eyes moving from one Silver Sleuth to another as if reassessing them. "That's an interesting combination of skills."

"You never want to watch mystery movies with us," Dottie said. "We always figure out who did it."

"We call ourselves the Silver Sleuths," Walt said, puffing out his chest slightly.

"Catchy," Beckett commented, but he was looking at me as if he were waiting to hear what my special skills were. I hated to disappoint him, but I didn't think he'd be too interested in my ability to do cross-word puzzles or how I can memorize song lyrics the first time I hear them. Neither of those things is helpful when watching mysteries on TV.

"Storm's coming in," I said for lack of anything better, nodding toward the windows where dark clouds were gathering on the horizon. "Looks like it could be a bad one."

Beckett followed my gaze. "You're right about that," he said. "Weather service issued a severe thunderstorm warning not long ago. You might want to wrap up your meeting early tonight."

"Nonsense," Deidre said dismissively. "We've weathered worse. Remember Hurricane Matthew?"

"I remember you showing up on my doorstep because you ate all your hurricane snacks before the storm hit," Dottie said.

Beckett turned to me. "What time will you close up here?"

"We usually finish at seven," I said.

He nodded. "You'll be cutting it close. You'll want to get home before it gets too bad."

"I'm just three blocks away," I told him. "The white corner house with the piazza at the end of Harbor Street. I'll have time before things get too bad. Those clouds are still a good ways off."

"You can predict the weather?" the sheriff asked, arching a brow.

"I'm my father's daughter," I said, and left it at that.

"Right." His eyes met mine with that dark, direct gaze that never seemed to waver.

He paid for his tea, leaving his usual generous tip in the jar by the register, and then he nodded to the group. "Enjoy your book club. Try not to solve too many crimes in one evening."

"No promises," Bea called after him as he headed for the door.

"Have a good night, Sheriff," I said.

He paused at the door, glancing back. "Dash," he corrected quietly. "After hours, it's just Dash."

Before I could say anything else, he was gone, the bell chiming in his wake.

Five pairs of eyes immediately swiveled to me.

"After hours, it's just Dash," Bea mimicked in a deep voice. "Well, well, well."

"Don't start," I said with a small smile. "It's just tea and manners. That's all."

"I certainly didn't notice any arthritis in his neck," Hank said observantly. "He was able to turn his head to look at Mabel just fine."

"Did you notice the scar on his jaw?" Deidre asked, leaning forward conspiratorially.

"Bar fight in Charleston," Walt declared.

"Knife fight with a drug dealer," Bea countered.

"Military," Dottie guessed. "He has the posture."

"You're all ridiculous," I said, returning to the table with a fresh pot of tea. "He probably cut himself shaving."

"No way," Walt shook his head. "That's a knife scar. Clean, deliberate. Man's seen action."

"I heard he's from Virginia originally," Deidre offered. "Old family, fell on hard times."

"I heard he was FBI before this," Bea said, not to be outdone. "Undercover work. Very hush-hush."

"I heard he's just a normal person trying to do his job without being the subject of wild speculation," I suggested.

"Boring," Bea dismissed. "My version is better."

"We should invite him to join the book club," Dottie suggested suddenly. "He seems interested in true crime."

"Occupational hazard, I imagine," I said dryly.

"No, it's perfect," Deidre agreed, warming to the idea. "We need fresh perspectives."

"And it'd give him a chance to stare at Mabel more," Bea added with a wink.

"He's probably very busy with sheriff duties," I said, adjusting my pearl pendant.

"Not too busy for tea, apparently," Deidre pointed out, patting my hand.

"Mabel should consider courtship," Hank announced to the table, as if I weren't sitting right there. "A respectable widow of her standing would be quite eligible."

Bea nodded sagely. "In my day, ten years was more than sufficient mourning period. I married my second husband six months after my first had been buried. Of course, Leonard and I had something of a past if you know what I mean."

"If you mean you were having an affair with him while Earl was alive then we know what you mean," Deidre said, shaking her head. "The whole island knew."

Bea pursed her lips tightly, but she didn't dispute it.

"Patrick would have wanted you to move on," Dottie said softly, using the exact phrase she'd repeated at years two, five, and seven.

Walt cleared his throat. "Sheriff seems like a decent sort. Responsible. Reliable pension. Good posture."

I glanced between them, fighting both amusement and exasperation. They'd decided my future with the same certainty they used to plan the church bake sale or determine who was stealing Mrs. Peterson's newspaper.

So I did what I always did when I didn't know what to say. I started singing.

*"Don't know why there's no sun up in the sky, stormy weather..."*

"Ethel Waters or Lena Horne?" Walt asked immediately.

"Lena," I said. "Though Ethel did it first."

"Good taste," he approved. "My Margaret loved Lena Horne. Saw her perform in New York once, before we were married."

And just like that, we were back on safe ground, with Walt launching into one of his stories about his late wife that somehow always involved either naval intelligence or jazz music, often both. The tension dissolved, and I found myself relaxing back into the familiar rhythm of their conversation.

Outside, thunder rumbled in the distance. I sipped my tea and half listened as Deidre started discussing the book, with frequent interruptions from the others. The storm was building, but in here, in this moment, everything felt comfortingly normal.

I'd spent ten years building this life—the tea shop, the routines, the careful distance I maintained from anything too emotional or complicated. Ten years as Mabel McCoy, young widow, tea shop owner, honorary senior citizen.

But as another rumble of thunder shook the building, I couldn't help wondering if maybe, just maybe, I was ready for a little storm in my life.

Not that I was thinking about Dash Beckett when that thought crossed my mind.

Not at all.

# CHAPTER
# TWO

Five minutes after I'd locked the door behind the Silver Sleuths, I was gathering my things and eyeing the roiling clouds nervously as I sang about Blue Skies under my breath. Chowder waited at the door, snuffling impatiently and glaring at me accusingly. He wasn't a fan of the rain.

"Sorry, Chowder," I told him, crossing to the hook where his yellow raincoat hung. "I know you'd prefer to drive, but we didn't bring the car today. It's only three blocks. Let's get you suited up."

Chowder's expression shifted from impatience to outright resignation. Ten years together had taught me his entire emotional range. For someone who lived rent free and liked to pee on hydrangeas, he had a lot of opinions.

I knelt beside him, wrestling the yellow raincoat around his substantial girth. The coat was a tight squeeze these days, thanks to my inability to resist his "I'm starving" eyes at treat time. His legs poked through the armholes with surprising cooperation, though the sound he made was pure martyrdom.

As I fastened the snaps under his belly, I made a mental list of things I needed to do as soon as I got home—order groceries, do laundry, organize Chowder's clothes closet. In all honesty, I didn't have a lot to do, so my night would probably look like most of my nights—in bed with a good book and a glass of Moscato.

Pretty pathetic when you think about it. Ten years was a long time to be alone, but I involved myself in things in the community and I had the tea shop. It was just the nights when I felt myself start to go a little mad. Not that I could share that bit of information with anyone. If you asked the citizens of Grimm Island, I was always perfectly presentable and put together, married to the memory of Patrick and the huge house he left me. I was Widow McCoy, and like a zoo animal, people would watch and wave and whisper at me as I sat in my rocker on my piazza, watching the boats pass by.

I sang louder, trying to drown out my own thoughts as I pulled on the green raincoat with little pink flowers and gathered my enormous pink umbrella. Umbrella, keys, purse, dog. The standard checklist for leaving anywhere.

"Ready for home, handsome?" I asked Chowder, who responded with a snort.

Outside, a light drizzle had begun, but it was nothing that warranted opening the umbrella yet, though I did pull up my hood. The evening air hung heavy with that particular coastal dampness that makes everything feel closer, more immediate. Harbor Street was quiet, the storefronts already darkened for the night, save for the warm glow of Grimm Island Books where Howard Miller was undoubtedly lost in his inventory sheets.

We headed down the sidewalk, Chowder's nails clicking against the concrete in a companionable rhythm. I let my mind drift back to *The Graves of Walter County*, excited to start the book for myself. Deidre had given me the extra copy she'd had in her bag. During their meeting, I'd learned more than I wanted to know about a body's decomposition when buried in a shallow grave in the woods. Why Dottie would keep pictures of cadavers from the Body Farm on her phone was a mystery to me, and I knew I'd be picturing them as I read, macabre as it was.

A loud crack of thunder electrified the air around me, and Chowder and I both jumped in surprise. Then the rain started, the drops fat and determined, landing with purpose on my raincoat. I fumbled with the umbrella clasp, muttering under my breath as the sky seemed to open up all at once.

"Good grief," I said, finally wrestling the umbrella open. But the wind immediately tried to turn it inside out. "Oh, for Pete's sake."

Chowder gave me a look that could only be described as accusatory, as if I had personally arranged the downpour to inconvenience him.

"Don't give me that look," I told him. "Just start walking."

The rain intensified with Hollywood-level dramatic timing, sheets of it now slashing through the glow of the streetlights. My vintage sea-green dress was already soaked at the hem and my shoes were a disaster. The hair around my face hung in wet ropes and stuck to my skin.

A passing truck sent a wave of murky water over my already drenched legs, and I let loose with a string of words that would have given the Grimm Island Ladies' Auxiliary collective heart failure. Growing up with a former merchant marine for a father had its linguistic advantages, even if I never deployed them in polite company.

"I think I mentioned that you'd be cutting it close," a familiar voice yelled out through the noise of the storm. "But now doesn't seem like the right time to say, 'I told you so.'"

"Generous of you," I said, gritting my teeth, but not turning to look at him. I blew out a slow breath. Of course Sheriff Beckett would be here now in time to see me looking like a drowned rat.

I finally turned to see his unmarked white Tahoe pulled up alongside us, window rolled down just enough to reveal his face.

"Sheriff," I acknowledged, trying to maintain some dignity as water dripped from my hood and down my collar.

"Get in," he said, nodding toward the passenger side. "I'll drive you home."

I hesitated, still thinking about his "I told you so" crack. Not to mention he was practically a stranger. Of course, stranger danger probably didn't apply to police officers. But he did look rather ominous. He was no longer in uniform, but wore a black long-sleeved T-shirt so he looked like he'd just come from a heist. He definitely looked like a man you wouldn't want to tangle with in a dark alley.

And then he smiled as if he knew exactly what I was thinking, and I shivered as another stream of water went down the neck of my coat.

Before I could give him my best Southern cold shoulder and continue walking, Chowder made the choice for both of us.

With surprising agility for a dog shaped like a loaf of sourdough, he waddled to the passenger door and sat expectantly, head tilted up toward the handle. The traitor.

"Your dog has more common sense than you do," Beckett observed, the corner of his mouth quirking up.

"He's not known for his loyalty," I said, squelching over to join my canine Judas. "Not when comfort's at stake."

I opened the door and gave Chowder a boost into the seat, and he scrambled toward Beckett with uncharacteristic enthusiasm, leaving muddy paw prints on the pristine seat.

"Oh, goodness gravy, I'm sorry about your upholstery," I said, cringing as I slid in after him, dripping all over the floor mats.

"It's a police vehicle," Beckett said with a shrug. "It's seen worse than a little rain and muddy paw prints."

"Well, that's terrifying," I said, trying not to imagine the variations of fluids that had come before me.

Beckett put the Tahoe in drive and pulled away from the curb. "End of Harbor Street, right? The big white house with the piazza?"

I raised an eyebrow. "You've got a good memory, Sheriff."

"It's my job to know the island," he said simply.

"It's your job to know where everyone on the island lives?" I asked, trying to wring some water from my hair without dripping all over his console.

"I'm doing my best to learn as many as I can," he said. "But with an island of more than ten thousand residents, it's a daunting task. But it just so happens you're the nerve center of the island gossip network. I was told by fifteen different people where you live my first day on the job."

I laughed despite myself. "I'm Switzerland in the gossip wars. Neutral territory. And it's unfortunate that my tea shop is literally right in the middle of the island. But the island gossips are amateurs. If you want the real scoop you'll ask the Silver Sleuths."

"Noted," he said, and he smiled, a real smile that reached his eyes.

It was a nice smile—disarming—and I almost relaxed.

Chowder had made himself completely at home, climbing over the center console to inspect the back seat before returning to sit directly between us, his bulging eyes fixed on Beckett with what appeared to be canine fascination.

"Your dog is staring at me," Beckett observed as we stopped at the island's only traffic light.

"He's assessing you," I explained. "Chowder's an excellent judge of character."

Beckett reached over and scratched behind Chowder's ears, earning a snort of pleasure from the little dog. "And what's the verdict, Chowder?"

"Jury's still out," I said, noticing the tattoo that was barely visible beneath his shirtsleeve.

"Maybe I should deputize him."

I scratched Chowder behind the ears and sighed. "He'd like that more than you could imagine. He loves to play dress-up. He's got a closet filled with more clothes than I have. I'm sure he'd love to add a badge to his collection. Though I should warn you, he's easily bribed."

Beckett was still smiling when he said, "It seems to be par for the course. I think that's one of the things that landed my predecessor and a few of his deputies in prison."

I didn't know whether to laugh or wince. The recent scandal our former sheriff had brought on the community was still fresh.

"Too soon?" he asked.

"Depends on the company," I said, shrugging. "People have long memories on Grimm Island. And they know how to hold a grudge."

"I'll remember that," he said.

The inside of the Tahoe was warm and dry, smelling faintly of coffee and something woodsy—cologne, maybe, or just Beckett himself. The rain hammered against the roof with increasing intensity, and I silently thanked whatever impulse had led the sheriff to drive by at that precise moment.

Despite my initial irritation with his appearance, good manners insisted I thank him for his hospitality.

"I'm grateful you came by when you did. That weather warning you mentioned was right on the money," I said, watching lightning flash over the harbor to our right. "I should have listened to you and left earlier."

"Forecasters occasionally get lucky," Beckett said with that dry tone I was beginning to suspect as his version of humor. "Though around here, I'm learning the locals are more reliable than any meteorologist."

"Let me guess," I said. "Someone told you their knee was acting up, so you knew to take the weather warning seriously?"

He chuckled, a low, warm sound that I hadn't heard from him before. "Something like that."

"How are you finding island life?" I asked, curious to know just one piece of information about the mysterious sheriff all the locals were clamoring to find out about.

"Different," he said after a moment. "Quieter, in some ways. Louder in others."

"The gossip, you mean."

He nodded. "I sneezed while in a meeting yesterday, and by the time I went to lunch, the waitress asked if I needed recommendations for allergy medicine."

I laughed. "That's Grimm Island for you. We lack privacy but make up for it in unsolicited advice."

"I've noticed," he said, slowing as we approached my house at the end of Harbor Street.

My home stood proudly against the stormy backdrop, a classic three-story Charleston single painted a pristine white that glowed softly even in the darkness. Black shutters framed each of the tall windows, their simple elegance a hallmark of Lowcountry architecture. The raised foundation elevated the main floor above potential floodwaters, with a set of white steps leading to the glossy black front door crowned by a fanlight window.

The house's most distinctive feature was its double piazza—the tiered side porches that ran the full length of the house, supported by slender white columns. The piazzas faced the river, and ferns and potted palms adorned the railings, creating the impression of a floating garden. Stately palm trees stood at the corners of the property, their fronds thrashing dramatically in the wind. The wrought-iron fence that surrounded the small front garden looked almost liquid in the rain, the camellias and azaleas behind it bending beneath the onslaught of the storm.

"Will you be all right getting in?" Beckett asked, nodding toward the front yard. "That's quite a river running down the sidewalk."

"We'll survive," I assured him, though the prospect of dashing across my front yard through the downpour was far from appealing. "Thanks again for the ride, Sheriff. It was very kind of you."

"Dash," he reminded me quietly. "And it was no trouble."

I gathered my purse and umbrella, preparing to make a run for it, when he placed a hand on my arm, so lightly I might have imagined it.

"Wait here," he said, then got out of the Tahoe and jogged around to my side, opening my door and extending his hand to help me out. He was soaked instantly, his dark hair plastered to his forehead, rain running in rivulets down his face.

His hand was warm despite the rain as he helped me from the car, and something electric shot through me at the contact—a sensation so foreign I nearly gasped. My body seemed to remember something my mind had forgotten, like muscles awakening after a long sleep. For ten years, I'd lived in a carefully constructed numbness, and this sudden awareness felt almost painful—a pins-and-needles tingling as circulation returned to a part of me I'd allowed to go dormant.

The guilt followed immediately, a familiar weight settling in my chest. Patrick's face floated in my memory, but strangely blurred around the edges. When had that happened? When had I stopped being able to recall with perfect clarity the exact shade of his eyes or the particular curve of his smile? The realization made my throat tighten even as my skin still hummed from Dash's touch.

"Thank you," I managed to say, pulling my hand away perhaps too quickly. The loss of contact felt both relieving and disappointing—another contradiction I wasn't prepared to examine.

"I'd walk you to the door, but I think your dog is anxious to get inside," Beckett said, nodding toward Chowder, who was already waddling at top speed toward the porch steps, ignoring the leash I'd attempted to put on him.

"He's a fair-weather dog in every sense," I confirmed. "But really, thank you for the ride."

"Before you go," he said, rain plastering his shirt to his shoulders, "I wanted to ask—those Silver Sleuths. They mentioned their backgrounds. Are they really as qualified as they claim to be?"

I smiled, pushing wet hair from my face. "More so, probably. They're the real deal. This country would be in better hands if they were running things, I promise you that."

"Good to know. Good night, Mrs. McCoy."

"Mabel," I corrected him, feeling bold. "After hours, it's just Mabel."

The smile he gave me then was brief but genuine, reaching all the way to his eyes. Then he was back in his Tahoe, pulling away with a wave as I splashed my way toward the porch where Chowder waited impatiently.

Inside, my house welcomed me with familiar shadows and the ticking of the antique grandfather clock in the hall. I peeled off my wet raincoat and boots in the mudroom, and looked down at my sodden dress and stripped that off too. I'd have to take it to the cleaners.

Standing in only my underwear and bra, I toweled off and then helped Chowder out of his yellow monstrosity. I toweled him dry while he grunted in protest.

"Don't be so dramatic," I told him, rubbing behind his ears the way Beckett had done. "You're the one who abandoned me for a ride in a warm car."

Once dried to his satisfaction, Chowder trotted off toward the kitchen, his nails clicking on the heart pine floors. I grabbed a vintage dressing gown in pale peach that I'd left hanging on the hook in the laundry room and tied it tightly around my waist. It had ridiculous wide bell sleeves and it was trimmed in fur. It made me feel like Rosemary Clooney until I caught sight of myself in the hall mirror and shrieked at the sight.

"Good heavens," I said, wiping at the mascara and eyeliner that had bled beneath my eyes so I looked like a raccoon. "Mortifying. Absolutely mortifying."

Chowder's nails clacked on the hardwood as he came back to check on me.

"Why didn't you say something?" I scolded. "I'll never be able to face him again."

Chowder snorted as if to tell me I was the one being dramatic now and went back to the kitchen to await his treat. I followed after him.

My house had been Patrick's wedding gift to me—a grand gesture that had both thrilled and intimidated me at the time. "Every Southern belle needs a proper home," he'd said.

I'd always found that statement to be a source of amusement and embarrassment, considering I was about as far from a true Southern belle as one could get. I'd grown up the daughter of a merchant marine and a glass artist. I'd been born here on the island, but my family wasn't *from* the island, if you know what I mean.

My mother was a fly-by-the-seat-of-her-pants kind of woman and a little flaky, but the constant moving around of military life was too much even for her spontaneous self, so she'd put her foot down when I was born and said she wasn't moving again. So my dad would go about his life, relocating to wherever he was told to go, and then he'd come visit me and my mom when he got the chance. It had been an arrangement that seemed to work for them. Then my dad died and Mom moved to Florida to be with her sister and make her glass with an ocean view, and I stayed on Grimm Island.

I'd met Patrick while I'd been working as a waitress at the country club, trying to pay for my last semester of college. We'd been something of a scandal in our own right, especially since Grimm Island was full of old money and tradition, and I lacked both of those things. But Patrick didn't care. He treated me like a queen and ignored the gossip. And I hadn't realized how I'd wanted a white knight to come in and rescue me, just like in the storybooks. He'd been my white knight. And then he'd been gone. I'd found that I was accepted on Grimm Island as Patrick's widow, much more than I had been as his wife.

This house was a reminder of him—the views of the water, the Lowcountry charm and grandness of the architecture, and the sycamore tree he'd planted himself in the side yard so one day, the sunlight wouldn't blast us in the face like a laser first thing in the morning.

I woke up one morning just last year and realized the sun no longer shone through our bedroom window like it once had. The sycamore had finally grown tall enough to cast the shade Patrick had promised it would. I had my shade, but I didn't have Patrick beside me to share in his small victory. I'd wept that morning—not the violent, consuming sobs of fresh grief, but something quieter, like rainwater finally spilling from a leaf that had held it too long.

That's how grief worked now, after ten years. It no longer crashed through me like a summer thunderstorm—sudden, overwhelming, leaving me gasping for air. Instead, it had aged into something more constant, a low hum beneath everyday moments, like the distant sound of waves you could only hear when everything else fell silent. The sharp edges had worn smooth like sea glass, still recognizable for what they once were, but transformed by time.

I could go days now without that familiar ache. But then some small thing—a song on the radio Patrick used to hum along with, the particular way light hit the harbor in late afternoon, or the whiff of his favorite aftershave on a passing stranger—would bring him back so vividly that for a split second, I'd expect to see him walk through the door. Those moments were becoming fewer, the images of his face less distinct, like a photograph left too long in sunlight. And that fading—

the gradual loss of what I'd already lost once—sometimes hurt worse than the original wound.

I'd built my life around his absence, each routine and habit carefully constructed like the walls of a fortress. The tea shop, the vintage clothes, the old music—they gave shape to days that might otherwise collapse under the weight of emptiness. I was Widow McCoy to everyone on Grimm Island, and I'd grown comfortable in that identity. It was safe. Predictable. What terrified me more than anything was the occasional, unwelcome question that whispered through my mind on nights when sleep wouldn't come: Who would I be if I ever stopped being Patrick's widow?

Now the house was just mine, its spacious rooms filled with a mixture of inherited antiques and my own more eclectic finds. The kitchen, at least, I'd renovated to my tastes—textured brick walls, exposed beams, butcher-block counters, and a giant farmhouse sink that could accommodate even my largest tea urns when I brought work home.

I poured myself a glass of Moscato and leaned against the counter, listening to the rain drum against the windows. Thunder still rumbled overhead, but it was moving away now, the storm passing over the island on its way out to sea.

Chowder sat expectantly by his food bowl, his expression suggesting I'd been neglecting him.

"You're shameless," I told him, but reached for the jar of homemade dog biscuits anyway. "Is this because Dash said he was going to make you a deputy? I'm sure you'll look very handsome in uniform. But you've got to stay clear of the badge bunnies. You're not equipped to handle women like that."

Chowder snorted, accepting the biscuit with delicate precision before carrying it to his bed in the corner.

I wandered into the living room with my wine, curling up in the window seat that overlooked the harbor. From here, I could see the lighthouse in the distance, its beam cutting through the stormy darkness in rhythmic sweeps. The rain tapped against the century-old glass panes, creating shadows that danced across the polished wood floors.

Patrick and I had spent countless evenings in this very spot, watching the lighthouse beam and making up stories about the ships that passed by.

But it wasn't Patrick I was thinking of tonight. When I tried to conjure his face in my mind it evaporated like mist in the wind, and despite the guilt that brought, all I could see was a man with dark hair, piercing black eyes, and a scar that conjured images of violence. A man who had a past and a darkness inside him caused by things I could never imagine. You could see it when you looked at him. And I knew as sure as anything he didn't belong on this island. A man like that couldn't survive without the occasional walk on the wild side.

I might not be very worldly, but I knew danger when I was looking it in the face. But his secret would stay safe with me. If he wanted to keep the illusion of being nothing more than a small-town sheriff, who was I to reveal it? I had illusions to maintain myself.

I sipped my wine and watched the rain, and Chowder, having finished his biscuit, waddled over to join me on the window seat, climbing into my lap with a grunt of effort.

"What do you think, Chowder? Is the sheriff as mysterious as everyone says? You think he's got some deep dark secrets in his past?"

Chowder responded by closing his eyes and beginning to snore.

"Helpful as always," I sighed, scratching his wrinkled head. "Maybe it's best to stay away from the sheriff."

Outside, the storm continued to rage, but in here, with my wine and my dog and the familiar creaking of the house around me, I felt safe. Still, as I gazed out at the rain-swept street, I realized that I'd never been very good at listening to my own advice.

# CHAPTER
# THREE

The morning after a storm always feels like a clean slate—air scrubbed fresh, streets glistening, the whole world somehow reset. At least that's what I told myself as I unlocked The Perfect Steep at precisely five thirty-seven, my usual opening routine thrown off by a restless night of dreams involving thunderstorms, lighthouse beams, and a certain sheriff with rain-soaked hair.

I decided a strong black tea was in order for myself this morning, minus the splash of milk I normally took, though I still gave myself two lumps of brown sugar. It seemed like the kind of morning for a strong dose of caffeine.

I'd deliberately chosen my favorite vintage dress for the day—a cherry-red fit-and-flare with tiny white polka dots. The sweetheart neckline and cap sleeves gave it a classic 1950s silhouette, and the full-circle skirt swished pleasantly around my knees as I moved. Sometimes clothing was the best armor a woman could have.

"We're not thinking about him," I informed Chowder, who hopped onto his window seat with the customary morning blend of enthusiasm and judgment. "Today is about tea, scones, and absolutely zero sheriffs."

Chowder snorted in a way that could only be described as skeptical.

"Don't give me that look," I said, flipping on lights and adjusting the thermostat. "I'm a grown woman who runs a successful business. I don't have time for distractions. I am perfectly comfortable living my life exactly the way it is. We're comfortable. And we have a routine."

I busied myself with the morning prep—measuring loose tea leaves, preheating ovens, and setting out the flour and my baking supplies. I baked the scones myself, but the other baked goods I got from Mrs. Wexler over on the mainland—muffins, beignets, and her killer cinnamon rolls were standards, and then she'd throw in a fourth option as a surprise. I checked the clock again, noting it was already after six, and wondering if she was okay. She'd usually made her delivery by now.

My morning regulars would arrive like clockwork—Howard from the bookstore at 6:45 for Earl Grey and a blueberry scone, Mrs. Pinkerton at 7:00 sharp for her chamomile with honey, the construction crew from the harbor renovation at 7:15 for black coffee so strong it could peel paint.

The routine was comforting. Predictable. Safe.

Which was why the knock at the door at half past six threw me completely off kilter.

Chowder barked once—his "someone's here" alert rather than his "danger" bark, which sounded remarkably similar but involved more snorting.

Through the glass, I could see Sheriff Beckett standing on my stoop, looking far too alert for this hour.

"Stranger danger," I muttered under my breath, giving Chowder a disapproving look he chose to ignore.

As the sheriff waited for me to open up, I took a moment to appreciate the view. He stood a couple of inches over six feet, with shoulders broad enough to suggest he spent his free time doing something more strenuous than paperwork. His uniform—light blue shirt and dark pants—was pressed to military precision, but it was how he filled it out that caught my attention. I was starting to have an unusual fascination with shoulders.

I was captivated by the thin scar that traced his jawline, starting just below his ear and running about two inches down. I had a feeling whatever had happened he was lucky to be alive.

"I'm not open yet," I called through the door.

"Official business," he replied, holding up a leather folder.

With a sigh that was only partially for show, I unlocked the door and stepped back to let him in. "Good morning, Sheriff. You're up early."

"Dash," he corrected.

"You said it was official business," I said, arching a brow.

He smiled in that slow, thoughtful way he had. "So I did. I'm sorry to disturb you before opening hours."

"No trouble," I lied, remembering how'd I'd looked when he'd last seen me and trying to push through the embarrassment, though I did look pretty spectacular in my red dress, so that had to count for something.

"Are you okay? You're looking kind of flushed."

"I'm fine," I said, feeling my face flush even more. "I'm just not used to law enforcement at dawn. Should I be worried?"

"Not unless you broke the law," he said, looking around the empty room. "But I do need a favor."

Chowder chose that moment to trot over, greeting the sheriff like he'd been sent a personal invitation with bacon treats attached.

"Chowder," I said. "Have some dignity." I blew out a sigh as Chowder rolled like a sausage onto his back for belly scrubs.

"He's just being friendly."

"You said something about a favor?" I reminded him, trying to keep things on track. "At six thirty in the morning?"

"I need to use your tea shop. For a meeting. Today, if possible."

"A meeting," I repeated, feeling like I was several steps behind in this conversation. "Here? The station doesn't have a conference room?"

"It does," he confirmed. "But this isn't an official meeting, and I'd rather not conduct it on government property."

My brows rose at that bit of information.

"When?" I asked, already mentally rearranging my day.

"After you close today?" He sounded almost apologetic. "Six o'clock? I know it's short notice, but—"

"Who's meeting?" I asked, curious despite myself.

Dash hesitated, then said, "The Silver Sleuths."

"I'm sorry, did you say the Silver Sleuths? As in, my Silver Sleuths? The geriatric crime enthusiasts who are bound and determined to find out everything there is to know about the mysterious new sheriff?"

He winced. "That's a terrifying thought," he said. "But yes. The very same. After our conversation last night, I did some research. Turns out their credentials are legitimate, and quite impressive."

"I told you so," I said, unable to resist repeating his words from the night before.

"You did." He nodded, then added, "I need their expertise."

I moved to refill my cup since my tea had gone cold. "For what exactly?"

Dash glanced toward the windows and looked out onto the empty street, then back at me, his expression serious. "A cold case. Something from before my time, but…something that needs resolving."

My curiosity was fully piqued now. "And you think five senior citizens and their true crime book club can help where the authorities couldn't?"

"Sometimes fresh eyes are exactly what a case needs," he said. "Especially eyes with their specific skills."

I studied him for a moment. There was something he wasn't saying, something in the tension around his eyes and the careful way he chose his words.

Chowder let out a soft woof and padded his way into the kitchen and the delivery entrance.

"That must be Mrs. Wexler with the pastry delivery," I said, setting my tea down again before I could drink it. "Do you need me to contact them?"

"If you don't mind," he said. "If they're busy we'll find another time."

"Oh, they won't be busy," I said. "Not for this."

"Thank you," he said. "I appreciate it."

"Don't thank me yet," I warned him. "You have no idea what you're getting yourself into with that bunch."

He smiled then, a real smile that reached his eyes. "I think I can handle a few enthusiastic retirees."

I laughed despite myself. "Famous last words, Sheriff. Famous last words."

———

I was so full of anticipation and nerves that I flipped the closed sign over fifteen minutes early and shooed out the last lingering customer, telling him I had a family emergency and to come back another day for a free pastry.

Walt arrived just as I was about to close the door.

"You're the first to arrive," I said.

"Shame," he said. "People have no consideration of time nowadays. On time is late. If I've said it once I've said it a thousand times." He wore a blazer with a crisp white shirt and carried a battered leather satchel that looked like it had survived at least two wars and a hurricane. "Where do you want us to set up?"

"Your usual table?" I suggested.

Walt shook his head. "Too exposed. We're sure to be the talk around town if people see us two nights in a row with the sheriff. The corner table is best." He pointed to the most secluded spot in the shop. "Less chance of someone peering through the window. You should get blinds. If you had blinds we could close them."

"Hmm," I said, because I couldn't think of anything better. Someone was getting a little too caught up in the sheriff's game.

Deidre was the next to arrive, her wild silver curls flying and her tote bag hitched over her shoulder. "Walt's in espionage mode, isn't he?" she asked, spotting him rearranging my furniture.

"I shudder to think what he's got in that briefcase," I said.

She sighed. "I brought a bottle of wine and some aspirin. I'm thinking we'll need both."

Dottie and Hank came in together like usual, arguing, like usual. I'd come to realize that was their own form of entertainment.

"—at least three weeks, based on the bloating," Dottie was saying.

"Unless there was unusual tidal activity," Hank countered.

"Do you two ever discuss normal things?" I asked. "Like weather or sports or literally anything that doesn't involve dead bodies?"

They both looked at me blankly.

"What's the fun in that?" Dottie asked, genuinely confused.

I just shook my head and went to put on a fresh pot of tea.

Bea swept in last, wearing turquoise pants and a flowing top with enough sparkly bits to function as emergency reflectors. Her arm jingled with at least a dozen bangles, and her oversized purse made a suspicious clinking sound.

"What's that sound?" I asked curiously.

"I brought ingredients to make sidecars," she said. "I figured we're going to need them. Walt tends to go overboard in these matters, and a little liquor will keep the rest of us from strangling him."

"Deidre brought wine."

Bea sighed. "Amateur."

And then she headed toward the group and began to set out the supplies from her bag on one of the other tables. She'd even brought her own knife and cutting board for the oranges.

At precisely six o'clock, the bell above the entrance jingled, and Sheriff Beckett entered. I noticed Walt look at the clock and shake his head in disappointment. To be on time was to be late. The sheriff wasn't exactly starting off in Walt's good graces.

Another man followed Sheriff Beckett inside. He was young, probably early twenties, with a smattering of freckles across the bridge of his nose.

"This is Deputy Harris," Beckett said by way of introduction. "He'll be assisting with some of the procedural aspects of the case."

"How long you been on the job, sonny?" Walt asked.

"I graduated from the academy two weeks ago," Harris said, his Adam's apple bobbing.

"Good call, Sheriff," Walt said, nodding approvingly. "He's untainted. Sometimes new blood is more needed than experience."

Sheriff Beckett's eyes shone with humor, but he nodded. "You can trust Harris. He reports only to me." He stood at the head of the table, a man who commanded attention. "Thank you for coming on such short notice. I'm sure you all have busy schedules."

"Sidecar?" Bea interrupted, swiping a lemon around the rim of a cocktail glass like a pro and then dipping the rim in sugar.

"They're on duty, Bea," Dottie said. "But I'll have one. Go heavy on the orange."

"I'll stick with tea," Walt said. "One of us needs to be clearheaded to hear why the sheriff called us here tonight."

Dash nodded, setting a thick file on the table. "I'm in need of an official posse. That includes you, Mrs. McCoy."

I bobbled Walt's teacup slightly before setting it down in front of him. "Oh, but I'm not...this isn't my area of..." I stammered.

"You know the island and the people on it," he said. "I want your perspective too."

Before I could protest further, Dottie patted the empty chair beside her. "Sit, dear. The sheriff has an excellent point."

With no graceful way to refuse, I took the seat, setting down my teapot.

"Now," Sheriff Beckett began. "I'm going to be upfront and let you know I've already done a cursory check on you all."

"You ran a background check on us?" Bea asked, smiling mischievously.

"Nothing so in depth," he said. "Not yet. But the internet has plenty to say about all of you. I'll have to run a background check if you're officially brought on to work the case."

Bea's lips twitched. "Don't believe everything you read on the internet, Sheriff. Sometimes the truth is much more scandalous." And then she winked at him.

"Ignore her," Walt said. "Everybody in the state knows Bea was caught in flagrante delicto with one of her snitches in the nineties. It made front page news everywhere." He waved a hand in dismissal. "No one cares, Bea. It was forty years ago."

"He wasn't a snitch," she said, lips pursed. "He was a senator."

"Same thing," Walt said. "Keep going, Sheriff. We've got nothing to hide."

"This case was officially closed decades ago, but I have reason to believe the investigation might have been compromised."

"By Sheriff Milton," Hank said immediately, his expression darkening.

The sheriff nodded. "Yes. And a few others."

"Not surprised," Dottie said, her lips pursed in disapproval. "That man was as crooked as they come."

"And now he's enjoying federal accommodations," Bea added, passing out sidecars like candy.

She handed one to me and I could've sworn Chowder arched a wrinkled brow at me. I took a small sip and watched the sheriff over the rim. I knew the hornet's nest he'd walked into after Milton's arrest couldn't be an easy one. The scandal had rocked our sleepy island community, leaving the department short staffed and under scrutiny. It would be a long time before people on the island trusted law enforcement again.

"The case I'm interested in goes back further than the recent issues," Sheriff Beckett said diplomatically.

"What's the case?" Hank asked.

"The drowning death of Elizabeth Calvert, summer of 1996."

A hush fell over the table. Even Bea, never at a loss for words, seemed momentarily silenced.

"Oh, I remember that one," Hank said. "Tragic."

"We all remember that one," Deidre said. "With the exception of Mabel, of course. Were you even born, dear?"

"Yes," I said. "And things like that don't happen often on Grimm Island. It was the talk of the town for years during my childhood."

Beckett placed a thick manila folder on the table.

"Hold on, young man," Hank said. "I know the law. Any case files or evidence is for law enforcement eyes only. You can't show us any of this legally."

Sheriff Beckett smiled and pulled out a single sheet of paper that looked very official. "Which is why I'm officially swearing you in. I told you I need a posse. Now raise your right hand and repeat after me."

I was too shocked to do anything but stick my hand up in the air and repeat the words the sheriff was saying. I'd had no idea posses still existed, and I'd never imagined that I'd be part of one. I didn't own a cowboy hat, and I'd never ridden a horse.

*"So help me God…"* we all repeated in unison.

"I need signatures from each of you," Sheriff Beckett said, "and then I'll file this with the clerk of court."

"Do we get badges?" Dottie asked.

"No," Beckett said.

"No matter," Bea said. "I've got a fake one somewhere. Used it once when I was working on a story."

"I didn't hear that," Beckett said.

"I need to buy more bullets for my gun," Dottie said. "I've only got four left." She reached into her bag and pulled out a silver .45 revolver with a pearl handle. And then she pulled out a makeup compact and opened it up. Inside were four bullets.

Sheriff Beckett opened his mouth to say something and then promptly closed it again. Probably a smart move on his part.

"What good is it to carry a gun around if it's not loaded?" Walt asked, incensed.

"I used to keep it loaded but I was digging around for a pen one day and accidentally pulled the trigger. Shot a hole right in the bottom of my brand-new Vera Bradley bag. So I took the bullets out and put them in here." She closed the makeup compact and rattled it for good measure.

"I've got a .22 you can use," Hank said. "That .45 will knock your teeth loose."

"Deal," Dottie said. "We can trade."

Deputy Harris winced and Sheriff Beckett shook his head, probably second-guessing his idea of making a posse that included five octogenarians and me. I had to admit, I was questioning his judgment as well.

He opened up the case file and spread out several photographs. I recognized the harbor shoreline, though the images were grainy and weathered with age. In one photo, something dark lay half submerged at the water's edge. I looked away quickly, my stomach clenching as the reality of what we were discussing suddenly hit home—not just an old case file but a young woman's life cut short.

"Elizabeth Calvert, twenty-two years old," he began, his voice taking on a clinical edge that I suspected helped him maintain professional distance. "Found floating near the pier on the morning of July 16, 1996. Top of her class at Charleston College, home for the summer before starting graduate school at Duke. According to the official report, she had been in the water approximately twelve hours."

"In 1996 I was working as a medical examiner for the state," Dottie said. "If I remember right it was the Charleston ME who did the autopsy. It was declared an accidental drowning."

"Accidental my foot," Walt snorted. "Girl was a champion swimmer. Won state titles three years running."

"Which was her father's argument and why he insisted foul play was involved," Dottie added.

Beckett nodded. "That's one of numerous inconsistencies I've found. The official cause of death was drowning, but the report contains several troubling details." He pulled out a photocopy of what appeared to be the autopsy report. "Bruising on both wrists, consistent with restraint. Blunt force trauma to the back of the head, which the ME claimed happened postmortem when the body struck rocks in the harbor."

"Defensive wounds?" Hank asked, leaning forward.

"None documented," he replied. "But the photos tell a different story than the written report." He pointed to another image. "Look at her hands. Those are clearly defensive injuries on her knuckles. They're mentioned in the initial examiner's notes but omitted from the final report."

The knowledge that we were looking at a dead girl's hands made my skin prickle with unease. My tea suddenly tasted too sweet in my mouth as I tried to reconcile the clinical terminology with the horror of what actually happened to this young woman.

"Toxicology?" Dottie asked.

"Showed alcohol in her system, but not enough to cause impairment for someone her size. No other substances." Beckett tapped another document. "The timeline is perhaps the most problematic element. Elizabeth was last seen leaving the library around six o'clock. According to witnesses, she appeared agitated but not intoxicated. The ME placed time of death between midnight and 2 a.m."

"So what happened in those six hours?" I asked, the question slipping out before I could stop it.

"Exactly," he said, meeting my eyes with an intensity that made my chest tighten. "Her car was found in the library parking lot, suggesting she never made it home. But her purse and belongings were missing and never recovered."

"There's got to be someone who saw her in those six hours," I said. "This is a small island."

"That's where you come in," he said. "People on this island have long memories. If the medical examiner's report has holes, we can assume the police report has holes too. There are just a handful of witness statements in the case file, and they're not well documented. Milton stated over and over again in the report that she must have been drinking, hit her head and drowned. He didn't bother too much with gathering facts."

"Makes sense," Hank said. "Milton wouldn't know the truth if it hit him in the face."

"Her father never accepted the ruling," Beckett said. "He insisted Elizabeth was a strong swimmer who knew the harbor currents. He believed she'd stumbled onto something related to her research."

"What was she researching?" I asked, curiosity piqued.

"Officially, she was working on a summer internship with the *Observer*," Beckett replied.

"Ooh," Bea said. "A journalist. Digging into people's secrets is a good way to get dead."

Dash nodded. "She'd been accepted into the master's journalism program at Duke. I found notes indicating she was specifically looking into financial irregularities related to several development projects in the area.

"The case was closed after three weeks, despite the father's objections, despite the inconsistencies in the physical evidence, despite the fact that Elizabeth's research materials were never found." He looked around the table, eyes settling on each of us. "Milton buried this case."

"Cover-up," Walt said grimly. "Classic Milton."

"There's more," Beckett said, pulling out another file. "I've been having our newly hired deputies going through old boxes of evidence. It's a mess. Deputy Harris found these notes shoved into another case box." Beckett opened the file folder and produced several yellowed papers. "Witness statements that never made it into the official report. Statements that contradict the accidental drowning theory."

"Why now?" I asked. "Why reopen this after all these years?"

The sheriff's eyes met mine, and something in them made my stomach tighten.

"I've worked a lot of homicides," he said. "And I know when I look at a case file and two and two don't add up to four. I need people who know this island's history, who understand its dynamics, and who aren't afraid to ask uncomfortable questions."

"People who aren't on the official payroll," Walt added shrewdly.

Sheriff Beckett didn't deny it. "I'm new here. There are connections I might miss, histories I don't know."

"And if it turns out a former sheriff was involved in a cover-up, it could reflect badly on the current department," Bea concluded.

"There's more," Sheriff Beckett said quietly. "Elizabeth Calvert's father is still alive. Cancer. Doctors give him weeks at best. His last wish is to know what really happened to his daughter."

I felt a lump form in my throat. This wasn't just about solving a case—it was about giving a dying man peace.

"So what exactly are you asking us to do?" I questioned, gesturing at the file. "We're not detectives."

"Speak for yourself, dear," Bea interjected, patting my hand. "I was an investigative journalist for years before I decided the social column had the juicier stories."

"I want you to review the case file and the evidence," he explained. "Talk to people who were around back then. See if memories have loosened with time, if people are more willing to speak now that Milton is behind bars. Retrace the steps of the investigating officer."

"Should be interesting," Hank said. "Milton's reach is far, even from the state penitentiary. He's still got more supporters than he should around here."

Deidre nodded. "A lot of people benefited from his arrangements."

"What's our operational timeline?" Walt asked, getting down to business.

"I can give you three weeks," Beckett said. "That's how long I can keep this under the radar before questions start getting asked."

"And our authority?" Hank inquired, ever the judge.

"None, officially," he admitted. "You're temporarily deputized volunteers having conversations. I'll handle anything that requires actual law enforcement."

"What about interference?" Dottie asked. "There will be those who won't want old cases reopened."

Sheriff Beckett's expression turned serious. "Her father wants it. But that's also why we're keeping this quiet. It's why I've brought you all in on this instead of bringing in outside investigators. An outsider would stick out like a sore thumb."

"And we're practically invisible," Bea said, cackling. "Nobody pays attention to old people asking questions. Especially around here. Everyone is nosy. And so little happens around here that the past might as well be the present."

"And me?" I asked, still not sure why I was included. "What's my role in all this?"

"You're essential," the sheriff said, his eyes meeting mine directly. "You're the legs of this operation."

"The legs?" I repeated.

"You've got youth on your side," Walt explained matter-of-factly. "You can cover ground faster than we can."

"And you can go places we can't without raising suspicion," Dottie added. "People talk to you differently."

"Not to mention your tea shop gives us legitimate cover for meetings," Deidre pointed out.

Bea patted my hand. "Face it, dear. You've just been drafted as our field agent."

I looked at Sheriff Beckett, who nodded. "I need you out there with them. Sometimes on your own, sometimes accompanying one of them."

"Plus you can run if necessary," Walt added pragmatically. "My sprinting days ended with the Reagan administration."

I couldn't deny a flicker of excitement at the thought of my involvement in the case. After ten years of predictable routines, I was ready for something different.

"So," Sheriff Beckett continued, looking around at our unlikely group, "are you in?"

The Silver Sleuths exchanged glances, some unspoken agreement passing between them in the way that only people who've known each other for decades can communicate. I found myself holding my breath, caught up in a moment that suddenly felt like a turning point—not just for the case, but for me.

"We're in," Walt declared, speaking for all of them.

I nodded, surprisingly certain of my answer. "I'm in too."

As I looked around the table at this band of senior citizen sleuths and the mysterious sheriff who'd brought us together, I realized I'd just agreed to dig up secrets that had been deliberately buried for decades. Secrets that powerful people would prefer stayed hidden. Secrets worth killing for.

What had I just gotten myself into?

WHEN YOU OPEN A TEA SHOP AT THE CRACK OF DAWN, midnight is practically the middle of the night. So when my doorbell rang just after midnight my first instinct was to pull the pillow over my head and pretend I hadn't heard it.

But then it rang again, more insistently this time, followed by three sharp knocks.

Chowder, who had been sprawled across half my bed despite his diminutive size, raised his wrinkled head and gave a half-hearted woof that clearly meant, "You're the human, you deal with this."

"Thanks for the support," I muttered, pushing back the covers and fumbling for my vintage peach silk robe with the extravagant feather trim. I slipped it on over my matching peach nightgown, the familiar weight of the silk a small comfort in the midnight darkness. I cinched it tightly at the waist and stumbled toward the stairs, pushing a mass of tangled blond curls out of my face.

By the time I reached my front door, I was awake enough to be properly annoyed. I peeked through the sidelight window, ready to give the midnight intruder a piece of my mind.

And there stood Sheriff Dash Beckett, looking tense and alert, with something tucked under his arm.

I pulled open the door just enough to peer out at him. "Somebody better have died."

His eyebrows rose slightly. "Excuse me?"

"The only reason you should be showing up at my door after midnight is if there was a murder. And even then, I'm not exactly qualified."

The corner of his mouth twitched. "No murder. Not yet, anyway."

I narrowed my eyes. "Are you threatening me, Sheriff?"

"Dash," he corrected. "And it sounds like you're threatening me." His grin widened. "Woke up on the wrong side of the bed?"

I crossed my arms over my chest, suddenly aware of how the silk of my robe clung to me in the night air. A traitorous heat crept up my neck at his proximity in the darkness—a heat that had nothing to do with the temperature and everything to do with the intensity of his gaze.

"Do you have any idea what time it is?" I managed, hoping my voice sounded steadier than it felt. My heart was suddenly performing a jazz drumbeat against my ribs, and I found myself fixating on the scar along his jawline, wondering how it would feel beneath my fingertips.

The thought ambushed me so suddenly that I nearly gasped. Where had that come from? I took a small step backward, trying to put distance between us that might cool whatever this was.

"No clue," he answered without checking his watch, those dark eyes still studying me with an attention that made my skin prickle with awareness. "I've pretty much been working twenty-hour days since I took over the job. May I come in? This is…sensitive."

It was then that I noticed his tension—the tight set of his jaw, the careful way his eyes scanned the street behind him. And I suddenly realized what this must look like—the town's new sheriff on a single woman's doorstep after midnight. Mrs. Pembroke lived on the opposite corner from me and she could see down our entire street from her drawing room window. She was known to suffer from insomnia and treated neighborhood surveillance as an Olympic sport.

"Get in here," I said, opening the door wider and practically yanking him inside by his sleeve, ignoring the electric current that seemed to jump from his arm to my hand. I shut the door quickly behind him, but not before catching a glimpse of a light flicking on in Mrs. Pembroke's house. "Brilliant. Just brilliant."

"Problem?" he asked, standing in my front hall like he wasn't quite sure what to do with himself. His presence seemed to shrink the space, making my normally spacious entryway feel suddenly intimate.

"You just guaranteed we'll be the main topic of conversation at Grits and Giggles by breakfast." I sighed, tightening my robe's belt again, painfully conscious of how I must look—hair a mess, dressed in my nightgown and robe. Not that I cared what Sheriff Beckett thought of my appearance. Not at all.

Yet even as I told myself this, I could feel my pulse fluttering at the base of my throat like a trapped moth, my breath coming just a little quicker than normal. Patrick had never made me feel so bewilderingly off kilter, so aware of every inch of my skin. The realization brought a sharp pang of guilt that twisted beneath my ribs.

Ten years a widow, and suddenly I was behaving like a teenager with her first crush—all because of a man who probably made all the women on Grimm Island feel this way with nothing more than that intense gaze and the quiet confidence he wore as comfortably as his badge.

"So what's so important it couldn't wait until a decent hour? At my tea shop. Where I work. In public," I said, focusing on irritation to mask the confusing symphony of reactions his presence was orchestrating in my body.

In response, he held out what I now saw was a worn leather-bound book. "This."

I took it gingerly, and as our fingers brushed in the exchange, a shiver ran up my arm, spreading across my shoulders like spilled water. I hoped he hadn't noticed, but the slight narrowing of his eyes suggested otherwise.

The binding was cracked and faded, the once-white pages yellowed with age. "What is it?"

"Elizabeth Calvert's diary."

That woke me up like an ice bucket challenge. "Her diary? Where did you—"

"Found it hidden in evidence storage. Behind a false panel in a filing cabinet that looked like it hadn't been opened since before I was born."

I stared at the journal in my hands, suddenly aware I was holding the private thoughts of a dead woman. "This wasn't in the case file."

"No, it wasn't," he confirmed, his voice grim. "Which raises some interesting questions, don't you think?"

"Why bring it to me?" I asked.

"I need you to read it. Immediately." He glanced toward the windows. "I can't be seen with it, and I can't take it back to the station."

I frowned. "Why not?"

"Because I technically shouldn't have removed it from evidence," he admitted. "Though I'm not sure it matters since it was never admitted as evidence in the first place. And because I don't know who I can trust at the department. Deputies Harris and Jackson have been working with me to sort through everything. They're not from the island and I hired them, so for now, I'm trusting them. But I've got thirty-eight other deputies who I inherited from Milton."

The gravity of what he was saying sank in. "You think someone there is involved in the cover-up."

He didn't confirm or deny, but his silence was answer enough.

"Coffee," I decided. "I need coffee before I can process any of this. Come on."

I led him through to the kitchen, where Chowder had already waddled his way after us, looking thoroughly put out about having his beauty sleep interrupted.

"Don't give me that look," I told Chowder as he snorted indignantly. "This wasn't my idea."

Dash watched our interaction with something like amusement. "Does he understand everything you say to him?"

"For the most part," I said, filling his water bowl since he was up anyway. "He's a very intelligent dog."

I busied myself with the coffee maker.

"You know," he said, breaking the awkward silence, "Since the neighbors are already talking, we might as well give them something real to talk about."

I nearly dropped the coffee scoop. "Excuse me?"

"Dinner," he clarified, and I could swear there was a hint of a smile playing at the corner of his mouth. "Tomorrow night. If you're free."

I turned to face him, coffee forgotten. "Like a date?"

"We don't have to call it that if it makes you uncomfortable," he said. "We could just call it dinner."

I studied him for a moment, trying to decide if he was serious. He met my gaze steadily, and I realized with a little jolt that he was completely sincere.

"I...ahh...haven't really dated," I said lamely.

"Have you eaten dinner?"

If a hole had opened up in the floor I would have gladly fallen through it, never to be seen again.

"I'll think about it," I finally said, turning back to the coffee. "After I've had caffeine."

He chuckled, a warm sound that seemed to surprise even him. "Fair enough."

Ten minutes later, we were seated at my kitchen table, steaming mugs of coffee between us, the diary laid out like a time bomb waiting to detonate. Chowder had settled at Dash's feet, the traitor, looking up adoringly whenever Dash absentmindedly reached down to scratch behind his ears.

I opened the diary carefully, mindful of its age. The first page had *Property of Elizabeth Anne Calvert* written in looping, girlish handwriting.

"She was twenty-two," Dash said quietly.

I nodded and began to flip through the pages. The early entries were what you'd expect from a young woman—complaints about professors and assignments, sorority parties and guys she'd dated but that never seemed to last long. She wasn't interested in college boys. She wanted someone who was mature and knew something about the world. There were more pages filled with her excitement about getting accepted into graduate school, and more gossip about friends. She never used their names. Only initials. But as I reached the entries from the weeks before her death, the tone changed dramatically.

"Listen to this," I said.

*Met with J again today. He says it's too dangerous, that I should let it go. But how can I? What they're doing isn't just wrong, it's criminal. The whole island is built on lies.*

Dash leaned forward. "What date is that entry?"

"July 2, 1996," I said. "Two weeks before she died."

I flipped forward a few pages and found another troubling entry.

*Sometimes I think I'm being followed. M's car was parked outside the library again today. Just sitting there. When I came out, he drove away without a word. Do they know? Have they figured out what I found?*

"M could be Milton," I said, frowning. "The former sheriff."

Dash nodded. "That makes sense."

I scanned the entry again. "As for J…I have no idea. I was just a toddler back then." I tapped my fingers on the table. "I've heard stories about the island's politics from that era, but it's all secondhand information."

"The Silver Sleuths might know," Dash suggested.

"Oh, they definitely will," I said, smiling slightly. "If there was a prominent J in 1996, they'll know exactly who it was and what they were hiding."

I continued reading, growing increasingly disturbed by Elizabeth's final entries.

*The men who run this island—they think they're untouchable. But I have proof now. Proof that would burn everything down. J says I'm being dramatic, that I should just leave town, go to Duke early and forget what I found. But he doesn't understand. This isn't just about politics or money. People died.*

That last entry was dated July 10, 1996—three days before her body was found floating in the harbor.

"She knew something," I said, looking up at Dash. "Something big enough to get her killed."

"But what?" he asked, reaching for the diary.

Before he could take the diary, my phone rang, startling us both.

I held up my phone so he could see the caller ID and then I answered.

"Deidre," I said. "Is everything okay?"

"I was about to ask you the same thing," she said. "Mrs. Pembroke just called. Says the sheriff's car has been parked outside your house since midnight."

I closed my eyes. "Of course she did."

"She seems to think you're in some kind of trouble. Are you in trouble, dear? Because I can call Walt—"

"I'm fine," I said, cutting her off. "Sheriff Beckett is here on…case business."

There was a beat of silence. "At midnight?"

"Yes."

"And did this case business require you to wear your nightgown, or was that just a bonus for the sheriff?"

I felt my face heat. "How does she even know what I'm—" I stopped. "Never mind. I'll explain tomorrow at the shop."

"We'll be there early," she promised, then added in a whisper, "And Mabel, dear? You might want to close your bedroom curtains. Mrs. Pembroke has her binoculars out."

I hung up and turned to Dash, who was failing to hide his amusement. "This is why I don't date," I muttered.

Dash raised an eyebrow. "The rumor mill works quickly here."

"You have no idea." I stood up, suddenly aware of how intimate this scene must appear—the two of us at my kitchen table in the dim midnight light, me in my nightgown and robe. "I need to try and get some sleep. I have to be up to open the shop in a couple of hours."

"Keep the diary with you," he said, coming to his feet. "Keep it hidden. I'll call you tomorrow to discuss what you find."

I nodded, clutching the diary. "What are you going to do?"

"Go home and get some sleep. It's the middle of the night."

I couldn't help the growl that came from low in my throat. Arrogant man.

He grinned at me and I stumbled over my own feet as I followed him toward the front door. That grin was a powerful weapon.

At the door, he paused. "Lock this behind me. And be careful, Mabel. Whoever killed Elizabeth might still be on this island."

"Cheery thought to end my night," I said dryly.

"Just being thorough." He glanced out the sidelight window. "Mrs. Pembroke is still watching."

"She'll be disappointed. No handcuffs or scandalous goodbye."

A hint of a smile touched his lips. "Good night, Mrs. McCoy."

"Good night, Sheriff," I replied.

I locked the door behind him and leaned against it, watching through the window as he drove away and humming Patsy Cline's "Walkin' After Midnight" under my breath. Chowder sat at my feet, his expression distinctly judgmental.

"Don't look at me like that," I told him. "It's just business."

His snort clearly communicated his disbelief.

"We've got work to do," I said, looking down at the diary in my hands. "And I've got a feeling things are about to get complicated."

# CHAPTER
# FIVE

I'D JUST REACHED THE BOTTOM OF THE STAIRS AT A quarter to five, dressed in my favorite yellow swing dress with white piping and pearl buttons. Chowder clicked down the stairs after me in his yellow vest and bow tie.

*"It don't mean a thing, if it ain't got that swing…shoo bop, shoo bop, shoo bop, shoo bop, shoo bop, shoo bop, shoo bop, shoo bop."*

I was trying to perk myself up after only a couple of hours of sleep, and I was praying the concealer I'd applied liberally was doing its job.

My phone rang just as I reached the mudroom to collect my handbag and keys—I decided to drive to work after Dash's warning. I didn't recognize the number.

"Hello?" I answered, wedging the phone between my ear and shoulder as I slipped on my white sandals.

"Sorry to call so early," Dash said.

"I should've known it was you," I said, scowling. "It's not even five o'clock in the morning. How did you get my number?"

"I'm a cop," he said dryly.

My lips pursed and I opened the mudroom door for Chowder. "You saw me three hours ago. What could you have possibly forgotten to say that you couldn't say in normal daylight hours? I thought you were going home to sleep? I thought—"

"Mabel," he said, cutting me off. "Listen, I need to—"

The line went dead mid-sentence.

"Sheriff?" I said, checking to make sure the call was connected. "Dash?"

Nothing.

A tendril of unease worked its way up my spine. I tried calling back, but it went straight to voicemail. Chowder whined softly at my feet, sensing my disquiet.

I unlocked the door of my mint-condition powder-blue 1959 Karmann Ghia convertible and Chowder hopped onto the white leather interior, making himself comfortable in the passenger seat.

I looked at my phone one more time, hoping to hear the phone ring again, but it stayed silent.

"It's probably nothing," I told him, not entirely convinced myself. "Dead zone. Or maybe his battery died."

I slid into the car and opened the garage door, and then I turned the key, listening to the purr of the engine as it came to life.

Chowder woofed softly and I looked over at him, so dapper in his bow tie. "You're right. Maybe he went back to sleep. He probably doesn't get enough rest. I'm sure being sheriff is a stressful job."

But the unease from the phone call didn't leave me.

The early morning was still dark, streetlights casting pools of light on the empty roads as I drove the short distance to The Perfect Steep. I parked behind the shop, unlocked the back door, and went through my normal opening routine on autopilot—turning on ovens, measuring loose tea leaves, and setting out supplies for the day's scones. My mind was still on Elizabeth's diary and Dash's strange call.

I'd just pulled the first batch of lemon scones from the oven when Walt knocked on the glass window of the back door, his Navy veteran cap perched precisely on his silver hair.

"You're early even by Walt-standard time," I said as I let him in. "Is everything all right?"

"Not here," he said quietly, glancing around despite the empty kitchen. "Too exposed."

I set down my oven mitts and led him into the small office at the back of the shop, closing the door behind us.

"Something's happened," Walt said once we were alone. "There was a break-in at the sheriff's office last night. Evidence room ransacked."

My stomach dropped. "How do you know this?"

Walt tapped the police scanner clipped to his belt. "Never leave home without it. Been monitoring police frequencies since '89. Heard the call come in about twenty minutes ago. Officers discovered the break-in when they arrived for the morning shift."

"So it happened sometime overnight?" I asked, trying to piece together the timeline.

Walt nodded. "Between when the night shift left and the morning shift arrived. Sheriff Beckett is down almost a dozen officers since Milton's arrest. Three more were arrested with him and several resigned, so Sheriff Beckett is working short staffed. They've been closing the sheriff's office for a couple of hours each night because there aren't enough officers to fill the gap. The break-in happened then."

I opened my bag and carefully unwrapped the leather-bound journal. "Sheriff Beckett brought me this last night. Elizabeth Calvert's diary. He found it hidden in the evidence room and didn't trust leaving it there."

Walt's eyes widened as he stared at the diary. "I was wondering what he was doing at your house so late. Deidre called me to let me know you weren't being harmed."

I shook my head in disbelief. "Good grief."

"You're a young woman who lives alone," he said. "It was good of Mrs. Pembroke to call and let us know. Eye-witness accounts are very important."

I narrowed my eyes at him. "Did you drive by my house?"

"You should get blinds for your kitchen windows," he said. "I could see the two of you plain as day."

I gasped. "You have to look over my fence to see in my kitchen windows!"

He nodded solemnly. "If I can do it, that means anyone can."

"Good grief," I muttered again. Walt was eighty years old. He could have broken a hip. That was the problem hanging out with senior citizens—none of them realized they were as old as they were.

He patted me on the shoulder like he was afraid I was going into hysterics. "That was wise of the sheriff to bring you the diary," Walt said. "He's got good instincts. That's something that can't be taught."

I let out a slow breath. There was no reason to be aggravated with Walt or any of them. The people of Grimm Island were who they were —a bunch of stubborn, know-it-all busybodies—and there was nothing that would change them save the Rapture.

"Sheriff Beckett said the diary was hidden in a false panel in a filing cabinet in the evidence room." I ran my fingers over the worn cover. "Someone must have discovered it was missing."

"That was fast work," Walt said. "And now the mayor knows about it, and word on the street is he's furious. I heard Mayor Cromwell called an emergency council meeting with Sheriff Beckett."

I remembered the abrupt end to our phone call earlier. "Sheriff Beckett tried calling me this morning, but the call cut off. I thought it was just a bad connection, but now…"

"Now we have to wonder what happened," Walt finished, his eyes sharp with concern.

"The diary must be what they're looking for," I said, clutching it tightly. "What should we do?"

Walt's expression grew serious. "First, we need to make a copy. If you trust me with it I'll take it over to the library and use the copy room. They open at seven, but hardly anyone is there first thing in the morning except old Mr. Verlander. He likes to have his coffee and a muffin at his desk every morning, so I don't think he'll give me too much trouble. I promise I'll bring it right back."

I bit my lip nervously. "I do trust you. But if someone broke into the sheriff's office looking for the diary then they might be willing to hurt whoever has it."

"Then I'll make copies for all of us," he said. "He can't hurt us all, and the more copies we have the more power we take from him."

I nodded and handed over the diary. He immediately put it in the inside zipper pocket of his windbreaker and zipped it up.

"Okay, but if you're not back in an hour I'm closing up and coming to look for you."

"Deal," he said. "I think we should call an emergency meeting of the Silver Sleuths. But not here—too many eyes. Your house, tonight."

I nodded, the seriousness of the situation sinking in. "I'll let the others know."

Walt headed for the door, then paused. "Take a different route home tonight. And Mabel?" His eyes were steel serious. "Watch your back."

With that cheery advice, he left, and I returned to my scones, my mind whirling. I went through the motions of opening the shop and serving my morning regulars, all while keeping an eye on the door, hoping Dash would walk in.

He didn't. But I'd at least felt the tension leave my shoulders when Walt had walked back in, almost exactly an hour later, and passed me the diary like we were doing an undercover drug deal.

When I still hadn't heard from Dash by midafternoon, I took matters into my own hand. I put the *Back in Fifteen Minutes* sign on the door, left Chowder napping in the window seat to stand guard, and drove to the sheriff's office.

The place was buzzing like an overturned beehive. Deputy Mark Reynolds was at the front desk, looking harried. When he spotted me, his usual easy smile flickered briefly through the stress.

"Mabel," he said, his voice warmer than his professional demeanor would typically allow. "This isn't the best time for your afternoon tea delivery."

"I need to speak with Sheriff Beckett," I said, trying to peek past him into the main office area. I happened to notice a hallway at the far backside of the large square room where desks were shoved together, and it was cordoned off with yellow crime scene tape.

Reynolds lowered his voice, leaning slightly over the desk. "He's been in meetings all day with the mayor and county commissioner. Something big's happening." His eyes showed genuine concern. "Everything okay at the shop? You look worried."

"Just need to talk to the sheriff," I said, not wanting to reveal too much, even to a friendly face.

He studied me for a moment, then sighed. "I can try to get a message to him when he's free. You know I'd help if I could, Mabel."

As Reynolds spoke, the door behind him swung open, and Deputy Larson stepped out, his perpetual scowl deepening when he saw me. Where Reynolds had been on the force for decades, a constant in the island's law enforcement landscape, Larson was relatively new—hired during the Milton administration about ten years ago. He was hard edged where Reynolds was soft, all sharp angles and rigid posture. The creases in his uniform were military precise, his dark buzz cut equally severe.

"Another tourist lost her way?" Larson asked.

"Mrs. McCoy's looking for the sheriff," Reynolds explained, his tone noticeably cooler toward his colleague.

"Join the club," Larson said, cutting his eyes toward me. "Seems our fearless leader had more important things to do than explain why someone broke into the evidence room on his watch."

The hostility in his voice was unmistakable.

"That's enough, Larson," Reynolds admonished quietly, his protective instinct flaring briefly as he glanced at me.

Larson's jaw tightened, but he backed off, turning his attention to me. "What's your business with Beckett, anyway? Someone file a complaint about those relics you sell?"

"I run a tea shop," I corrected, forcing a pleasant smile. "If you have questions about my shop you should come in or ask Jennifer. She comes in on Mondays and Thursdays every week like clockwork."

Reynolds' eyes got big and he went into a coughing fit, though I could've sworn I heard some laughter in there.

Larson colored slightly, and I knew I might have gone too far, which was not at all like me. Proper Southern women weren't confrontational. But there was something about Larson that just rubbed me the wrong way, and the words popped out of my mouth before they'd barely formed in my brain.

Everyone on the island knew Larson and his wife were trying to "work things out." But it didn't take a rocket scientist to know that wasn't going to happen as long as his cruiser was parked on the side street of Jennifer Newsom's home twice a week.

Something flickered across Larson's face—so brief I almost missed it—but I had a feeling I'd just made an enemy.

Reynolds shifted uncomfortably, giving me an apologetic look. "I'll tell the sheriff you stopped by. Maybe try back later? Or I can drop by the shop when my shift ends if you need something urgent."

"You're the best," I said, not ready to leave empty handed. I gestured toward the crime scene tape visible in the back. "What happened here? The whole island's buzzing with rumors."

Reynolds hesitated, then leaned forward. "Break-in last night. Evidence room hit. Sheriff's had us all running in circles trying to figure out what was taken."

"Specifically from the cold case section," Larson added, watching me closely.

My expression remained neutral, but internally my pulse quickened.

"When will he be back?" I pressed, deliberately ignoring Larson's bait.

"No idea," Reynolds sighed, his familiar face showing genuine regret. "But the mayor looked ready to skin someone alive when they left. Never seen him so angry."

Larson checked his watch with exaggerated impatience. "I've got patrol. Reynolds, make sure Mrs. McCoy signs the visitor log before she leaves." He glanced back at me, his eyes cold. "Department policy. We keep track of everyone who comes around asking questions these days."

The threat was subtle but unmistakable.

After he left, Reynolds seemed to deflate slightly. "Don't mind him, Mabel. Larson's been on edge since the break-in—we all have."

"Thanks," I said, turning to leave. "If you see Sheriff Beckett, please tell him I need to speak with him."

"Will do," Reynolds promised, already turning to answer a ringing phone. "See you tomorrow for my usual," he called after me.

"See you then," I replied, though my mind was already racing ahead to what the break-in might mean.

I hurried back to my car, a sense of urgency propelling me. As I pulled out of the parking lot, I noticed a dark sedan I hadn't seen before, idling across the street with its engine running. The windows were tinted, making it impossible to see who was inside, but something about it sent a chill straight down my spine.

"Not a coincidence," I whispered, my mouth gone suddenly desert dry. The reality of being followed—actually followed—hit me like a physical blow, turning my insides to ice water. This wasn't some movie thriller. This was my life, and someone was watching me because of a decades-old diary.

The sedan stayed with me for two more turns, and with each one, my heart hammered harder against my ribs until I could feel the pulse in my throat like a trapped bird. My palms grew slick against the steering wheel, leaving damp prints on the polished surface. A prickling heat crawled up the back of my neck, while a contradictory chill spread through my limbs. I forced myself to breathe—in through my nose, out through my mouth—but each breath felt shallow and insufficient, like I was trying to pull air through a coffee stirrer.

*"Yes, we have no bananas, we have no bananas today!"* I sang at the top of my lungs, forcing a cheerfulness I didn't feel. The old tune was my go-to for anxiety, but today the forced optimism only highlighted my fear, sending a violent shiver down my spine.

On a hunch, I took a deliberate wrong turn instead of heading directly back to the shop, my fingers trembling so badly I had to grip the wheel with both hands to steady them. I checked my rearview mirror without being too obvious. Sure enough, the sedan pulled out and followed, maintaining a precise three-car distance.

A wave of nausea rolled through my stomach, acidic and insistent. I swallowed hard against it, tasting bitter fear at the back of my throat.

The familiar streets of Grimm Island suddenly seemed alien and threatening, each turn a potential trap, each intersection a decision that might lead me closer to whoever was inside that car. My vintage Karmann Ghia, usually my pride and joy, now felt fragile and exposed —a powder-blue target moving through hostile territory.

Heart pounding, I managed to lose the sedan by cutting through the grocery store parking lot and doubling back. My ears rang with rushing blood, and I found myself checking the mirror every few seconds, flinching at shadows and slowing cars. By the time I returned to the tea shop, the top of my dress was sticking to my back with cold sweat, and my legs felt rubbery and unreliable as I hurried inside, locked the door behind me, and withdrew to the office where I could think. Chowder followed and lay down on my toes to show his support, his solid warmth gradually helping to anchor me back to reality.

The break-in, Dash's abruptly ended call, and now someone following me—it all had to be connected to Elizabeth's diary. I pulled it from my bag and carefully opened it again, this time focusing on the final entries I hadn't had time to fully examine earlier.

*If anything happens to me, the proof is in the lighthouse. They'll never think to look where I've hidden it. J doesn't even know. It's safer that way.*

The lighthouse. Elizabeth had hidden something in the lighthouse.

I stood and moved to the window, where I could just make out the distant silhouette of the Grimm Island Lighthouse standing sentinel at the harbor entrance. Whatever secret Elizabeth had discovered—whatever had gotten her killed—the proof was still there.

Waiting to be found.

Whether that would be by me or by whoever had been following me remained to be seen.

# CHAPTER
# SIX

BY THE TIME I CLOSED THE SHOP AND HEADED HOME, THE sun was beginning to set, casting long shadows across the island. Following Walt's advice, I took a circuitous route, watching carefully for the dark sedan in my rearview mirror. My eyes darted between the road ahead and the reflection behind me, tension coiling in my shoulders with each passing minute.

When I arrived home, I pulled into the garage and waited for the door to close completely before getting out. Chowder hopped down and immediately began his security patrol of the premises, sniffing along the perimeter with the seriousness of a trained K-9 unit. He paused at the side door, barking once to be let into the yard, where he promptly celebrated our safe arrival by lifting his leg on my prized hydrangeas.

"Really? Those are just starting to bloom," I said with a sigh.

I unlocked the door, stepped into the mudroom, and secured the dead bolt behind us. Then I immediately started checking windows and drawing curtains, humming "Mind Your Own Business" by Hank Williams under my breath. Nothing like a pointed musical warning to set the mood for a clandestine meeting about murder.

The phone rang just as I finished closing the living room drapes.

"Mabel, dear, is everything all right?" Mrs. Pembroke's voice crackled through the line, her concern as transparent as plastic wrap. "I couldn't help but notice you're drawing all your curtains. At six thirty in the evening. On a Saturday night. You never close your curtains."

"Everything's fine, Mrs. Pembroke," I said, moving to close another set of curtains while I talked. "Just getting a headache and wanted to keep the light out."

"A headache? Are you sure you're not preparing for a gentleman caller? I saw the sheriff's car drive by twice earlier."

I rolled my eyes. "No gentleman callers, Mrs. Pembroke."

"Well, if you need anything—aspirin, a casserole, an alibi—you just let me know."

After hanging up and changing into my favorite high-waisted navy swing trousers with white side buttons, a soft white button-down, and white tennis shoes, I tied my hair back with a red scarf. Comfort with a dash of vintage—my at-home armor for facing conspiracy.

I had just finished setting out glasses for Bea's inevitable bourbon when I heard someone pull into my driveway, followed by the sound of multiple car doors slamming.

"Showtime," I muttered.

The doorbell chimed three times in quick succession—a pattern that could only be Walt.

I opened the door to find all five Silver Sleuths on my porch, looking like they were ready for battle.

"You're late," Walt announced, checking his watch as he breezed past me.

"I live here, Walt. I can't be late to my own house," I replied, accepting Deidre's kiss on the cheek.

"Did you know Mrs. Pembroke's at her window with what appears to be opera glasses?" Deidre asked.

"She said it was for my protection," I said, trying not to grimace.

Dottie shuffled in behind Deidre and handed me a tin of home-made cookies. "Those contain dark chocolate. Good for the heart."

Her hair was as black as an inkpot and I wondered if she'd been to the salon earlier in the day.

Everyone had been to my home enough times that they felt comfortable going through my cabinets for plates and cups. Bea swept in with a large casserole dish of jambalaya, and Walt arrived carrying what appeared to be surveillance equipment.

"Walt made us all meet at the library and condense to one vehicle in case we were being followed," Dottie explained as they settled around my dining room table. "Took us twenty minutes to get here because he took every back road on the island."

After everyone had filled their plates with Bea's excellent jambalaya, Walt pulled out a manila envelope and slid it across the table to me like a scene from *Mission: Impossible*. Nervous laughter bubbled up inside of me, but I managed to tamp it down so no one thought I was insane.

"Your copy so you don't have to use the original," he said. "I delivered everyone else's copy earlier so they had time to review it before this briefing."

"And what fascinating reading it was," Bea said, her brash voice cutting through the room. "Poor girl. So young, so bright. A woman who knew what she wanted and what she liked." Bea waggled her eyebrows. "Especially in bed. Some of those pages were quite racy."

"She had the makings of a fine romance novelist," Deidre agreed. "I read the juicy parts twice."

"Who cares about that crap?" Dottie said. "Some poor fella whose name starts with C is cemented in history as an enthusiastic, but quick, lover. And the guy whose name starts with a J was a stallion." Dottie dug into her jambalaya. "I skimmed most of those pages so I could get to the good stuff. That last entry about the lighthouse gave me chills," she said, shivering delicately. "Poor girl was scared down to her toes."

"Which is why we need to keep these diaries hidden," Walt said. "If Elizabeth hid something in the lighthouse then we can bet it's something her killer doesn't want us to find. Trust no one."

"Not even each other?" Bea asked, arching a perfectly penciled eyebrow.

"Especially not each other," Walt replied without a hint of irony.

"Bunch of baloney, Walt," Dottie muttered. "Maybe you need to ask Doc Givens to adjust your medication before you turn into a full-blown conspiracy theorist."

"My medication is fine, thank you very much," Walt said stiffly.

"Oh, lighten up, Walt," Deidre said. "You know she's teasing. And obviously those of us in this room can trust each other. Right?"

Deidre gave Walt a pointed stare and he glowered at her, caught between his training and good Southern manners. His eyebrows came together like a long bushy caterpillar and he sucked in his cheeks as he stared Deidre down.

"Fine," he said. "I'll trust on a case-by-case basis."

"Good," Deidre said. "Now we can get down to business." She wasted no time clearing the table and spreading blueprints across the mahogany surface, anchoring the corners with crystal candlesticks that had been a wedding gift from Patrick's side of the family.

"The lighthouse plans," she announced. "Original construction from 1879 and renovations from 2002."

"Six years after Elizabeth died," I noted.

"Exactly," Deidre nodded. "She says in her diary she hid something there in 1996. We need to figure out what spaces might have existed then but been changed during renovation."

"Or what might still be there that no one's noticed," Dottie added.

I turned through the copied pages Walt had given me until I got to the section I was looking for and then I read—"*If anything happens to me, the proof is in the lighthouse. They'll never think to look where I've hidden it. J doesn't even know. It's safer that way.*

"So we know she hid something in the lighthouse, but I'm more curious to know who J is. If we can figure it out maybe he could give us some clues as to what we're looking for."

"Oh, that's easy," Bea said immediately. "Jason Brooks. If I remember right, and I always do, they were seen together quite a lot that summer. There was a lot of speculation over their relationship, especially since she'd recently broken up with her boyfriend of several years. The Harrington boy."

"Harrington," I said, the name ringing a bell. "Clint Harrington?"

"The very same," Bea said. "Harrington Construction. Junior took over the business a few years after Elizabeth's death. Built this island into the juggernaut it is today."

"I guess now we know who C and J are," Dottie said, shaking her head. "Poor Clint."

Bea scoffed. "Poor Clint? You mean poor Brenda," she said, referring to his wife. "She's the one who has to be married to Mr. Speedy. No wonder the woman always looks so grumpy."

"Maybe he learned a thing or two over the last thirty years," Deidre said, though the frown on her face indicated she doubted it. "He was always a smart kid if I remember right."

"He's also rich, powerful, and connected," I said. "Was he close to Milton?"

"They detested each other," Walt said. "Which shows Harrington has a heck of a lot more sense than his father did. If I remember right old Clinton Sr. did some business with Milton in the early days. Land development stuff, but all that ended when the son took over."

"But he and Elizabeth were lovers," I said. "We can't take him off the suspect list. So what about Jason Brooks? I don't recognize that name."

"Ah, the stallion," Bea said lasciviously.

"You probably wouldn't recognize him," Hank said. "Brooks was the assistant DA for the island at that time. Young and brilliant. Good looking like a Kennedy. Built for politics. Wasn't he a distant cousin or whatnot of yours, Bea?"

"He was the cousin of my second husband Leonard's niece," Bea said offhandedly. "I don't think they were blood relatives, but at least he had a tie to the island so it gave him an in when he started at the DA's office. We should put him on the suspect list too, even though he is family. No allowances can be made. That's how Milton got in the pickle he was in."

"Among other things," Dottie said slyly. "I think the problem was his pickle was getting dipped in too many jars."

Deidre snorted out a laugh and Hank downright guffawed, slapping his hand on his knee until he turned red in the face. The corner of Walt's mouth quirked in what could have been a smile. I realized at that point how little I knew about the goings-on around the island.

"I just want it noted that I broke several scandals about Milton over the last forty years and the people on this island chose to ignore them," Bea said indignantly. "Told me I had no credibility because I was just a gossip columnist. Didn't I have pictures of him shimmying out the window of Sharon Carter's bedroom window? And the very next day all the charges against her son were dropped. Biggest drug dealer on the island and everyone knew it."

"Well, Milton's first wife must have believed your reporting," Deidre said. "Because everyone remembers the morning Lucinda Milton packed her bags into the sheriff's Cadillac and drove right through his prized flower beds on her way out of town."

"They lived next door to me," Dottie said. "I got a front row seat from my bedroom window. Of course, I got a front row seat to a lot of things happening in that house. Milton wasn't the only one sneaking in and out of windows in the middle of the night. Can't believe you missed that, Bea."

"Oh, I knew," Bea said, waving a hand. "But I always liked Lucinda. And figured she deserved what happiness she could get considering she had to wake up next to that bloated know-it-all of a man every morning. Roy Milton probably looked like a stuffed sausage naked. I couldn't help but feel sorry for her."

"Maybe if we could get back to more important matters," Walt said primly. "I want to know if Mabel has heard from our sheriff."

"Wouldn't mind seeing him naked," Bea muttered under her breath and I choked on my water.

I coughed and sputtered while Hank pounded on my back. "Not since his call cut off this morning," I replied, eyes watering. "I went by the station, but he was in meetings with the mayor."

"Probably getting his behind chewed over that break-in," Hank observed. "Mayor Cromwell's been looking for an excuse to undermine Beckett since he arrived. You know the county council went over Cromwell's head and appointed Beckett without his input after Milton was arrested. The mayor wanted to install one of his cronies, but the corruption ran too deep. You know Cromwell and Milton had been fishing buddies for decades."

"Dollars to donuts Cromwell loses the election in November," Dottie added. "Too much stink on him from Milton's scandal. No direct evidence against him, but mud sticks when you play in the pigpen too long."

"Cromwell knows it too," Bea said with a knowing nod. "That's what makes him dangerous. Nothing worse than a politician with nothing to lose."

"Speaking of dangerous," I said, lowering my voice despite being in my own home, "Someone tailed me today after I left the station. Dark sedan, tinted windows, the whole cliché."

Five pairs of wizened eyes widened simultaneously.

"Did you get a plate number?" Walt demanded, suddenly all business.

"No. I was a little busy trying to outmaneuver him."

"Amateur," he muttered.

Dottie patted his hand. "We can't all be James Bond in orthopedic shoes, Walt."

Walt looked like he might argue but couldn't quite deny the accuracy of her description.

"I can only assume it's connected to Elizabeth's diary," I said.

"Someone should talk to Jason Brooks," Hank said. "He's still an attorney in Charleston. If anyone knows what Elizabeth was investigating, it would be him."

"Sounds like you need to make a trip to Charleston, Mabel," Bea said, her bangles jingling as she reached for the bourbon bottle.

"Me? Why me?" I asked.

"You're the least conspicuous," Walt pointed out. "Young, attractive widow paying a courtesy call versus five senior citizens showing up asking questions about a decades-old death."

"I know Jason Brooks," Hank said, straightening in his chair. "He appeared in my courtroom from time to time. He's a good attorney. I could arrange an introduction, go with you as backup."

"Who's going to run my tea shop?" I asked. "I only have part-time help."

"We will," Dottie and Deidre said together, their smiles indicating they saw working at the tea shop a new adventure.

"Don't look at me, dear," Bea said. "I like being served. Not serving others. My husbands spoiled me rotten. I know where my giftings lie."

Since I actually wanted to keep customers and make money, I was fine with Bea bowing out of running the shop.

Just then, Chowder's head snapped up and he rolled to his feet.

Walt immediately went for the weapon he was undoubtedly hiding in his jacket. "Intruder," he whispered.

I held my breath as the distinctive sound of my mudroom door opening echoed through the house.

# CHAPTER
# SEVEN

A RUSH OF COOL EVENING AIR CARRIED WITH IT THE SCENT of cedar and leather.

"It's just me," Dash called out, his voice low and steady.

I let out a sigh of relief, but Walt's hand didn't leave his pocket.

Dash appeared in the doorway like a shadow materializing, dressed in a plain black T-shirt that stretched across his shoulders and jeans that had seen better days. His badge glinted on his belt and his weapon was holstered—the only signs of his official position. Gone was the pressed uniform I was accustomed to seeing him in. If I had to judge by the expression on his face and the set of his shoulders, I'd say his day probably hadn't been one of the better ones since he'd taken the job as sheriff.

My fingers fumbled with the teacup I was holding, nearly spilling its contents. The domesticity of him standing there in my dining room struck me with unexpected force, as if the sheriff had momentarily transformed into just a man—one whose presence suddenly made the room feel smaller, more confined.

Despite the exhaustion evident in the slight shadows beneath his eyes, there was a watchful intensity in his posture that made me think of the panthers that sometimes prowled the island's wildlife sanctuary —economical in movement, deliberate in stillness.

A flush crept across my collarbones, rising up my neck like an incoming tide. I turned away, busying myself with straightening papers on the table, hoping the dim evening light concealed the color I could feel blooming on my skin. My body was reacting to him in ways I hadn't experienced in years—hadn't allowed myself to experience. Every sense seemed heightened—the ticking of the grandfather clock suddenly too loud, the bourbon too fragrant, the room too warm.

"How did you get in?" I demanded, letting irritation coat my words to mask the flutter of nerves beneath. I needed the distance of formality between us, needed to remember that he was Sheriff Beckett, not the man whose hands I'd found myself watching when he held his coffee cup earlier that day.

"Parked three streets over, cut through the Wilsons' backyard, and hopped your fence," he said with casual confidence, as if scaling fences was standard procedure. He crouched to greet Chowder, who was beside himself with joy. "Your garden gnome with the sailor hat makes a convenient key holder."

My mouth fell open. "Captain Barnaby? You figured out how to open him?"

"Hey, I watch QVC late at night too," he said, rising to his full height. "Hollow ceramic figurines aren't exactly Fort Knox." In the soft light of my dining room, the angles of his face seemed sharper, more defined. "You might as well leave a key under the welcome mat."

I wanted to be properly outraged at his intrusion, at the presumption of finding my hidden key. Instead, I found myself wondering what other secrets of mine he could uncover with that watchful gaze. The thought sent a ripple of something dangerous down my spine—not quite fear, not quite anticipation, but a disconcerting blend of both.

Patrick had been steady, reliable, safe—his love as comfortable as a well-worn quilt. But there was nothing comfortable about the way Dash Beckett made me feel. His presence was like standing at the edge of deep water, the tension between staying safely on shore or diving into unknown depths.

"Who knew I needed a state-of-the-art security system on my garden decorations?" I retorted, clinging to indignation like a life preserver.

A hint of a smile played at the corner of his mouth, a brief crack in his otherwise guarded expression. That small softening of his features shouldn't have affected me, but it did—like catching a glimpse of something rare and unexpected.

"Oh, honestly," Bea interjected, eyeing Dash with unabashed appreciation as she passed him a tumbler of bourbon. "The man just scaled a fence in the dark to avoid detection. I'd say that deserves a drink rather than a lecture on garden ornament protocol."

Dash accepted the glass. "Thank you, ma'am."

"Oh, don't ma'am me, young man," Bea said with a delighted shimmy of her shoulders. "I'm still young enough to appreciate the view when it walks through the door."

Hank barked out a laugh. "The only thing you're too young for is that centurion cruise that leaves from the harbor next month."

"Hush, Hank," Bea said. "If you tell me I look anything but half my age then I'll start to think all that plastic surgery wasn't worth the money. And then I'd have married Randolph for nothing. What do you think, sugar?" Bea winked flirtatiously at Dash. "Did he do a good job?"

"Bea!" Deidre admonished, but her eyes sparkled with amusement. "You'll embarrass him."

"I don't embarrass easily," Dash said, taking the empty seat next to me.

He settled beside me, and I breathed in the scent of sandalwood and something more masculine. My hands suddenly felt clumsy and too large, the distance between our elbows measured in molecules rather than inches. After ten years of carefully maintained solitude, I'd forgotten how to navigate this particular form of proximity—the consciousness of another person occupying your space, breathing your air.

"Where have you been all day?" I asked, focusing on the blueprints rather than the barely there brush of his sleeve against mine as he leaned forward. The innocuous contact shouldn't have registered, certainly shouldn't have sent a current across my skin like static electricity, but my body seemed determined to betray me in new and mortifying ways. "Your call cut off mid-sentence this morning, and no one's heard from you since."

The humor in his eyes vanished, replaced by something harder, colder. When he spoke, his voice was controlled in a way that suggested he was carefully measuring each word.

"Mayor Cromwell and some of his friends on the city council have been taking turns trying to question my investigative priorities," he said, swirling the bourbon in his glass without drinking it. "Seems they think I orchestrated the break-in to drum up drama. They forget I don't answer to them."

"Did you?" Bea asked bluntly.

"Bea!" Deidre admonished.

"What? We're all thinking it." She turned to Dash without an ounce of shame. "Did you stage the break-in to cover taking the diary?"

"No," he said firmly, meeting her gaze. "The hidden panel where I found the diary was left open, so they know it's gone. Then they ransacked the room to make it look like part of a larger theft."

"How bad is it?" Hank asked.

"Bad enough. Evidence from three cases gone, filing cabinets ransacked. Professionally done—no prints, security cameras disabled." Dash's eyes found mine. "They're looking for the diary."

"I was tailed today," I told him, watching his expression darken. "Dark sedan followed me after I left the station this afternoon."

His jaw tightened. "That changes things. You're not safe here alone."

"I've got Chowder," I said, as the dog in question rolled onto his back at Dash's feet, stubby legs waving in the air. "He's very intimidating once you get past the ridiculous snoring and pathological need for belly rubs."

"I can see that," Dash replied, the corner of his mouth quirking up as he obliged Chowder with a quick scratch. "He'd definitely strike fear into the heart of any intruder with carryout food."

I smiled despite myself. It was almost disorienting how quickly he could shift from intense to charming and back again. The room felt warmer with him in it, and I wasn't sure if that was comforting or concerning.

"So," I said, clearing my throat and tapping the papers on the table, "Now that we're all caught up on break-ins and threats, we should probably talk about why we're really here. Elizabeth's last diary entry mentions the lighthouse. We need to search it."

"The lighthouse is county property under Coast Guard jurisdiction," Dash said. "We can't just walk in."

"Well, technically..." Deidre began, then stopped when we all looked at her. "I may have a key."

"You what?" I asked, nearly choking on my bourbon.

"I'm on the historical preservation committee," she explained. "We have access for documentation purposes."

"That's...convenient," Dash said slowly.

"I think the word you're looking for is illegal if we use it without authorization," Hank pointed out.

"Only if we get caught," Bea countered cheerfully.

"No one is breaking any laws," Dash stated firmly. "I can get us access officially. I'll file the paperwork for an evidence search."

"That could take days," Walt objected. "And it would alert whoever broke into the station."

"I have a better idea," I said, the plan forming as I spoke. "The historical society is hosting a fundraiser tomorrow night. Lighthouse tours are part of the package."

"We'd all need tickets," Dottie pointed out.

"I have tickets," I said. "Patrick served on the board. They still send me invitations every year."

"That could work," Dash conceded. "But it's still risky. The entire island social circle will be there."

"Which makes it the perfect cover," Walt countered. "No one would suspect us of searching for evidence at a public event."

"And who's going to notice a few senior citizens wandering away from a tour?" Deidre added. "We're practically invisible. People just see gray hair and assume we're confused."

"I've never had a gray hair on my head," Bea said, patting her flaming-red coiffure.

"God wouldn't know your real hair color if he had to pick it out of a lineup," Deidre said without malice.

"I can only bring one guest with my ticket," I said, looking around the table.

"It should be Dash," Walt said immediately. "He's got training."

"It absolutely should not be Dash," I countered. "Everyone on the island knows who he is. He'd stick out like a peacock at a penguin convention."

"I'll be there anyway," Dash explained. "The historical society sent me an invitation as soon as I took office. Apparently, the sheriff is always on their guest list for these fundraisers."

"How convenient," I said.

"For once, yes," he agreed. "I can mingle with the guests while keeping an eye on things. No one will question why I'm there."

"Deidre already has a ticket because she's a board member," I said.

"I have a ticket because I'm a donor," Hank said. "I donate to all kinds of things. I'm always getting invited places that have a dress code and want me to bring my checkbook. I never go, but I'll make an exception this once as long as I don't have to donate more money."

"I can get my own ticket," Bea announced, looking at her red manicured nails. "I still have connections. I'll show up about fifteen minutes late so no one thinks we're all together."

"Hogwash, Bea," Dottie said. "You know you like to make a grand entrance."

Bea smiled. "So what if I do?"

"That leaves Dottie and Walt who don't have tickets."

"I'm afraid I'm going to have to pass on attending the event," Walt said. "I've got plans tomorrow evening that can't be changed."

"What plans?" Bea asked nosily.

"Personal plans," Walt said pursing his lips.

That was probably the wrong thing to say. There wasn't a personal anything that Bea hadn't been able to find out.

"So that leaves Dottie," I said. "You can have my second ticket."

"Thank you, dear."

"And I'll pick you up," Hank told her. "I have to pass your house to get to the lighthouse."

I raised my brows at that, but didn't say anything. Hank and Dottie had been spending an awful lot of time together lately.

"Could you pick me up, dear?" Deidre asked me. "You know I don't drive as well at night as I used to."

"You don't drive as well in the daytime either," Walt said, "But you never bring that up."

"Hush, Walt," Deidre said, waving her hand at him.

"Of course," I said, knowing that Walt was right. Deidre was a terrible driver. "I'm happy to."

"You all need to be careful," Dash warned, suddenly serious. "If Elizabeth was killed because of what she discovered, whoever did it might still be on this island. And they've already shown they're willing to break into the sheriff's office to cover their tracks."

"Don't worry about us," Walt said confidently. "We've been handling ourselves since before you were born, son."

"We're always armed, you know," Bea added casually. "This is the South. Even my mailman wears an ankle holster."

"Please do not bring weapons to a public fundraiser," Dash said, looking alarmed.

"Can't make any promises, Sheriff," she said. "Everyone else will be armed too. A girl's got to protect herself."

"Have another sidecar, Bea," Dottie said. "You're scaring the sheriff."

"What about this Jason Brooks?" I asked, redirecting the conversation. "When should we talk to him?"

"Let's get through tomorrow night first," Dash said. "If we find the evidence, we'll need it before approaching someone with his connections."

The planning continued over second helpings of jambalaya and refills of bourbon. I noticed Dash checking his watch periodically, a slight tension in his shoulders that hadn't been there before.

"Something wrong?" I asked quietly while the others argued about whether Dottie's arthritic knee would prevent her from climbing the lighthouse stairs.

"Just cautious," he replied, his voice low. "I wasn't followed here, but I can't stay long. Someone is bound to notice my vehicle parked where it is and Larson's been watching me like a hawk."

"Larson? Why am I not surprised," I said, remembering his cold stare at the station. "That man practically radiates resentment."

"He's having trouble with the transition," Dash said. "He'll either fall in line or he'll be out of a job. Change is hard for some people."

Larson had always struck me as someone who enjoyed wielding authority more than actually protecting and serving.

"I should go," Dash said, rising from his chair. "The longer I'm here, the more suspicious it looks."

"How will we communicate if something changes?" I asked, walking him to the mudroom.

"I'll call you," he said, pulling out his phone and frowning at it. "My battery's dead. Been in meetings all day without a chance to charge it."

"You can use my charger if you want to stay a bit longer," I offered, then immediately regretted it when I saw the slight quirk of his eyebrow.

"Thanks, but I should go. Just be at that fundraiser tomorrow night. Dress up, blend in, and keep your eyes open."

"I always dress up," I said, slightly offended. "I don't own sweatpants."

A hint of a smile touched his lips. "I've noticed."

Before I could process that comment, he was gone, slipping out the mudroom door and into the gathering darkness.

I returned to find Bea watching me with a knowing smile.

"Don't," I warned.

"I didn't say a word," she replied innocently.

"You didn't have to. Your face said plenty."

"All I'm thinking," she said, leaning closer, "Is that man moves like someone used to staying in the shadows. Very mysterious. Very sexy."

"We're investigating a potential murder, Bea. This isn't a romance novel."

"The best mysteries always have a little romance," she replied, patting my cheek. "And darling, the way he looks at you is definitely a mystery worth solving."

I rolled my eyes, but couldn't quite suppress the little flutter that had started in my stomach. That was the problem with sheriffs who showed up unannounced and complimented your fashion choices—they had a way of making a girl forget she was supposed to be focused on murder rather than the way his eyes crinkled when he smiled.

The Silver Sleuths departed an hour later, armed with an elaborate plan for tomorrow's lighthouse mission.

"Remember," Walt said at the door, "Constant vigilance."

"I'll try to stay alert between opening the shop at dawn and running a business all day," I promised.

After locking up behind them, I moved through the house, checking windows and doors one more time before heading upstairs. Chowder waddled up beside me, his nails clicking on the hardwood stairs.

"What do you think, Chowder? Are we completely crazy for getting involved in this?"

Chowder snorted, which I took as emphatic agreement.

As I changed into my nightgown, I couldn't help peering out my bedroom window toward the harbor, where the distant lighthouse beam swept rhythmically through the darkness. Somewhere inside that tower, Elizabeth Calvert had hidden something important enough to die for.

Tomorrow night, we'd find out what it was.

*"Into each life some rain must fall,"* I sang softly as I climbed into bed. *"But too much is falling in mine…"*

I patted the bed beside me, and Chowder made his way up the small pet stairs I'd placed there years ago. With a grunt of effort, he nestled against my side. Within minutes, he was snoring softly, completely unburdened by thoughts of murder and conspiracy.

"Must be nice," I whispered, stroking his wrinkled head.

As I lay in bed, I found myself staring at the diary on my nightstand. Only a few days ago, my biggest worry had been whether Mrs. Wexler would remember the extra cinnamon in my beignet order. Now I was searching for clues in a lighthouse with a team of surprisingly formidable senior citizens and a sheriff who seemed to carry as many secrets as answers.

"What would Patrick think of all this?" I whispered to the empty room.

For the first time in years, I realized I couldn't quite picture his response. That thought should have troubled me, but instead, I felt something unexpected—a flicker of anticipation for tomorrow.

# CHAPTER
# EIGHT

By Sunday evening, my bedroom looked like a vintage clothing store had exploded and died a tragic death. I'd tried on more outfits than a backup dancer at a Vegas revue, and I was no closer to finding something appropriate for a night of casual lighthouse breaking and entering.

The day had started normally enough at St. James Baptist Church, where I'd fidgeted uncomfortably in a modest floral dress with a Peter Pan collar while Pastor Bruce delivered a sermon about "the lust of the eyes and the pride of life." I'd tried to focus on his words, but my mind kept traitorously drifting to a certain sheriff with broad shoulders and mysterious scars.

Mrs. Pembroke had leaned over and whispered, "He must have seen the sheriff leaving your house the other night," which had sent me sinking lower in the pew, and made me wish I'd slept in and done laundry on the Lord's day.

The service had been packed—everyone wanted to be seen as concerned, upstanding citizens while simultaneously fishing for gossip about the break-in at the sheriff's office. I'd caught several people watching me, no doubt wondering if I had insider information courtesy of my late-night visitor.

It hadn't helped matters that Sheriff Beckett had also been in attendance, standing at the back with arms crossed, observing rather than participating. Our eyes had met briefly during "Amazing Grace," and he'd given me a slight nod that caused Mrs. Wilson to clutch her pearls and swivel her head between us like she was watching tennis.

Now, hours later, I was standing in my closet in my underwear, wondering what dress would knock Dash's socks off.

"This is ridiculous," I told Chowder, who was sprawled across my bed like a furry, judgmental ottoman. "I'm not going to this thing to impress the sheriff. What's the dress code for solving a murder while pretending to care about historical preservation?"

Chowder snorted, which I took as his professional opinion that I was overthinking things.

I finally settled on a vintage black silk dress with cap sleeves and a lace bodice that said "respectable widow" but had pockets deep enough to hide stolen evidence. The kind of dress that could transition seamlessly from charity function to felony—every Southern woman's wardrobe staple.

"How do I look?" I asked, giving Chowder a little twirl.

His expression clearly said I looked like trouble, which was exactly the vibe I was going for.

The drive to Deidre's took me past the island's most prestigious addresses, but none compared to the Whitmore mansion. The Greek Revival beauty stood like a monument to old shipping money, its columns and sweeping steps declaring that the Whitmores had been somebody long before being somebody was fashionable. Two stately palm trees flanked the entrance like sentinels, while meticulously maintained flower beds added splashes of color against the soft sage green of the façade. It was the kind of house that had weathered hurricanes, economic downturns, and family scandals with equal dignity, emerging each time looking like it had stepped out of *Southern Living* magazine.

This was old Grimm Island—the kind of wealth that whispered instead of shouted, that came with trust funds older than some countries and social obligations that stretched back generations. The Whitmores hadn't just lived on the island, they'd helped shape it, one shipping contract and charitable donation at a time.

Deidre emerged from the house looking like royalty. Her navy gown with silver threading caught the evening light perfectly, and she moved down those imposing steps with the confidence of someone whose great-grandfather had helped founded half the businesses on the island. Despite being well into her late seventies, she possessed that straight-backed posture and sharp gaze that had intimidated generations of noisy children during her fifty-year reign as head librarian.

It was funny how she'd traded a shipping empire for a library, but somehow both suited her perfectly. Knowledge was power, whether it came from cargo manifests or card catalogs, and Deidre Whitmore had always understood that better than most.

"Ready for our little adventure?" she asked, settling into my passenger seat with the same grace she'd probably used to board the family yacht.

"Ready as I'll ever be," I replied, though looking at her elegant composure, I couldn't help but wonder if I was bringing a butter knife to a gunfight.

The drive to the lighthouse took us along Harbor Street as the sun painted the sky in watercolors—soft oranges bleeding into deep purples, with streaks of gold that turned the Spanish moss hanging from the live oaks into something magical. Under different circumstances, it would have been breathtakingly romantic. Tonight, it felt more like nature was setting the stage for whatever drama we were about to unleash.

"Daddy used to bring me here when I was little," Deidre said, gazing at the lighthouse with something like nostalgia. "Said the Whitmores had a responsibility to preserve the island's maritime history." She gave me a sideways look. "I suppose that's what we're doing tonight, in a way. Though I doubt he had breaking and entering in mind."

"Well, when you put it like that, we're practically performing a public service," I said.

"Exactly. Very civic minded of us." She nodded toward the crowd. "Now, shall we go mingle with the enemy before we rob them blind?"

We made our way through the crowd of people who thought roughing it meant staying at a hotel without a concierge. I smiled and nodded at faces I recognized, my palms already sweating. I wasn't made for a life of deception.

"There's the sheriff," Deidre whispered as we approached the entrance. "Nine o'clock, talking to Judge Calhoun."

I followed her gaze across the lawn and nearly choked on my champagne. Sweet Mary and Joseph. Dash stood across the room in a charcoal suit that transformed him from small-town sheriff to something altogether more refined and infinitely more dangerous.

The fine linen stretched across his shoulders as he leaned in to speak with the judge, the tailored lines revealing what his uniform had only hinted at. In the golden glow of the twinkling lights, he looked like he belonged among the island elite, yet somehow apart from them too—a wolf who'd learned to wear fine clothing but hadn't forgotten how to hunt.

In that moment, I realized the danger Dash Beckett posed had nothing to do with his badge and everything to do with how he made me feel—awakened, unbalanced, alive in ways I'd forgotten were possible.

As if sensing my scrutiny, his eyes lifted, meeting mine across the crowded room with an intensity that made my knees weaken beneath my carefully chosen dress. For a moment, everything else—the mission, Elizabeth's diary, even Deidre standing beside me—faded to insignificance. The sounds of the crowd receded to a distant hum. There was only the hammering of my pulse at the base of my throat and the dark intensity of his gaze locked on mine.

His lips curved slightly—not quite a smile, but an acknowledgment, intimate as a touch.

A decade of carefully cultivated widowhood—of defining myself through Patrick's absence—wavered like a mirage in the desert. Patrick had been safe harbor, a sheltered cove of calm waters. But Dash—he was the open ocean with all its unknown depths and dangers. The recognition filled me with equal parts longing and guilt.

"You're staring, dear," Deidre murmured, the amusement in her voice dragging me back to reality. Her words felt like being doused with cold water, and I blinked rapidly, trying to regain my composure.

"I was just…assessing the situation," I said lamely, smoothing my hands down the front of my dress as if I could wipe away the evidence of my thoughts.

"Mmhmm," Deidre said, clearly unconvinced. "The 'situation' does look quite appealing in that suit."

I ignored her comment and focused on our mission. "Remember the plan. We mingle and act inconspicuous and then join the first lighthouse tour at eight. Dash will create a distraction at the second level while we search the third."

"I may be old, but my memory's just fine," Deidre said, patting my arm. "Now, let's go charm some potential suspects."

I scanned the area, searching for familiar faces. Dottie and Hank were engaged in animated conversation with the historical society president, Mrs. Elvina Whitaker, a formidable woman in her sixties whose family had been on the island since before the Civil War.

"Mabel, darling!" Mrs. Whitaker exclaimed when she spotted me. "How lovely to see you this evening. You're looking radiant as always."

I allowed her to envelop me in a cloud of Chanel No. 5 and air-kisses. "I wouldn't miss it, Elvina. The lighthouse preservation fund is so important to the island's heritage. It was a passion project of Patrick's."

"Rest his soul," she said, touching her hand to her bosom. "And speaking of preservation, have you met our new sheriff? Such a dedicated public servant. He's been asking the most interesting questions about the lighthouse's history. Too bad he's an outsider."

My gaze traveled back to Dash, who was now speaking with Mayor Cromwell. The mayor's face was flushed, his hand gestures growing more animated by the second. Whatever they were discussing, it clearly wasn't pleasant small talk about the weather.

"We've crossed paths," I said neutrally. "He seems very... thorough."

"Indeed," Mrs. Whitaker replied, lowering her voice conspiratorially. "Between us, I think Mayor Cromwell is feeling a bit threatened. The new sheriff doesn't play by the old island rules, if you catch my meaning. I'm trying to arrange a time for him to meet my daughter."

I made a noncommittal sound. Josephine Whitaker had been a few years behind me in school, and she was a sweet girl, but she didn't have the sense that God gave a goose. Of course, I didn't really know a thing about Dashiel Beckett. He might have a fondness for empty-headed nitwits.

"There you are!" Bea's voice rang out, causing heads to turn as she made her entrance—fifteen minutes late, exactly as planned. She glided toward us in her signature turquoise raw silk cocktail dress, the peacock feathers at the collar pluming dramatically around her neck and framing her face. Her red hair was styled in an elaborate updo that caught the light like a flame.

"I was beginning to think you weren't coming," Deidre said, giving Bea a knowing look.

"Darling, one must time these things perfectly," Bea replied, adjusting one of her enormous turquoise earrings. "The first fifteen minutes of any party are dreadfully dull. Besides, an entrance is wasted if everyone isn't already there to appreciate it."

"That dress is certainly an attention-getter," Deidre said. "How many peacocks had to die for you to look that silly?"

"Oh, shut up, Deidre," Bea said good-naturedly. "At least I don't look like I'm going to a funeral for a tinsel maker."

I rolled my eyes and let out a sigh. One thing I'd learned about older people since hanging out with the Silver Sleuths was they never held back on their words and it was almost impossible to insult them.

"Did you see Mayor Cromwell's face when you walked in?" I asked, interrupting their bickering. "I don't think he's a fan of yours, Bea."

"Oh, I imagine not," Bea said with satisfaction. "I can't stand that blowhard. And I've still got juicy stuff on him I never put in print."

"Bea," I said, covering my mouth to hide my laughter. "Be nice."

"Good Lord, what for?" she said, grinning. "Nice girls never have any fun. Remember that, darling." She glanced toward the lighthouse and pitched her voice louder than usual. "The first tour starts soon. We should all go together."

"Subtle," I murmured as she swept past.

"Subtlety is for people under seventy," she whispered back. "I don't have time for it anymore."

As eight o'clock approached, I excused myself from a mind-numbing conversation with Dr. Peterson about his recent gallbladder surgery and made my way toward the lighthouse entrance.

Dash intercepted me before I reached the gathering tour group.

"Everything's set," he said quietly, falling into step beside me. "Dottie created a small diversion in the museum. Knocked over a replica of an antique sextant that was precariously balanced on its display stand. They'll be busy examining it for damage for at least fifteen minutes."

I winced, thankful it was only a replica. "I think you've created a monster. They're really getting into this."

We reached the lighthouse entrance where a small crowd had gathered for the tour. The historical society docent, a retired schoolteacher named Mrs. Collins, was explaining the lighthouse's construction and operational history.

"...and the Fresnel lens, installed in 1925, can be seen up to twenty-one nautical miles in clear conditions," she said. "Now, if you'll follow me inside, we'll begin our ascent. Please stay together, and remember there are 167 steps to the top."

"Goodness gravy," Bea said loudly. "I stopped doing steps in the eighties when I threw my StairMaster to the curb. I'll stay down here."

Deidre rolled her eyes. "I guess I'm going up."

"Any idea where in this tower Elizabeth might have hidden something?" Dash whispered as we filed in behind the others. "That's a lot of ground to cover."

I shook my head, the enormity of our task suddenly daunting. "Her diary just said 'in the lighthouse.' We'll have to search every level without looking like we're searching."

The interior of the lighthouse was cool and dim, with whitewashed brick walls and a spiral staircase that wound upward along the curved interior. Mrs. Collins led us upward, stopping periodically to share historical tidbits while I frantically scanned each level for any sign of a hiding place.

The base level contained the original keeper's quarters, now converted into a small museum with glass display cases and educational placards. Nothing here seemed likely—too public, too frequently disturbed by renovations and visitors.

"The keeper's quarters were modernized in 1952," Mrs. Collins explained, confirming my suspicions. "Very little of the original structure remains in this section."

We began our climb up the spiral staircase, the steps worn smooth by generations of keepers' boots. My dress suddenly felt conspicuous against the weathered brick and rusted metal, its deep pockets weighted with purpose. Every whisper, every footstep echoed against the curved walls, magnifying my anxiety.

The second level housed the oil storage room—a small circular chamber with the original storage tanks now serving as additional display cases.

"This is where they kept the whale oil, and later kerosene, that fueled the light," Mrs. Collins explained. "During renovation in 1985, workers found newspapers from 1879 stuffed between these walls for insulation."

I exchanged a glance with Deidre. Elizabeth had been a history major—would that detail have caught her attention? But the renovation predated Elizabeth's death by over a decade. Whatever she'd hidden, she'd done it after this space had been restored.

As we moved up to the third level—a watch room with logbooks under glass—I felt my nerves start to fray around the edges. We'd already covered two levels with no luck, and Mrs. Collins was keeping a brisk pace. The group would reach the top before we had any chance to search thoroughly.

"The watch room is where the keeper would maintain detailed

records," Mrs. Collins was saying. "Weather conditions, ships passing, any distress signals…"

Something about her words triggered a memory. Elizabeth's cryptic warning from her diary about choosing a hiding place no one would suspect echoed in my mind.

"Mrs. Collins," I asked, trying to sound like a casual tourist, "when was the last major renovation of this lighthouse?"

"The most extensive work was completed in 2002," she replied. "Though there were plans being discussed as early as 1995. Budget issues delayed the start for several years."

1995—the year before Elizabeth died. She would have known renovations were coming. She'd have chosen somewhere that would remain untouched…

"Now, if you'll follow me," Mrs. Collins continued, "we'll head up to the mechanical room, which houses the original clockwork mechanism that once rotated the light."

As we climbed the increasingly narrow staircase to the fourth level, something clicked into place. Elizabeth's internship had been with the *Observer* and she'd been working on a story about island development—which meant research into construction, contracts, funding. She would have seen the renovation plans. She would have known which parts of the lighthouse were scheduled to be preserved rather than restored.

"It's in the mechanical room," I whispered to Deidre as we reached the landing. "Elizabeth would have known it was the one section they planned to preserve intact as a historical exhibit."

Deidre's eyes widened in understanding as we entered the mechanical room—a larger space dominated by massive brass gears and clockwork that once rotated the powerful lens above. The air here felt different—thick with dust and the metallic tang of old machinery.

"This magnificent mechanism—" Mrs. Collins gestured to the imposing brass assembly, "—is completely original to the 1879 construction. It was considered such a marvel of engineering that the renovation committee specifically voted to preserve it exactly as it was."

That was it—this room had remained untouched even during renovation. The perfect hiding place for something you wanted to remain undisturbed for years. Most of the crowd was winded now that we were on the third floor, and no one seemed to care too much about the historical significance of the machinery.

Dash caught my eye from across the room and gave an imperceptible nod toward Mrs. Collins. On cue, he spoke up.

"Excuse me, Mrs. Collins," he called out, his voice carrying above the general murmur. "I'd read on one of the Grimm Island history plaques downstairs that in 1911 the hurricane waters got so high and were so strong it broke out one of the windows in the lantern room. Is that even possible?"

Mrs. Collings looked delighted at the question and she said, "Let's go up and take a look, shall we?"

There were some murmured groans from some of the other tourists as they started up the stairs to the lantern room, and I spied a few people sneaking away from the group and going back down to the bottom floor.

Deidre and I eased our way to the far corner of the mechanical room, putting deliberate distance between ourselves and the tour group.

"The clock's ticking," Deidre whispered.

"Look for anything that doesn't look original or seems out of place." It wasn't a large room, and I scanned the bricks, searching for something—anything.

"The walls," I whispered, turning my attention to the brickwork surrounding the large windows. "The mortar looks different here—newer in some spots."

We both moved to different sections of the curved wall, running our fingers along the mortar lines. The rough texture scraped against my fingertips as I methodically felt each brick, searching for anything unusual.

"Nothing on this side," Deidre reported, frustration evident in her voice. The sounds from the tour group upstairs were shifting—Mrs.

Collins was wrapping up her presentation. We were running out of time.

I worked faster, my fingers pressing and probing each brick near the window. Then I felt it—one brick protruded slightly more than the others, the mortar around it subtly different in color.

"Deidre," I whispered urgently, "This section looks tampered with."

She joined me as I pushed gently on the brick. It moved slightly then caught. The ancient mortar crumbled slightly under my fingertips, leaving dusty residue beneath my manicured nails as I tried again, harder this time.

The footsteps on the stairs grew louder. I could hear Mrs. Collins announcing for everyone to take a final look at the view and then watch their step as they started back down the stairs. We had a minute tops. Maybe just seconds.

"Together," I whispered, lining my fingers up with Deidre's against the stubborn brick. "One, two, three."

We pulled in unison, and the brick slid outward with a soft scrape that sounded thunderous to my hyperalert ears. It revealed a small cavity behind it, just large enough to hold—

A Ziploc bag, yellowed with age, containing what appeared to be a small notebook and several folded papers. The bag had protected its contents from the decades of dampness and salt air.

I extracted the package with trembling fingers and nestled it into the deep pocket of my dress, the plastic crackling softly. I could hear footsteps on the metal stairs above.

In our haste, we'd left the brick displaced, a dark gap in the wall announcing our tampering to anyone who looked closely. Deidre's eyes widened in alarm.

As the tour group began their descent, I pressed the brick back into place and gave it a good whack with my fist so it would go back into the slot. A wave of dizzying relief washed over me as I felt it slide smoothly into position.

"Thank God I wore black," I whispered to Deidre. "I'm sweating like a racehorse."

"Are you all right, dear?" Mrs. Collins asked, noticing that Deidre and I were waiting for the group. "You're looking flushed."

"Just a little lightheaded from the climb," I said, forcing a smile. "All these stairs!"

"Take your time coming down," she said. "I don't want any accidents on my watch."

Dash appeared at my elbow as we joined the group and made our way back down. "Find something?" he murmured, his voice barely audible.

I gave him a slight nod, trying to control my breathing. My hands were still shaking, adrenaline coursing through my veins like electricity. Whatever we'd just recovered had been important enough for someone to kill Elizabeth Calvert. And now it was in my possession.

I was a mess of emotions, and I could barely focus. Dash had moved off when one of the men in the group had started asking him questions about noise ordinances, and I was just trying to put one foot in front of the other.

I was so focused on appearing normal that I nearly collided with Deputy Larson at the bottom of the stairs.

"Enjoying the tour, Mrs. McCoy?" he asked, his beady gaze piercing into mine.

"Very much," I replied, fighting to keep my voice steady. "I had no idea how complex the mechanical systems were."

His gaze dropped briefly to my hands. "You've got dirt on your hands. Must have found something interesting up there."

Ice seemed to crystallize in my veins, but I summoned a casual smile. "It's an old place. I'm sure we're all bringing a little bit of it back with us."

His eyes narrowed slightly. "Some things are worth leaving in the past."

I met his gaze without flinching, though my breaths came quick and shallow. "I disagree. I love the past. We can learn a lot from history. And a lot from the secrets that are buried there."

"Just make sure you don't get buried with them."

I gave him a thin smile, but I maintained my composure as I

brushed past him, the proof of Elizabeth Calvert's final discovery burning like a brand against my skin.

I found Deidre across the room looking pale. "Are you okay, dear? You don't look so good. Was that Deputy Larson?"

"Yes, that's him," I answered. "And I'm fine."

"Does he suspect something?"

"I don't know," I said. "The only reason he'd have to suspect anything is if he knows about the diary."

"Good point," she said.

"We need to get out of here," I said, feeling the weight of Elizabeth's secret grow heavier with each passing moment. "Regroup somewhere safe."

"Your place?" Deidre suggested.

I shook my head. "Too obvious. If someone's watching us, that's the first place they'll look."

"The tea shop, then," Deidre decided. "Back entrance. One hour. I'll tell the others. Be right back."

I nodded, watching as she moved casually through the crowd before making her way to where Bea was holding court with a small group of society matrons.

I caught Dash's eye across the lawn and gave him a slight nod toward the exit, and then held up my phone so he'd know to check my text message. He acknowledged with an almost imperceptible tilt of his head, then deliberately turned to engage Mrs. Whitaker in conversation, providing cover for our departure.

"Let's go," I whispered as soon as Deidre came back. "Act like we're leaving because you're tired from all those stairs."

"I don't need to act," she grumbled, rubbing her knee. "I'm going to feel this tomorrow."

We made our goodbyes to a few key people, playing our parts as innocent attendees departing an ordinary fundraiser. As we walked to my car, an irresistible impulse drew my gaze back to the lighthouse, its rotating beacon punctuating the twilight with rhythmic flashes.

Elizabeth had trusted her secret to that tower, believing it would be safe until someone came looking for the truth. Now, twenty-eight years later, we'd found it—but I couldn't shake the feeling that we weren't the only ones searching.

As we drove through town, I took several unnecessary turns, doubling back and changing directions until I was confident no one was following us.

"I feel like I'm in one of those spy movies Walt is always watching," Deidre commented as I made a third circuit around the town square.

"Better safe than sorry," I replied, finally turning down the alley that led to the back entrance of The Perfect Steep. "I haven't noticed that car that was following me before."

"Maybe he got bored," Deidre said. "You don't really do a lot."

"Thank you," I said dryly. "All I know is that whatever's in this package got Elizabeth killed. I'd rather not join her."

I parked behind the shop and used my key to unlock the back door. The comforting aroma of bergamot and cinnamon that lingered even after hours of closure greeted us as we stepped into the darkened kitchen.

"I'll put on some tea," I said, flipping on the lights. "The others should be here soon."

But before I could fill the kettle, the kitchen door swung open, and Sheriff Beckett stepped in. His suit jacket was gone, his tie loosened, and his expression serious.

"Did you find something?" he asked without preamble.

I nodded, pulling the plastic package from my pocket and handing it to him. "Hidden behind a brick in the mechanical room, just like Elizabeth's diary suggested."

Dash carefully took the yellowed plastic bag, examining it under the light. "This could be exactly what we need." His eyes gleamed with anticipation as he placed it on the counter. "When will the others arrive?"

"They should be here shortly," I said, filling the kettle.

I moved to put on some tea, my mind racing with possibilities about what might be inside the package. My fingers still felt the phantom weight of the evidence through the fabric of my dress pocket.

Whatever had been in there had threatened someone powerful enough to kill for it twenty-eight years ago. Elizabeth's words from her diary echoed in my mind: *The men who run this island—they think they're untouchable. But I have proof now.*

Three quick knocks sounded at the back door.

"That's Hank," Deidre said, moving toward the door.

I opened it to find Hank and Dottie waiting outside. Bea swept in behind them dramatically, the silk of her turquoise dress whispering against the doorframe as she entered.

"Did you find it?" Dottie asked without preamble.

I nodded, pointing to the package Dash was still holding. "Hidden behind a brick in the mechanical room."

"Well, don't just stand there," Bea exclaimed, making a beeline for the teapot. "Open it! But first, who wants a little pick-me-up in their tea?" She grabbed the bottle of bourbon she kept under my counter.

"Sign me up," Deidre said. "My knees are aching something fierce. Do you have any ibuprofen?"

"Look in the top right drawer of my desk," I told her, and she shuffled off to the office.

"I'll take a hit too," Hank said. "But just a small one. I'm driving. I need something to take the edge off. I can't stand those things. A bunch of uppity know-it-alls."

"Most of those people have been your circle of friends your whole life," Dottie said scoldingly.

"Didn't say I didn't like 'em," Hank said. "Just said they're a bunch of uppity know-it-alls."

Dash carefully placed the package on the table. "It's been preserved surprisingly well."

"Plastic bag," Dottie noted with approval. "Smart girl."

"You have plastic gloves?" Dash asked.

"Of course," I said, moving behind the display counter where I kept bakery items during opening hours. I handed him the gloves and he put them on with ease.

Dash opened the yellowed ziplock. Inside was a small notebook and what appeared to be several pages of financial ledgers. He gently removed them, placing them on the table.

I moved to the counter where the kettle had begun to whistle. As I prepared a pot of Earl Grey, I couldn't help stealing glances at the table where they all huddled over Elizabeth's hidden treasure. I arranged the teacups on a silver tray, adding sugar and milk for those who took it.

"It looks like accounting records," I said, leaning closer as I passed out the cups.

"Not just any records," Dash replied, his voice low. "These appear to be from the Harbor Development Corporation. And look at these notations in the margins—RM, PC. Initials."

"Roy Milton," Hank said immediately. "Our former crooked sheriff."

"And PC could be Paul Cromwell, the current mayor's father," Deidre added. "He was on the city council back then."

"There's a third set of payments here," Dash said, pointing to a column of figures with no initials beside them. "Regular amounts, substantial ones, but no identification."

"These unmarked payments could be what Brooks was warning Elizabeth about," I said, recalling our earlier discussion about Jason Brooks. "If he knew these payments were happening…"

"He's definitely our next stop," Hank agreed, examining the papers closely. "These ledgers show money moving through shell companies, payments to officials. Elizabeth was onto something big."

"We need to talk to him as soon as possible," Deidre insisted.

"I'll call him first thing tomorrow," Hank said, adjusting his glasses. "We served on a judicial panel together back in '03. He'll take my call." He tapped his finger on the ledger. "I'll tell him it's about Elizabeth Calvert. If he has any conscience at all, that should get his attention."

"This is just a piece of the puzzle," Dash cautioned. "These records suggest impropriety, maybe financial fraud, but they don't prove Elizabeth was murdered because of what she found."

"No," Dottie said, leaning in to study the pages. "But they give us a clear direction. If Brooks was warning her about the danger of investigating these payments, he might know who silenced her permanently."

"Let's not jump to conclusions," Dash warned. "These documents are nearly thirty years old. We need to build this case carefully, interview people who were around back then. This is just the first step."

"Well," Bea said, raising her teacup that now smelled more of bourbon than tea, "To first steps and finding justice for Elizabeth Calvert. After thirty years, it's about time someone finally looked for the truth."

We all raised our cups in a solemn toast, the weight of what we'd found settling over us. Through the darkness outside, I could see the lighthouse beam sweeping across the harbor, circling endlessly as it had the night Elizabeth died.

Whatever secrets that light had witnessed all those years ago, we were finally on the path to uncovering them.

# CHAPTER
# NINE

THE DRIVE TO CHARLESTON WAS PLEASANT ENOUGH, though my nerves made it difficult to appreciate the verdant marsh views as we crossed the causeway connecting Grimm Island to the mainland. My vintage Karmann Ghia hummed contentedly along the highway while Hank sat beside me, his panama hat perfectly positioned on his silver hair, dressed in a seersucker suit that practically screamed retired federal judge.

"You're grinding the gears, Mabel," he commented mildly as I downshifted with perhaps more force than necessary. "This old girl deserves better treatment."

My hands tightened on the steering wheel as we drove through the congested streets. "I feel like I should have practiced an interrogation technique or two. My experience is limited to asking customers if they'd like another scone."

"This isn't an interrogation," Hank said, his voice carrying the measured tone that had likely calmed countless courtrooms. "It's a conversation with a potentially valuable witness."

"A conversation about a thirty-year-old murder that was covered up by half the island's power players," I pointed out. "Hardly afternoon tea."

Hank's eyes crinkled at the corners. "In my experience, the most effective legal strategy is often just good conversation paired with careful listening. Save the dramatic table-pounding for television courtrooms."

"Is that what made you such a feared judge? Your conversation skills?"

"That," Hank replied with a hint of a smile, "and an unerring ability to spot a liar at twenty paces. Forty-three years on the bench, you learn to be precise with language." He glanced at me. "Besides, we have no evidence connecting Brooks to Elizabeth's death. Just what we assume is his initial in her diary."

I nodded, focusing on the road ahead as Spanish moss-draped oak trees gave way to the outskirts of Charleston. The morning sun glinted off the Cooper River as we crossed the bridge into the historic downtown.

"Take King Street," Hank directed. "Brooks' office is in that fancy new building near Marion Square. The one that looks like a glass spaceship landed on top of a brick warehouse."

"I know the one," I said, maneuvering through the increasingly congested streets. Charleston always felt like stepping into another century—until you hit traffic. Then it felt like being trapped in purgatory with tourists wielding selfie sticks.

As we drove, I snuck glances at Hank, realizing how little I knew about him despite all the years he'd been coming to my tea shop. Judge Henry "Hank" Hardeman was something of a legend in South Carolina legal circles, but he rarely spoke about his career or personal life.

"How well do you actually know Jason Brooks?" I asked, breaking the companionable silence.

Hank's expression grew thoughtful, the lines around his eyes deepening. "Well enough to know his reputation. Smart man. Ambitious. Always calibrating which way the wind was blowing before he'd offer an opinion."

"That doesn't sound like someone who'd risk his career to help a college student investigating corruption."

"People are rarely all one thing, Mabel," Hank said, adjusting his cuff links—sterling silver scales of justice that had been a retirement gift from his clerks. "Brooks was different back then. Younger, more idealistic. Sometimes the years sand down our sharp edges, make us more accommodating."

There was something in his tone that suggested personal experience, and I found myself curious about the man behind the judicial façade.

"Is that what happened to you?" I asked, unable to stop myself. "Did you become more accommodating with age?"

Hank barked out a laugh that filled the small car. "Good Lord, no. Just ask anyone who's known me longer than a decade. I've only grown more obstinate with time."

I smiled, thinking of the stern but fair-minded man who'd been a fixture at my tea shop for years. "Eleanor always said you were stubborn as an old mule," I remarked, remembering his late wife fondly. She'd been a regular at my shop in its early days.

A shadow crossed Hank's face at the mention of her name. "She would know better than anyone."

"I still miss seeing her at the shop," I said quietly. "Her book club was one of my first regular gatherings."

"Forty-four years we were married," he said, his voice softer than I'd ever heard it. "She was my third time at the altar, you know."

"Third?" I couldn't hide my surprise. Growing up on Grimm Island, I'd only ever known Hank with Eleanor. The idea that he'd had a life—marriages, even—before moving to the island was strangely jarring.

"Most folks on the island only know us from after I was appointed to the federal bench," he said, seeming to read my thoughts. "But I was a practicing attorney in Charleston for years before that. Eleanor and I bought our weekend house here on Grimm Island in '76, but I commuted to Charleston until my appointment in '83. That's when we moved here permanently."

"So you had a previous life?" I prompted, intrigued by this new side of someone I thought I knew well.

"First was Catherine," he said, a nostalgic smile playing at his lips. "College sweetheart. Married right after law school when I was twenty-five. Lasted less than two years. She wanted a husband who came home for dinner. I wanted to change the world one case at a time."

"Then came Vivian," he continued, gazing out the window at the historic homes we passed. "Brilliant attorney. We met while I was clerking for a judge and she was working at the DA's office. Another brief experiment—all passion mixed with the excitement of law—a year of working together, living together, fighting together. We burned too bright too fast."

"That sounds contentious," I observed, turning onto Meeting Street.

"Most civilized divorce in Charleston history," Hank replied. "We drafted the agreement over a bottle of Macallan 25 and parted as friends. She's a state supreme court justice now."

"I had no idea," I said, reconciling this new information with the Hank Hardeman I thought I'd known all my life. "You never mentioned them."

"Grimm Island knows me as the man I became with Eleanor," he said simply. "We met when I was thirty, and suddenly I understood what marriage was supposed to be. After she got sick with cancer, I finally retired from the bench. She'd been after me to do it for years." His voice caught slightly. "Wish I'd done it sooner, spent more time with her."

I knew those feelings of regret all too well. Patrick had been thirty-six, in the prime of his life and healthy. We were ready to start a family. And then all of a sudden, he was gone. He'd had a massive heart attack on the ninth hole of the golf course at the country club. I'd been told he'd died instantly.

"She was the one who taught me to appreciate tea," Hank added, his eyes distant with memory. "Always said coffee was for lawyers in a hurry, but tea was for judges who needed to contemplate the weight of their decisions."

That explained his loyalty to my tea shop, I realized. It wasn't just about the Silver Sleuths or the scones—it was a connection to Eleanor.

As we crossed the Arthur Ravenel Jr. Bridge, Charleston's skyline came into view—a mixture of church steeples, historic buildings, and modern glass towers rising against the blue harbor backdrop. The city where Hank had begun his career was now our destination to uncover more pieces of Elizabeth Calvert's story.

"There it is," Hank said, gesturing toward a striking building where traditional brick met contemporary glass. "Brooks' office is on the twelfth floor of that architectural identity crisis ahead. Park in the garage around back. I called ahead—he's expecting us at eleven."

I navigated into the parking garage and found a spot close to the elevators so Hank wouldn't have to walk so far.

"Ready?" Hank asked as I shut off the engine.

"As I'll ever be," I said, reaching for my vintage leather satchel. Inside was a notebook, Elizabeth's diary (the copy, not the original), and copies of the ledger pages we'd found in the lighthouse.

I caught my reflection in the mirrored doors of the elevator—navy linen dress with white piping, matching navy heels, and my hair pinned back with vintage barrettes.

We took the elevator to the twelfth floor, where Brooks, Holloway & Winters occupied a corner suite with sweeping views of the Charleston harbor. The reception area screamed old money and new technology—heart pine floors and exposed brick walls contrasting with sleek glass partitions and modern art.

The receptionist, a polished young woman in a perfectly tailored designer suit, smiled with practiced warmth. "Judge Hardeman? Mr. Brooks is expecting you. May I offer you coffee while you wait?"

"Tea, if you have it," Hank replied.

"Of course," she said smoothly. "And for you?" She glanced at me with barely concealed curiosity.

"The same," I said.

We were shown to a seating area where *Charleston Magazine* was prominently displayed alongside legal journals and financial publications. The coffee-table book showcasing South Carolina's historic courthouses was a nice touch—probably meant to impress visiting judges like Hank.

"How much do you know about Brooks' career after the DA's office?" I asked quietly as we waited.

"Followed the standard trajectory for ambitious attorneys in this state," Hank replied. "Left the DA's office around '98, joined a private firm, made a name representing developers and business interests. Started his own firm about fifteen years ago." He nodded toward a wall of framed photographs showing Brooks with various politicians and business leaders. "Made all the right connections. Never went into politics like he'd wanted to in his early years. I always wondered why. He was ripe for it."

Before I could ask more, a door opened, and Jason Brooks himself emerged. He was tall and trim, with salt-and-pepper hair that seemed deliberately styled to project distinguished authority rather than age. His custom suit hung perfectly on his frame, and his smile revealed teeth that had definitely benefited from cosmetic dentistry.

"Judge Hardeman," Jason greeted, extending his hand. "What an unexpected pleasure. I was sorry to hear about Eleanor."

"That's kind of you," Hank said, shaking his hand firmly. "And how's Christine and the kids."

"Not kids anymore," he said. "I've got one at Georgetown Law School and the other is a sophomore at Stanford. As far as Christine —" He shrugged his shoulders and looked a bit sheepish. "We've been divorced about five years now. She wasn't a fan of lawyer's hours."

"I'm sorry to hear that," Hank said.

"It's just one of those things," he said. "Probably for the best. Now I'm able to fully focus on the firm, the kids are taken care of, and when I get a few days off I pack up my fishing gear and head to Costa Rica to fish. I have no complaints. So to what do I owe the pleasure?"

"I appreciate you making time on such short notice," Hank said. "This is a friend of mine. Mabel McCoy."

Brooks turned to me, his politician's smile in place, and then it warmed considerably when he took a good look at me. He was a handsome man and obviously took very good care of himself, and after his hand lingered a little longer than was usual on mine I had to wonder if his divorce had anything to do with the flirtatious charm that seemed to emanate from his pores. I found myself a little flustered when I took my hand back.

"Ms. McCoy," he said, smiling. "Hank keeps beautiful company. Please, both of you, come with me to my office."

It was a short walk down a slate-tiled hallway and small glass offices that looked out over the city. We took a left down another hallway, but this one had plush carpet and a quiet opulence that bordered on extravagant. A separate reception area opened up and there was a woman sitting behind a large curved desk that blocked the door to Brooks' office.

"My personal admin, Lena," he said as he ushered us into his office.

"I must admit I was intrigued by your call," Brooks said, gesturing for us to take seats in leather chairs positioned in front of his desk. "You mentioned an old case from Grimm Island? I wouldn't have expected you to be digging into anything there, Hank. As far as I know, Grimm Island has never had a big problem with crime. At least the violent kind."

"Elizabeth Calvert," Hank stated, getting straight to the point. "Her father is dying. His last wish is to know what really happened to his daughter."

The change in Brooks was immediate—like watching ice form across a pond in winter. His posture stiffened, and his shoulders tensed visibly.

"Elizabeth Calvert," he repeated, the name emerging deliberately, as if he were testing a delicate instrument. "That's a name I haven't heard in many years. The official ruling was accidental drowning."

"We found her diary," I interjected. "And in it, she mentions someone named J who warned her that her investigation was dangerous—that she should let it go. It's been mentioned by several people that the two of you were involved that summer."

Brooks stared at us for a long moment, then reached forward and pressed a button on his desk phone. "Lena, hold my calls for the next hour. And would you please bring in tea for my guests?"

He rose and walked to his office door, closing it with a soft click. From his desk, he pressed another button that engaged a privacy film over the glass walls of his office, instantly turning them opaque.

When he returned to his seat, his professional veneer had visibly faltered. "How did you come across her diary after all this time?"

"It was found hidden in evidence storage," Hank explained. "The new sheriff is reopening the investigation into her death," I said.

"Investigation?" Brooks echoed. "It was ruled an accidental drowning."

"You and I both know there was nothing accidental about it," Hank said, his voice carrying quiet authority. "Nothing about her death set right then and now that we've seen the case file it definitely doesn't set right."

Brooks exhaled slowly, raking a hand through his styled hair. For the first time, he looked like a man rather than a carefully constructed professional image.

"I always wondered if she'd left evidence somewhere," he admitted finally. "She was too smart not to have backup."

"So, does that mean you're J?" I asked.

He straightened his tie, his composure returning. "Yes. Elizabeth and I...we were romantically involved that summer. Not intentionally. It was just one of those things."

"She'd been dating the Harrington boy for a while if I recall," Hank said.

Brooks cleared his throat. "Like I said, it was just one of those things. I knew she was still dating Clint. I knew she was going to break it off with him. She didn't want to be tied down before she left for Duke. And I was comfortable with the idea of a summer fling, nothing serious. At least that's how it started. We were both young. Elizabeth was adventurous and impulsive and I was working a hundred hours a week at the DA's office and looking for fun."

"I take it Clint found out about the fling?" I asked.

"Oh, yeah," he said. "And it wasn't pretty. Three days before she died he showed up to her apartment unexpected and I happened to be there. There was a confrontation—heated words exchanged, a physical altercation. I sustained minor injuries—black eye, busted knuckles. Clint was a big guy, but he didn't get away unscathed." He smiled at that, looking down at his knuckles as if the marks would still be there. "Elizabeth was shaken. I think she saw a side of Clint she'd never seen before."

"What exactly did Clint know about her research?" Hank inquired.

"Initially nothing," Brooks said. "Elizabeth was careful to keep her investigation separate from her relationship with him, especially once she began suspecting his father's involvement. But during the confrontation, he saw some of the documents on her coffee table—Harbor Development Corporation contracts with his father's company. I think he was intoxicated, volatile. He demanded to know what she was doing, grabbed some of the documents and started going through them. Even then he was being groomed to take over the business. He knew what he was looking at."

Brooks' voice remained steady, but a muscle in his cheek twitched involuntarily. "Clint threatened to tell his father about what she was doing, and he threatened to damage my career, which he could have done. I had political ambitions back then. Clint told her she'd regret making a fool of him and then slammed out."

A knock at the door interrupted us, and his secretary entered with a silver tea service on a tray. Lena poured three cups with precision, adding a splash of milk to Jason's without being asked—clearly she'd served him before. She offered a plate of shortbread biscuits that no one touched, then departed quietly, closing the door behind her.

Brooks waited until she was gone before continuing, his poise now gone. He lifted his cup but set it back down untouched.

"What exactly was she investigating?" I queried, connecting the threads. "The financial records we found showed payments to Milton and Cromwell, but what was she hoping to expose?"

Brooks leaned back in his chair. "Elizabeth believed she'd uncovered a systematic pattern of corruption—bribes to officials in exchange for development approvals, falsified environmental impact studies, manipulated zoning changes. The triumvirate of Milton, Cromwell, and Harrington Sr. controlled virtually every major development project on the island."

"But Elizabeth threatened to expose them," Hank postulated.

"And someone silenced her permanently," I added.

Brooks nodded, throat working visibly. "I always assumed it was Milton who arranged it. He had the authority, the connections to cover it up."

"But Milton's in prison now," I pointed out. "And someone broke into the sheriff's office looking for Elizabeth's diary. Someone who's still very interested in keeping these secrets buried."

"Paul Cromwell is dead," Brooks contemplated aloud. "Milton's locked up. That leaves—"

"Clinton Harrington," Hank finished. "Or his son, who took over the business."

Brooks ran his thumb along his jawline before nodding. "Harrington Construction has flourished since Clint Jr. took over. He's transformed it into one of the largest developers on the coast."

"Let's back up a moment," I suggested, watching Brooks intently. "What happened after Clint confronted the two of you?"

Brooks drummed his fingers lightly on his desk blotter. "After he left that night, Elizabeth was shaken but also more determined than ever."

"And the last time you saw her?" Hank asked.

"She came to my office on July fifteenth," Brooks recounted, his gaze drifting briefly to the harbor view. "She was different—calmer—almost resolute. Said she'd taken precautions in case something happened to her. I told her we should have dinner and talk it over, but she said she had things to see to." His voice remained steady, but his knuckles whitened around his pen. "The next morning, she was found in the harbor. I never did find out what precautions she'd taken."

A heavy silence fell over the room. Brooks reached for his tea, taking a small sip before setting it down again.

"What happens now?" he finally asked, looking between us.

Hank straightened in his chair. "Now we build a case. Elizabeth deserves justice, even after all these years."

"Her father is dying," I contributed. "This might be his last chance to know the truth."

Brooks was silent for a long moment, conflict evident in his expression. Finally, he opened a drawer in his desk and withdrew a business card, writing something on the back before handing it to me.

"This is my private number," he revealed. "Not the office line. If you find something concrete—something that can't be dismissed or buried—call me. I should have helped Elizabeth when I had the chance. Maybe I can make up for that now." He handed me the card.

Hank studied him for a moment, his gaze thoughtful rather than accusatory. "Twenty-eight years is a long time to carry this burden, Jason."

Brooks glanced at the photographs on his wall—the smiling images of himself with powerful men. "It was only supposed to be a fling." The was sorrow and regret in his voice. "But I fell in love with her. It was impossible not to. It's time to right any wrongs I may have committed. I've spent nearly three decades building a career on the foundation of my silence," he confessed quietly. "I'd like to spend whatever years I have left being able to sleep at night."

▭

As we made our way back to the car I asked Hank, "Do you think he was telling the truth?"

"Too early to draw conclusions," he cautioned. "Right now, all we have is his word that there was a relationship between them. We need corroboration and evidence. That's how justice works—facts, not speculation."

We made our way back to the car in silence, each lost in our own thoughts. As we pulled out of the parking garage into the bright Charleston sunshine, I checked my rearview mirror, half expecting to see the dark sedan that had followed me before.

"Clint Harrington Jr.," I declared as we merged onto the highway heading back to Grimm Island. "We need to talk to him."

"Agreed," Hank concurred, buckling his seat belt. "But we need to be careful. If Brooks is right, and Elizabeth was killed for what she found, Harrington might be more dangerous than we thought."

"Let's talk to Sheriff Beckett and see what he thinks," I said, the idea sending a thrill of anticipation through me.

"Good idea," Hank said. "I'm afraid I have more questions than answers after that meeting. After nearly thirty years, why is someone still desperate to keep Elizabeth's discovery hidden? Financial fraud has a statute of limitations. Murder doesn't."

"The question is what exactly did she find?" I pondered, gripping the steering wheel tighter. "What secret was worth killing for then—and still worth protecting now?"

We fell silent for a while, both lost in thought as the highway stretched before us. The weight of it all—a young woman's death, a father's dying wish, a decades-old cover-up—settled around us like a heavy fog. To calm my nerves, I found myself doing what I always did when anxiety threatened to overwhelm me.

*"You must remember this—A kiss is just a kiss,"* I sang softly, the familiar melody soothing my frayed nerves. *"A sigh is just a sigh…"*

Hank smiled faintly, his eyes on the road ahead. *"Casablanca,"* he said. "Eleanor's favorite. We saw it on our first date."

I glanced at him, surprised by the coincidence. "Patrick's too," I admitted. "We had our first kiss during that scene.

*"The world will always welcome lovers,"* I continued singing softly, *"As time goes by…"*

The lighthouse appeared in the distance as we crossed the causeway back to Grimm Island. Its beam swept steadily across the harbor waters where Elizabeth's body had been found all those years ago.

The island looked peaceful in the afternoon light, its oak-lined streets and pastel houses picture perfect against the coastal backdrop. But beneath that polished surface lay secrets buried deep—secrets someone was still willing to kill for.

I couldn't shake the feeling that we were heading straight into danger. I was just a tea shop owner, and I had no business chasing down clues or confronting powerful men with dangerous secrets.

As I turned onto Harbor Street, I caught a glimpse of headlights in my rearview mirror. A dark sedan, hanging back just far enough to seem innocent, but close enough to keep us in sight.

My hands tightened on the steering wheel as the reality hit me like a physical blow. They knew. Whoever had killed Elizabeth, whoever had spent twenty-eight years keeping her secrets buried, they knew we'd found what we were looking for.

But if they thought a little intimidation would make me back down, they clearly didn't know Mabel McCoy.

# CHAPTER
# TEN

DEATH HAD A WAY OF FOLLOWING ME HOME—LIKE GUM stuck to the bottom of my favorite vintage pumps. I slammed the *CLOSED* sign against the door with more force than necessary, sending the silver bell into a frantic jingle that matched my heartbeat. Charleston had left me with more than just answers—it had awakened old ghosts and created new ones.

"Some partner you are," I muttered to Chowder, who was sprawled in his window seat, paws twitching in doggy dreams. "I'm chasing down murderers while you're napping in the sunshine."

At the sound of my voice, one eye popped open. He snorted, then rolled over, presenting me with his wrinkled backside.

"So that's how it is," I said, turning back to the espresso machine. "Just remember who controls the treat jar."

My hands moved in a familiar rhythm, cleaning the gleaming silver surface until I caught myself humming "Someone to Watch Over Me," the irony not lost on me. The memory of Brooks' haunted expression flickered behind my eyes. *It was only supposed to be a fling, but I fell in love with her. It was impossible not to.*

The bell above the door jingled, snapping me from my dark reverie. My heart did a ridiculous little skip before I forced it back to a respectable pace. Right on schedule—so predictable I could set my watch by him—and yet somehow the sight of him still managed to surprise me every time.

"We're closed, Sheriff," I called over my shoulder, unable to hide the smile in my voice as I arranged the clean cups. "Even for Grimm Island's finest."

"Seems I've developed a habit of catching you after hours," he replied, his voice carrying a husky note that sent a bolt of electricity straight down my spine.

I spun around, retort ready on my lips, but the words dissolved on my tongue. He stood in the doorway, sunset backlighting him like he was posing for a magazine cover. Instead of his usual pressed uniform, he wore a gray suit that made him look more like a Wall Street executive than a small-town sheriff. The jacket stretched across his shoulders in a way that made my mouth go dry. His tie hung loosened at his neck, collar unbuttoned like he'd been slowly strangling all day and had finally broken free. His dark hair was mussed, as if he'd been running his hands through it in frustration, and the effect was devastating.

"Bad day with the press?" I asked, gesturing to his formal attire, hoping my voice didn't betray the sudden desert in my mouth.

He raked a hand through that already disheveled hair, the movement causing his jacket to pull tight across his chest.

Sweet mercy.

"Let's just say I prefer criminals to journalists," he said with a grim smile that would have sent lesser women to their fainting couches. "At least with criminals, you know where you stand." His eyes found mine as he moved deeper into the shop. "You never did give me an answer about dinner."

Heat crept up my neck as I remembered his earlier invitation. Between break-ins, mysterious stalkers, and treasure hunts, I'd conveniently forgotten to respond. "Been a little busy," I said, fumbling with a teacup that suddenly seemed determined to leap from my grasp. "The new sheriff is a real taskmaster."

The corner of his mouth curved upward, a small chink in his

professional armor. "I'll put in a good word for you. Everyone needs to eat. What do you say? Tonight? I was hoping we could talk somewhere more private."

My pulse betrayed me, but then I remembered the case. Of course he'd want to talk somewhere more private.

"Right," I said, trying not to sound disappointed. "No one knows we're working on this case. Where did you have in mind?"

"I was thinking my place," he said, watching me carefully.

"You cook?" I asked, my pulse going back into overdrive at the thought of being with him in his home. Alone.

He grinned and tugged at his tie again. "I'm a champion at takeout. I already know all the best places on the island."

I was having trouble getting enough spit in my mouth to swallow. "That is a bad, bad idea." My voice came out in a croak.

"Why?"

"Because my reputation would be shot," I said. "There is no mercy on this island. Denise Gruber got caught going to third base with her boyfriend when I was a senior in high school and she's been labeled damaged goods ever since. Couldn't get a date to save her life after that. She had to move to Colorado and start over. Finally found a husband last year, but I hear she's had to pay a fortune in therapy to get her self-esteem back."

"You're kidding," he said.

"This is the South," I said. "There are expectations."

"Who sets the expectations?"

"I have no idea," I said, having wondered the same thing my entire life. "It's the way it's always been."

"That makes no sense," he said. "I've been here less than a month and I already know more scandals about the people on this island than I've ever known anywhere else I've lived."

"So you've moved around a lot?" I asked, curiously.

He arched a brow and said, "Nice try."

"I thought so." And then I sighed. "Every family on this island has scandals. But everyone pretends they don't know about them. So they're secret scandals."

"Except everyone does know about them," Dash said.

"Yes, but there are rules. You talk about that kind of stuff behind people's backs. You don't bring it up in the middle of a dinner party. Unless someone has had too much to drink. That's happened from time to time. But then the next day everyone pretends the drunk person wasn't drunk and that whatever they brought to light never happened. It's how we function here."

"That's absolute insanity," Dash said, looking at me like I was from outer space. "So won't everyone pretend they don't know you're at my house for dinner and then talk about it behind your back? Why aren't you allowed a scandal?"

"Oh, I've had my fair share," I said, my lips pinching involuntarily. "Just ask anyone what they thought about Patrick marrying the McCoy girl."

"I thought McCoy was your married name," he said.

"No, Patrick's family name is DuBose," I said. "I'd planned to change my name, but we travelled for a lot of the first year we were married, and then when we came back to the island and bought the house I got busy with making it a home. I figured I'd get around to changing my name eventually, but then Patrick died. We were only married two years."

"I'm sorry," he said, and the sincerity in his voice almost brought tears to my eyes.

"Thank you," I said. "It was a difficult time. And my family doesn't have the island pedigree. The only reason I'm accepted now is because I'm Patrick's widow. In a lot of ways, it's a lot easier to be his widow than it was to be his wife. But there are behaviors that are expected along with that position. I can't just waltz into strange men's homes at night without facing the consequences."

"You think I'm strange?" he asked, smiling.

I felt heat rush to my face. "That's not what I meant. I just don't need to be tomorrow's headline at Grits and Giggles."

"You're a grown woman who'd be coming for dinner," he said. "I'm not asking you to show up naked and make us fried chicken."

"Well, that would be a terrible idea," I said. "I'd never make fried chicken naked. At least not without an apron."

He laughed, his eyes crinkling, and in that moment, I couldn't have told him my name if he'd asked.

"Now that's an image I won't get out of my head anytime soon," he said. "Come on. We'll go out to dinner instead. How come you're not worried about my reputation?"

"Oh, you're an outsider," I said. "You're expected to have a sordid reputation. It's practically a requirement."

"I had no idea there were so many expectations on this island," he said, studying me with those dark eyes.

"You haven't seen anything yet," I said. "There's a steakhouse on the edge of the island—The Salt House. I've heard it's good."

"Yeah, I've heard that too," he said. "We can stop by your house first to drop off Chowder."

I hesitated, suddenly imagining Mrs. Pembroke's opera glasses trained on us from across the street, her fingers already dialing the island gossip hotline.

"That would be nice," I said, the words emerging surprisingly steady.

Chowder's head popped up so fast I worried he'd given himself whiplash. His bulging eyes darted between us with an expression of pure canine calculation.

"Don't worry, boy," I said, scratching his wrinkled head. "I'll feed you dinner first."

After locking up, we walked into the parking lot and I noticed his Tahoe parked next to my car. "I'll follow you home," Dash said, his voice a dark promise that sent a shiver down my spine.

Ten minutes later, I stood in my bedroom, looking in the mirror and barely recognizing the woman staring back at me. I'd chosen a royal-blue dress that had been hiding in the back of my closet for years. The fitted bodice hugged my curves before flaring into a full skirt that swished satisfyingly when I moved. A matching fabric belt cinched my waist, tied with a small bow that added a touch of whimsy to the classic silhouette.

I'd painted my lips a deeper red than usual and pinned my hair in soft waves that framed my face. Pearl earrings caught the lamplight as I tilted my head, examining this strange creature in the mirror. Her cheeks were flushed, her eyes bright with something I hadn't seen in years—anticipation, excitement, life.

The blue made my blond hair seem brighter, my skin more luminous. I looked...awake. Like someone had finally tugged aside the heavy curtains I'd been hiding behind and let the sunlight pour in.

"Get it together, Mabel," I whispered to my reflection, catching myself humming "Fly Me to the Moon" as I adjusted an errant curl. "This is just dinner to discuss the case." The lie tasted sweet on my tongue, easy to swallow but impossible to believe.

I met Dash downstairs five minutes later, my pulse fluttering when his eyes traveled over the blue dress in unhurried appreciation. We took his car for the short drive to the restaurant, the silence between us comfortable yet charged with anticipation.

The Salt House was a white clapboard building nestled among ancient live oaks dripping with Spanish moss just before the expressway that led into Charleston. Twinkling lights wound through the tree branches, casting golden pinpricks against the deepening twilight sky. The scent of jasmine hung heavy in the air, mingling with the salt breeze off the water.

A hostess with a neat blond ponytail greeted us at the door. "Welcome to The Salt House. Do you have a reservation?"

"No," Dash said. "A quiet table if you have one."

She fluttered her eyelashes at Dash and gave him a flirtatious smile. "We have patio seating available. Right this way."

She led us through the dimly lit restaurant and out onto a pergola-covered patio. The roof was covered in trailing jasmine and the tables overlooked the water. The soft light of a candle glowed from each table.

"Enjoy," the woman purred at Dash, placing leather-bound menus on the table and lingering longer than she should have.

Dash never glanced at her, but instead held out my chair for me, his hand briefly grazing my back, and waited for me to sit down. That simple touch sent sparks shooting across my skin like electricity finding a new conductor.

"This is beautiful," I murmured, relieved to be outside and away from any prying eyes. I'd seen at least three people I knew on our walk through the restaurant.

"You look...different," he said, the word carrying unexpected weight.

"Different good or different bad?" I asked, suddenly self-conscious, spreading my napkin to give my hands something to do besides fidget.

"Different good," he confirmed, a slight smile playing at his lips. "I don't think I've seen you in that color before."

"I was saving it for a special occasion," I replied, then immediately wanted to kick myself. "Not that this is a special occasion. You want to talk about murder and the case. I just mean, I don't get out much so I wanted to wear it."

"Why do we wait for special occasions for the things we want?" he asked. "Why not wear the dress because you want to? Or drink the expensive wine that's meant for a celebration?"

"Are you a sheriff or a philosopher?" I asked.

"Being a cop means knowing a lot about human behavior and how people think," he said.

A sommelier appeared with the wine list. "Good evening. Can I start you with something to drink?"

"What wine do you suggest for celebrations?" Dash asked, his gaze never leaving mine.

I saw the humor there, but also something more—something deeper and darker that I had no idea how to handle. I was way out of my league with a man like Dash Beckett, and girlish fantasies weren't going to cut it.

"I have the perfect selection," the sommelier said. "I'll be back in a moment."

After he'd gone, Dash raised his water glass, the crystal catching the candlelight. "To unexpected partnerships."

I hesitated and then picked up my glass and clinked it against his. "To finding the truth."

It was only moments before the sommelier returned to the table and filled our glasses. The wine was velvet on my tongue, dark cherries and spice and something deeper, more mysterious. I took a second sip, feeling the tension of the day begin to loosen its grip on my shoulders.

"So what was your impression of Brooks?" Dash asked, his voice pitched low for privacy. "You've not mentioned your visit with him today."

"My impression is that he's been carrying the weight of Elizabeth's death for nearly thirty years," I replied. "And that he's lived with fear for just as long. His whole career was built on a foundation of silence and secrets."

Dash nodded, his expression darkening. "Men in power get very comfortable protecting each other. Break that pact, and the consequences can be severe."

"Is that why you're so interested in this case?" I asked, leaning forward slightly. "Because of corrupted power?"

Something flickered in his eyes, a shadow passing over deep waters. "Partially," he acknowledged, running his thumb along the rim of his glass. "I've seen what happens when the people meant to uphold the law decide they're above it."

There was a story there—something personal and painful—but before I could probe further, the server returned with a platter of antipasti that could have fed half the island. We spent a few moments selecting olives, cheeses, and cured meats while discussing the next steps in our investigation.

"We should talk to Clint Harrington," I suggested, spearing a marinated artichoke heart. "Based on what Brooks told us, his father was deeply involved with Milton and Cromwell. And Clint knew about Elizabeth's investigation into the development corporation."

"Harrington's not going to talk to us voluntarily," Dash pointed out. "He's one of the most powerful men in the state now. We need more leverage before we approach him. What about Milton's ex-wife?"

"Which one?" I asked. "He's got two. Though Dottie did say there was quite a scandal while Milton was married to his first wife, Lucinda. Apparently she lives on the mainland now."

Our conversation paused as the server delivered our entrées—grouper piccata for me, and a steak for Dash that made my mouth water just looking at it. The food was exquisite, but I found myself more intrigued by the man across from me than the meal before me.

I'd been watching that thin silver scar on his jaw since the first day he'd walked into my shop. The way it caught the light, how it somehow made him more real than the polished authority figures I'd known all my life. My curiosity finally got the better of me.

"Can I ask you something?" I ventured, setting down my fork.

He looked up, wariness darkening his eyes like gathering storm clouds. "I don't know," he said. "Depends on if this is a date or a business meeting. I figure on a date you can ask a personal question or two."

"Sneaky," I said.

"Thank you."

"Fine. It's a date. The scar on your jaw," I said, gesturing with my fork. "I've been curious since the first time I saw you."

His fingers went to it reflexively, tracing the silvery path as if confirming it was still there. Candlelight caught the movement, illuminating the slight ridges and valleys that marked where flesh had been torn and mended. For a moment, I thought he'd deflect the question, but then he took a deliberate sip of wine and set his fork down with precision that spoke of carefully maintained control.

"I worked undercover for the DEA," he said, his voice dropping so low I had to lean forward to catch the words. "Spent four years investigating a group of corrupt cops in New Orleans who were running a drug ring."

My fork clattered against my plate. "Four years?" The enormity of it struck me like a physical blow—four years living someone else's life, surrounded by people who would kill you if they discovered the truth.

He nodded, his gaze suddenly distant, seeing something far beyond our intimate table. "Deep cover. New identity, new background, new life. I was supposed to infiltrate the operation, gather evidence, and get out."

"But something went wrong," I said softly, the food forgotten between us.

Shadows seemed to gather around him, the scar deepening as his jaw tightened. "I was close to making a deal that would have implicated one of the ringleaders—a detective named Vidrine. We met at a warehouse by the docks. I was wearing a wire, but my backup was stationed too far away."

His fingers traced the scar again, following the path of a memory etched permanently into his skin. "Vidrine got paranoid. Started asking questions I couldn't answer. Then he pulled a knife—faster than I could react." His voice dropped to little more than a whisper. "Said he wanted to see what I was made of."

A chill raced down my spine despite the restaurant's warmth. My hand rose unconsciously to my own jaw, fingers ghosting over smooth skin as I imagined the blade slicing through his. I could almost taste blood in my mouth, copper and salt mixing with the lingering notes of wine.

"How did you get away?" I asked, hardly daring to breathe.

"I fought for my life until backup finally realized something was wrong and stormed the place," he said, his expression guarded in a way that told me there was more to the story—darker moments he was deliberately leaving in shadow. "You don't walk in shadows like that without walking out with scars."

The scar was no longer just a physical feature—it was the visible edge of a much deeper wound, the tip of an iceberg whose true mass lay hidden beneath the surface.

"So that's where you're from? New Orleans?" I asked, hungry for any scrap of information about this enigmatic man.

A smile touched his lips briefly before vanishing, like sunlight glinting off a wave before it's swallowed by the depths. "No," he said simply, taking another bite of his steak and effectively closing that line of questioning. "You can ask me more questions on our next date. Now it's your turn."

"My turn for what?"

"To tell me something about yourself," he clarified, setting down his utensils and giving me his full attention. The intensity of his focus was almost tangible, like being caught in a spotlight I couldn't escape. "Something I don't already know."

I laughed nervously, taking a sip of wine to buy myself time. "There's not much to tell. I'm not exactly exciting or mysterious."

"Try me," he urged, waiting with a predator's patience.

The wine had loosened my tongue, and once I started, the words tumbled out like water through a broken dam. "Well, I spend most of my time at the tea shop. I do crossword puzzles—always in pen, never pencil. I read mostly mysteries and historical fiction. I love old music, as you might have noticed, and I only like movies that have explosions or car chases. I crochet, but badly—my blankets always end up as trapezoids instead of rectangles."

I couldn't seem to stop myself. "I have a black thumb—every plant I touch dies a spectacular death. I can't dance to save my life, though I love to try when no one's watching. And I—"

"You're hiding," he interrupted, the words soft but sharp enough to slice through my rambling.

My fingers tightened around the stem of my wine glass. "Excuse me?"

"Behind all those little details," he continued, his gaze never wavering. "You're hiding who you really are."

Heat bloomed across my chest and crept up my neck, not from embarrassment but from the startling sensation of being truly seen— like he'd peeled back layers I'd forgotten were there.

"And who am I really?" I challenged, my voice emerging huskier than intended, betraying emotions I couldn't name.

He leaned forward, those dark eyes fixed on mine with an intensity that made my lungs forget how to function. The restaurant around us seemed to recede—the clink of silverware, murmured conversations, even the soft music playing in the background faded until there was nothing but the charged space between us.

"You tell me, Mabel McCoy," he said, his voice low and intimate.

"Who are you when you're not being Patrick's widow? When you're not being the proper tea shop owner everyone expects you to be?"

The question hit like a punch to the solar plexus, so precisely targeted it knocked the breath from my lungs. In all the years since Patrick died, no one had ever asked me that. I'd been so busy becoming what everyone expected—grieving widow, community business owner, proper Southern lady—that I'd forgotten there might be someone else beneath those carefully constructed layers.

"I don't know," I admitted, the honesty scalding my throat like strong whiskey.

"I think you do," he said, leaning closer until I could smell his aftershave mingling with wine and steak, a heady combination that made my head swim. "I think you've wrapped yourself in a cocoon of vintage dresses and perfect manners and widow's weeds. But the real Mabel McCoy is in there, waiting to break free."

My heart hammered so hard I could feel my pulse in my fingertips, my throat, behind my eyes. He'd somehow looked past all my careful defenses and seen a truth I'd been hiding even from myself.

"And who do you think she is?" I whispered, barely able to force the words past the tightness in my throat. "This real Mabel McCoy?"

His eyes held mine, dark and knowing. "I'm not sure yet. A free spirit? A rule-breaker? Someone wild and unpredictable?" His mouth curved into a smile that sent a shiver cascading down my spine like falling dominoes. "But I'm looking forward to finding out."

The moment stretched on, electric and dangerous. His hand rested on the table between us, and I had the overwhelming urge to reach out and touch it, to bridge the small physical distance that suddenly seemed to represent so much more.

The server materialized at our table, breaking the spell. "Everything is delicious, yes?" he asked, smiling between us.

I nearly knocked over my water glass as I leaned back, grateful for the interruption that allowed me to catch my breath. "Everything is perfect," I managed, though I could barely remember what I'd been eating.

We declined dessert and Dash paid the bill with a discretion and ease that showed me he wasn't a stranger to fine dining. Who was this man? Every moment I spent with him made me more curious.

Outside, stars scattered across the velvet sky like diamonds on black silk. The night air was heavy with jasmine and salt and possibility.

"We should go back to your place," Dash said as he opened the passenger door of the Tahoe and helped me in.

My pulse spiked embarrassingly, but before I could formulate a response, he added, "To work on the case. We need to make an evidence board, organize what we know so far. I can't do those things during regular work hours, and I can't keep it at the station."

"Right," I agreed, feeling like a dummy. "That makes sense."

The drive home was mercifully short, giving me little time to over-think the evening. Chowder greeted us at the door with suspicion that quickly morphed into betrayal when he recognized Dash, waddling over like he'd been waiting all night for him to return home.

"Traitor," I muttered as Dash crouched to scratch behind his ears.

"He just knows quality when he sees it," Dash replied with that half smile that did dangerous things to my equilibrium. "Let me bring in some things from the car. I wouldn't say no to some tea if you've got any."

I looked down at Chowder when he went back out the door. "Did he seriously just ask me if I've got tea?"

Chowder grunted and then waddled into the kitchen. I followed after him and started the pot boiling.

Dash brought in a large corkboard, along with colored pins, index cards, and string that reminded me of a middle school project I'd once done, and he spread them out over the dining room table.

"Very official," I observed.

"Law enforcement 101," he replied. "Visual organization helps see connections we might otherwise miss."

For the next few hours, we mapped out the case like generals plan-ning a battle. Photos, names, and dates covered the board in a web of colored threads and stark reality. We created categories of players—the deceased (Paul Cromwell, Clinton Harrington Sr.), the incarcerated

(Sheriff Milton), the potentially involved (Clint Harrington Jr., Lucinda Milton, Jason Brooks), and witnesses who might have seen something the night Elizabeth died.

"We should also talk to Vanessa," I said, making another card.

"Vanessa?" Dash raised an eyebrow.

"Milton's second wife," I explained. "They married not six months after his divorce from Lucinda was final. The ink was barely dry on those papers. Big scandal back then, not just because of the timing but because she was young enough to be his daughter—early twenties when he was pushing fifty."

"That would have been around '97 or '98?" Dash asked, making a note.

"Not long after Elizabeth died," I said. "The timeline's interesting. Lucinda was still his wife when Elizabeth died, but she left him shortly after. Then he married Vanessa." I tapped my pen thoughtfully. "They were only married a few years, but she still lives on the island."

"Any theories about that?" Dash asked.

"Island gossip suggested she got a generous divorce settlement," I said. "She opened that little boutique on Driftwood Street—Coastal Chic. The startup money had to come from somewhere."

"Another person of interest," Dash agreed, adding a thread connecting Vanessa to Milton.

I added more names to our list—potential witnesses who had been around in 1996, island residents who might have seen Elizabeth the night she died, former employees of Harrington Construction who might have known about the bribes and kickbacks we'd found in the lighthouse ledgers.

"I'm going to have Deputy Harris search through the old witness statements he found," Dash said, writing Harris's name on the board. "See if any of them match the names we've collected here. I've got him going through all the old boxes one by one. He may find more hidden evidence."

"Can you trust him?" I asked, remembering how Dash had mentioned he wasn't sure who at the department he could rely on.

"He's new," Dash said, though his expression remained guarded.

"Came in after the Milton scandal. No connections to the old guard. I've vetted him thoroughly and keep him on a need-to-know basis." He paused, a shadow crossing his face. "Trust but verify—a lesson I learned the hard way."

I nodded, feeling a surge of hope that we were actually making progress in uncovering the truth about Elizabeth's death.

"This is overwhelming," I said. "Look at all of these people. We haven't even scratched the surface."

"The Silver Sleuths need to divide and conquer," Dash said. "They've been deputized. If most of these people still live on the island they could have statements finished over the next couple of days."

"You realize once we start asking questions on the island you have no hope of keeping this under wraps."

"Yeah, I realize that," he said. "And we're going to use it to our advantage. It's pretty obvious someone doesn't want us digging into these old cases. They've already trashed the evidence room and sent someone to follow you. Now it's time to poke the hornet's nest."

By the time we finished, the grandfather clock in the hall had long since tolled midnight, its sonorous chimes the only sound in the sleeping house besides our voices.

I stretched, muscles protesting after hours bent over the evidence board. "I should probably call it a night. This is way past my bedtime. I have to be up in just a few hours."

"Yeah, me too," he said, collecting his jacket from the back of the chair. I walked him to the door, Chowder waddling alongside us like a furry chaperone. "You're going to have to explain to me again how it's okay for me to be here without ruining your reputation, but not for you to come to my house."

"Because I'm right here where anyone who wants to see what's going on can," I said. "Walt even climbed my fence so he could look in the windows when he heard you'd come by in the middle of the night. It's like having chaperones. We're basically sending out a signal to the community that no matter what time you come here, everything is aboveboard and no funny business is happening."

"The logic is mind blowing," he said. "Is there a rule book or something I can buy about Southern decorum?"

"It's a learned art," I told him. "You'll figure it out."

"So you're telling me that because we're being wide open about my being here in the middle of the night, that no one will assume the worst because people could be looking through your windows to check on your behavior?"

"Well, when you put it like that it does sound odd," I said, very nervous all of a sudden.

He turned to face me, one hand still on the doorknob. The hall light cast half his face in shadow, emphasizing the sharp angles of his cheekbones, the curve of his mouth as it lifted in a slow smile.

"If your reputation is already safe," he said softly, the words hanging in the air between us like a question. "We might as well push the limits a little. See if we can find the Mabel McCoy who breaks the rules and tests the boundaries of what's been built around her."

A thrill of excitement shot down my spine at his words, and I found I wanted to test the boundaries very, very much. He stepped closer, his hand coming up to cup my face with a gentleness that stole my breath. He gave me time to step back, to say no.

I didn't.

His lips met mine, and the world tilted on its axis. The kiss was gentle at first, almost questioning, but when I made a small sound of surprise, it deepened into something more urgent, more demanding. His hand slid to the nape of my neck, fingers tangling in my hair as his other arm wrapped around my waist, drawing me closer until I could feel the solid wall of his chest against mine.

I found myself responding with an enthusiasm that would have mortified me if I'd had the capacity for rational thought. My hands gripped the front of his shirt like I was drowning and he was the only thing keeping me afloat. The taste of him—wine and tea and something uniquely, intoxicatingly him—flooded my senses until I could hardly remember my own name.

When we finally broke apart, we were both breathing as if we'd run a race. His eyes were darker than I'd ever seen them, pupils dilated in the dim light of my entryway.

"I think that cocoon of yours is starting to crack, Mabel McCoy," he said, his voice rough with something that made my knees threaten to buckle beneath me.

Then he was gone, the door closing quietly behind him, leaving me standing in my hallway with my fingers pressed to lips that still tingled from his touch. My pulse thundered in my ears, each beat sending a wave of heat through my body until I felt feverish with it.

Chowder waddled up beside me, looking up with what could only be described as canine judgment, his wrinkled face somehow more disapproving than usual.

"Not a word," I told him, my voice unsteady, barely recognizable as my own. "Not one word."

He snorted and turned, heading toward the stairs with a dismissive swagger that clearly communicated his opinion on the matter.

I stood frozen for a moment longer, listening to the sound of Dash's car as it started and pulled away from the curb. Through the window, I watched his taillights disappear down Harbor Street, wondering what exactly I'd just gotten myself into. Ten years of carefully constructed widowhood, shattered by a single kiss that felt more real and forbidden than anything I'd experienced.

As I moved through the house turning off lights and straightening chairs that didn't need straightening, I couldn't help the smile that kept tugging at my lips. Snippets of melody escaped as I belted out "I Feel the Earth Move" by Carole King all the way up the stairs. I had no idea where it had come from. My music memory didn't really extend past the 1950s.

I stripped out of my dress and touched the silk of my nightgown, but I left it hanging over the back of the chair and fell face first into bed naked. I might not know exactly who Mabel McCoy was beneath all those carefully constructed layers, but for the first time in a very long time, I was looking forward to finding out.

# CHAPTER
# ELEVEN

My lips were still tingling when I unlocked The Perfect Steep at five thirty the next morning. I'd gone to bed with the ghost of Dash's kiss branded on my mouth and woken up with it still there, like a secret I couldn't quite keep to myself. Every time I thought about it—which was approximately every thirty seconds—my stomach performed elaborate somersaults.

The early morning routine helped ground me as I prepared for another day of serving tea while apparently also becoming an amateur detective. The scent of cinnamon and bergamot wrapped around me like a comforting blanket as I moved through the pre-dawn quiet, measuring loose tea leaves and warming ovens. By the time I'd finished baking scones and setting out the displays for the day, my regular morning customers had begun filtering in—Howard from the bookstore for his Earl Grey, Mrs. Pinkerton for her chamomile, and the construction crew from the harbor renovation seeking coffee.

For ten years, I'd been Widow McCoy, keeper of Patrick's memory and purveyor of fine teas. It was a role I knew how to play, comfortable as my vintage dresses and just as carefully preserved. But last night, standing in my foyer with Dash's hands cupping my face, I'd felt something crack open inside me—something wild and unfamiliar that had nothing to do with being a widow and everything to do with being a woman.

And it terrified me more than finding a cockroach in my lingerie drawer.

*"I've got you under my skin…"* I sang softly as I measured loose tea leaves with precision, trying to focus on the familiar rhythm of opening tasks rather than the memory of Dash's voice, rough with something primal, saying he was looking forward to watching me break free of my cocoon.

Chowder waddled in from the back room, where I'd set up his bed for the early mornings. He ignored me completely, making a beeline for his food bowl, snuffling and grunting with single-minded purpose. His entire wrinkled body communicated one clear message—breakfast trumped whatever human drama I was experiencing.

"Well good morning to you too," I said, pausing my tea measurements to fill his bowl. "At least one of us has priorities straight."

Chowder didn't even look up, his focus entirely on inhaling his kibble like it might escape if he didn't eat it immediately.

"Romance isn't on your radar, is it, buddy?" I asked, returning to my tea. "Smart dog."

The bell above the door jingled as Walt pushed his way in at ten o'clock, after the morning rush had cleared out. His Navy veteran cap was perfectly positioned, giving him an air of military discipline that even his eight decades couldn't diminish.

"The sheriff called us for a Silver Sleuth reconnaissance update," he announced, making his way to his usual table by the window with purposeful strides. "The others should be here momentarily."

"Morning, Walt," I said, setting down a cup of his usual Earl Grey, the steam curling upward like a question mark. "How was your morning?"

He eyes swept the room with practiced efficiency. "Good. We

should operate with an abundance of caution. Have you noticed anyone paying particular attention to the shop this morning?"

"No one's been lurking around or paying special attention to us," I assured him.

"During my time in Naval Intelligence, we learned that the most effective surveillance often happens in plain sight. The KGB once maintained a monitoring post in a Finland coffee shop that could pick up conversations in Moscow."

Before I could respond, the door chimed again as Dottie swept in, immaculately dressed in pants that were patterned like my Spode tea set and a white button-down tied in a knot at her waist. Her jet-black bob sat on her head like a helmet.

"I've reviewed those autopsy notes from the Calvert case," she announced, setting down her purse. "Cause of death was listed as drowning, but the bruising patterns on the wrists indicate restraint prior to submersion. There's clear evidence of perimortem trauma that was deliberately downplayed in the report."

"Morning, Dottie," I said. "Tea?"

She glanced up, momentarily distracted from her medical analysis. "Oh, yes. Thank you, Mabel." Her clinical gaze assessed me quickly. "You look flushed. You have a fever?"

My hand flew to my face. "Busy morning."

"Hmm," she replied, clearly unconvinced by my explanation but too polite to press further.

The bell jingled again as Hank and Deidre entered together, followed closely by Bea, who was wearing an eye-catching turquoise pantsuit with peacock-inspired accessories.

"My word, Mabel," Bea exclaimed, zeroing in on me immediately. "You're positively glowing this morning. I haven't seen that particular look since Margaret Wilson got caught with the tennis pro in the country club sauna. You're looking all hot and bothered."

"I just finished telling Dottie that it's been a busy morning," I said, arranging teacups. "Clarissa called in sick, so it was just me to deal with the morning rush. Genevieve is going to come relieve me in about an hour. I've got to hire a couple of more people. We're busy enough that I can justify it, and Clarissa isn't always reliable. Not to mention the tourist traffic has already gotten bad and summer hasn't even started."

While the thought was in my head I looked in the drawer under the register and found the *Help Wanted* sign, and I went to put it in the window.

"Clarissa is always sick," Dottie said, waving her hand in a dismissive gesture. "She's Junie Miller's granddaughter you know, so that explains a lot. This generation doesn't know how to work. Get a sniffle and then they're out for the count. Probably home playing video games. I remember working a double shift once when I was assistant medical examiner. I had high fever and chills. But I did my job because those people had loved ones who were relying on me."

"Good thing the dead don't care if you're contagious," Bea said dryly. "Before Dottie gets too high on her soapbox, I got a call from Mrs. Pembroke at the crack of dawn." Bea set her Louis Vuitton on the table with deliberate slowness. "She said the sheriff's car was parked outside your house until after midnight."

"We were working on the case," I said, realizing how incredibly lame that sounded.

"Of course you were," Deidre said encouragingly. "Otherwise Sheriff Beckett wouldn't have called us all in for an emergency meeting. I'm sure you discovered something very important."

"Like whether or not he's had a tonsillectomy," Bea said, waggling her drawn-on brows. "Lord, if I were forty years younger, I'd be climbing that man like a magnolia tree."

"Come now, Bea," Deidre chided, though her eyes sparkled with laughter. "Mabel's personal life is her own business."

"In this town?" Bea scoffed. "Sugar, there is no such thing. Especially when it involves Emma Jean Pembroke. That woman could spot a lipstick smudge on a collar from two counties over. Her nose for scandal is sharper than a hound dog on a jailbreak. She was one of my sources for years."

I was saved from further interrogation by the arrival of Dash himself, looking ridiculously handsome in his pressed uniform. Our eyes met briefly, and the memory of last night's kiss sent warmth creeping up my neck.

"Good morning, everyone," he said, his voice steady and professional. "Mabel."

"Morning," I managed, focusing on the teapot.

"Well, well, well," Bea murmured, her gaze bouncing between us. "Isn't this interesting."

"Thanks for coming on such short notice," he said, bulldozing ahead so not to give Bea a foothold in the conversation. "I've got a county budget meeting at eleven thirty, but I wanted to review what Mabel and I discovered last night with our evidence board."

I gave Bea and Dottie an "I told you so" look.

"Based on our mapping of Elizabeth's connections and the corruption timeline, I've identified key individuals each of you should focus on. The sooner we divide and conquer, the faster we'll get answers."

I poured tea for everyone, grateful for the familiar task as Dash opened a folder of documents that contained photocopies of our evidence board.

"Walt, I'd like for you to follow up with these former Harrington Construction employees," Dash said, sliding a list across the table. "Your background gives you the best chance of getting them to open up about the harbor project Elizabeth was doing research on."

Walt nodded, reviewing the list quickly. "I don't know some of these names. Transient workers most likely."

"Possibly," Dash said. "I had my admin go ahead and pull current addresses and phone numbers for you. All but one name on the list still lives in the Charleston area."

Walt nodded. "I'll crack these guys like an egg. If there's information to be had, I'll get it. Did you know I used to teach interrogation classes when I was in the military?"

"I saw that in your file," Dash said. "You're a scary man, Walt."

Walt seemed pleased, so I assumed he took it as a compliment.

"Deidre," Dash continued, "the evidence board pointed to missing records. I need you to dig into the historical archives of the Harbor Development Corporation. Property transfers, permit applications, anything related to the wetlands project Elizabeth was investigating."

Deidre's eyes lit up. "The county archives have everything from 1990 to 2000 in the basement. I've already called in a favor with the clerk to pull those boxes."

"Dottie," Dash continued, "your medical expertise is crucial. Can you analyze the autopsy report more thoroughly? Look for anything that contradicts the official drowning ruling."

"I've already started," Dottie replied. "I've identified three separate inconsistencies so far in the postmortem examination. The pattern of petechial hemorrhaging alone suggests asphyxiation prior to submersion."

Hank leaned forward, interested. "Would that be consistent with strangulation before entering the water?"

"Precisely," Dottie said, clearly pleased. "The hyoid bone also showed microfractures consistent with manual strangulation. I could tell that just by looking at the pictures. If you could exhume the body I could be even more thorough."

Dash winced. "I'd hate to put more stress on Elizabeth's father. Let's wait on that and see if you can find everything you need through other means." His gaze moved to Hank. "Hank, we identified the country club as a key information hub last night. Can you work your connections there? See if there's anyone with loose lips who remembers Elizabeth's death."

"Consider it done," Hank agreed. "I have a standing tee time with Judge Calloway tomorrow morning. Man's been a member for forty years and knows every skeleton in every closet on this island. He tends to become particularly talkative around the third hole when he's had a Bloody Mary or two."

"And Bea—" Dash turned to her, "—your social connections are invaluable for this investigation."

"You mean I know where all the bodies are buried," she said with a knowing smile. "Metaphorically speaking, of course."

Dash nodded. "The more Mabel and I searched through files and witness statements, the more connections we came across. But the statements left in the case file are incomplete at best. Some of them refer to statements taken, like Clinton Harrington, but his statement isn't in the file at all. We need information about the relationships between Milton, the Harringtons, and the Cromwells. Focus on the time period just before and after Elizabeth's death. I want all the dirt on all of them."

Bea's eyes lit up. "I'll dig through my files. It's going to be juicy. I remember that summer. This island was a hotbed of scandal. If I remember right, that was the same summer Cromwell's wife had an affair with Clinton Harrington."

"I don't think so," Deidre said. "I think that was several years before Elizabeth was killed."

"I've got pictures somewhere," Bea said. "If I'm right you have to let me go shopping with you to pick out some new clothes. And you have to pay for them."

"I have no desire to look like a lady of the night at my age," Deidre said. "I'm a Whitmore."

"Don't pull that lord of the manner attitude with me, Deidre Whitmore. I remember your Aunt Phyllis. Woman knew the inside of every bedroom on Grimm Island. And your Uncle Josiah married his first cousin."

"That's ancient history, Bea," Deidre said, sucking in her cheeks.

My eyes had grown wider as the conversation progressed, and everyone was quiet. None of this was ancient history to me, so I watched with fascination.

"Chicken," Bea said.

"Fine, you've got a deal."

Satisfied, Bea made herself at home behind the counter and poured herself a drink.

Dash turned to me last. He looked a little shell shocked, but he continued on with the briefing. "Mabel, you and Dottie should follow up with both of Milton's ex-wives as we discussed. See if you can jog their memories or shake loose information that we might not have in official reports."

"I have Lucinda's number, so I'll give her a quick call," Dottie said.

"We were friends when she lived on the island. But I haven't spoken to her since she moved away."

As the meeting broke up, each Silver Sleuth heading off with their assigned tasks, Dash lingered at the counter while I refilled the coffee carafe.

"You doing okay with all this?" he asked quietly.

"Sure," I said, smiling. "I'm living out my Nancy Drew fantasies and helping a group of octogenarians keep their minds active. Seems like a win in my book."

He smiled, but his eyes remained serious. "About last night—"

"We don't have to talk about it," I interrupted quickly, heart hammering. "It was just…"

"Just what?" he prompted, his voice dropping and his gaze dropping to my lips.

Before I could answer, Walt approached us with purposeful strides, interrupting the moment.

"I've got a plan of attack," he said, holding up his list. "Wish me luck."

As Walt left I turned back to Dash. "I'm pretty sure he's going to interrogate those construction workers like they're enemy combatants."

Dash chuckled. "He's formidable. I'd have loved to have someone like him on my team when I was in Afghanistan. He'll be a great asset for this case."

My eyes widen at the bit of information he let slip about himself, but I didn't say anything, hoping he'd reveal more. "None of them are to be underestimated. They've all had impressive careers, and now they're channeling all that expertise into this case."

"I'm starting to realize that," Dash said as the group filed out, each with their assigned mission.

"I better get to that budget meeting," he said reluctantly. He hesitated, looking like he wanted to say more, but instead simply nodded and headed for the door. Just before exiting, he turned back.

"By the way," he said, those dark eyes finding mine across the room, "you look nice today."

And then he was gone, leaving me with a fresh wave of butterflies and the unmistakable feeling that my carefully constructed widowhood was crumbling faster than I could shore it up.

"I got through to Lucinda," Dottie announced, making me jump. I'd forgotten she was still in the tea shop. "It just so happens she's coming to the island tomorrow to visit her sister. She'll meet us for lunch at The Blue Crab at eleven o'clock."

"That's great," I said. "We can head over to Vanessa's boutique now. I've never met her."

"You're not missing out on much," Dottie said, rolling her eyes. "Milton deserved every bit of that horror show."

I laughed and served sandwiches while we waited for Genevieve to show up to take the afternoon shift.

Dottie and I walked down Harbor Street and took a right onto Driftwood toward Vanessa's boutique. I intentionally slowed my pace some to make sure Dottie could keep up, but I ended up having to lengthen my stride. She was spry for a woman her age.

"So you're friends with Milton's first wife?" I asked.

"Oh, I've known Lucinda since we were girls," Dottie said. "Her maiden name is Conroy. She comes from one of the founding families. Those Conroy girls were something else back in the day. They were wild as wild could be, but they were fun. Everyone on the island wanted to be invited to a Conroy party. I think that's why Milton wanted Lucinda. He was always about having a good time. The dummy. Never did grow up."

"Amazing he was ever elected sheriff in the first place," I said.

"Lucinda's daddy helped with that," she said. "Wanted to make sure he could support his baby girl. Then Lucinda's sister Marjorie ended up marrying one of Roy Milton's cousins, but they divorced not long after Roy and Lucinda split up. Marjorie has pretty severe MS and can't travel easily, so Lucinda comes back to visit and check on things. But Roy burned her pretty badly."

"I'm surprised Lucinda moved away if her roots run that deep," I said.

Dottie nodded. "She's still got a lot of family here. And she owns property here. But being married to Milton must have been too much for her to bear, and she made her escape when she could. Family ties are hard to break here."

"Then good for her," I said.

Dottie looked at me with an intuitive gaze that made me uneasy. "You're thinking of the ties to your own family?" she asked.

I shrugged and said, "Families like the ones on Grimm Island fascinate me. Generations upon generations of the same last names and family properties. I never knew my grandparents. My mom's parents were divorced and she took off to marry my dad when she was barely seventeen. They didn't approve so she never talked to them again. Both of my dad's parents died in a car wreck when he was fifteen and he was swept into the foster care system. It's why he joined the military. It's just such an odd feeling to live in a place where you know you'll always be an outsider."

"And then you married Patrick and got an instant family with deep ties to the island," she said.

I grimaced, remembering the scandal. "I didn't have a lot of friends when the announcement was made that Patrick and I would be married, even though I'd grown up on the island. But once we got engaged, I had even less friends and a whole lot more enemies."

"Oh, I remember," Dottie said, chuckling. "Patrick's grandmother and I were contemporaries of sorts, but in all honesty I never cared for her much. She was a bit high in the hoof for a woman who'd been the daughter of a cotton farmer. Maybe that's why she was so hoity toity. But once she married Andrew DuBose you'd have thought she was the Queen of Sheba. She was a formidable woman, and she wouldn't have approved of anyone for Patrick unless she'd picked the woman herself."

I chuckled, remembering that Patrick had told me she'd tried to do just that.

"I had to give credit to Patrick though," she continued. "He took one look at you and it didn't matter a twig what his family said. They even threatened to cut him off you know."

"Yes, I know," I said softly. "He didn't care. He'd made his own way in the world and he was proud of that. He didn't need his family's money." I couldn't keep the pride from my voice.

"There you go," Dottie said. "Patrick was good people. And once the two of you said your vows, the family came around and they accepted you."

"Accepted might be a strong word," I said, laughing. "But the vows certainly made things easier. And for a time, it was nice to have a family." I sighed, realizing I couldn't remember the last time I'd seen Patrick's mother around town. His grandmother had passed on the year after Patrick had died. She'd taken his death very hard.

Dottie squeezed my hand affectionately and said, "Well, I've always been a firm believer that a family isn't necessarily the one you're born with, but the one you make."

The words hit me with unexpected clarity, like the first notes of a melody I'd known all my life but had somehow forgotten. Looking at Dottie's lined face, I realized I'd spent so many years defining myself by what I'd lost that I'd nearly missed what I'd found. The Silver Sleuths with their bickering and bourbon, their wisdom and war stories—they'd become my makeshift family when I wasn't looking. Walt's paranoia, Dottie's medical musings, Bea's outrageous gossip, Hank's judicial temperament, and Deidre's meticulous research— they'd filled the empty corners of my life with something that felt remarkably like belonging.

"You might be onto something there," I said, my throat suddenly tight with emotion I hadn't expected.

Dottie patted my arm knowingly, then straightened her shoulders.

"Now, let's go see what that viper Vanessa has to say for herself."

We approached Coastal Chic, a charmingly renovated storefront with large display windows showcasing resort wear in breezy pastels. A hand-painted sign in elegant script promised *Sophisticated Coastal Style for the Discerning Lady*.

"You said that Milton got what he deserved when he married Vanessa," I said. "Did you know her before she married him?"

Dottie snorted, the sound surprisingly delicate coming from her. "She was Judge Garfield's granddaughter. Everyone knew Vanessa. She was barely twenty-one and Garfield had gotten her a job working for the county clerk's office. That's when Milton honed in and decided she needed a mentor if she was going to make it in city government. Judge Garfield liked to have had a fit when he found out. And believe me, it didn't take long for everyone to find out. Their affair wasn't exactly a secret. They once got caught going at it in the public records office when they thought everyone had left for lunch. Much to Milton's chagrin the county clerk's office has cameras everywhere."

I winced. "And Lucinda found out?"

"It would have been impossible for her not to know. Milton didn't even try to keep it a secret. He wore that scarlet letter loud and proud." She shook her head. "That man weaponized humiliation like no one I've ever seen."

I pushed open the boutique door, setting off a delicate wind chime. The interior was a masterpiece of coastal chic—whitewashed wood, seagrass rugs, and artfully arranged displays of linen dresses and statement jewelry. The air smelled of an expensive sea-inspired perfume that was being pumped through the vents in the ceiling.

A woman emerged from the back room. She was tall, at least five ten, and she had honey-blond hair that waved artfully down her back. She had high cheekbones, full lips, and suspiciously smooth skin that suggested regular appointments with Charleston's finest cosmetic surgeons. She wore white linen pants and a gauzy blue top that exactly matched her eyes, accessorized with enough gold jewelry to sink a small rowboat.

"Welcome to Coastal Chic," she greeted with Southern warmth. "We just got in the most fabulous new…" Her voice trailed off as she registered Dottie, and her perfect smile flickered for just a moment. "Dorothy Simmons, isn't it? I haven't seen you in years. You haven't changed a bit."

Dottie smiled, showing a lot of teeth, and said, "Hello, Vanessa. This is my friend Mabel McCoy. Mabel, this is Vanessa Milton."

"Garfield," Vanessa corrected. "I went back to my maiden name after my divorce. Mabel McCoy." She stared hard at me, narrowing her eyes in thought. "I know that name from somewhere, but I can't place it."

"She was Patrick DoBose's wife," Dottie said, touching a beaded blouse that looked terribly uncomfortable.

"That's me," I said, instantly disliking Vanessa.

"So tragic," she said, her eyes looking suspiciously moist. "Patrick was a couple of years younger than me in school you know."

Since Patrick had been twelve years older than me I wasn't at all surprised to hear this. I'd known none of the friends he'd gone to school with when we got married.

"He had quite the reputation with the senior girls, even as an underclassman." She sighed dramatically and then giggled as if we were all sharing a joke. "We were all just shocked when he married you. Thought for sure you had to be in the family way."

I realized what Dottie had been talking about. Vanessa was as crazy as a possum in a knapsack.

"No," I said, my smile sharp enough to cut glass. "I guess it was just love."

"Hmm," she said, her eyes full of malice. "Do you still run the little tea shop?" She smoothed her hair back from her face. "It was so good of Patrick to leave you with money so you could dabble in your interests. You came out quite well, didn't you?"

"Except the part where my husband died."

Dottie sniffed and said, "You're one to talk, Vanessa Milton. Didn't Roy give you a nice settlement so you could open this store?"

The change was immediate. Vanessa's smile hardened into something brittle, and her hands dropped to her sides.

"I haven't been married to Roy in twenty years," she said coolly. "And I have no interest in discussing him now."

"Not even to help solve a murder?" Dottie asked.

Vanessa's eyes widened fractionally before she controlled her expression. "What murder? I don't know what you're talking about."

"Elizabeth Calvert," Dottie said. "The two of you would've been the same age."

"She was a year older," Vanessa said. "But I knew her. Thought she was smarter than everyone because she was going off to a fancy college. But she liked to party and she liked men. Discarded them like tissues all through high school."

"Doesn't mean she deserved to die," Dottie clapped back. "If it did you'd be six feet under."

"Well, I never—"

"Yes, you have," Dottie cut in.

"Sheriff Beckett is reopening the case," I said, wondering if Vanessa was the kind of woman who'd punch a senior citizen. I decided she probably was.

Vanessa laughed, but it held no humor. "And he sent you two as his emissaries? That's the most pathetic thing I've ever seen. What a loser. He won't last long around here. Though he is fine to look at."

"*Whore*," Dottie coughed.

I pushed Dottie behind me in case things got physical and said, "I'll let him know your opinion on the matter. But we've been deputized. Officially." I had to say I enjoyed the flicker of disbelief that crossed her perfect features.

"Like I said, pathetic. Now if y'all aren't going to buy anything, maybe you can go harass someone else."

"We came to ask questions about your good-for-nothing husband," Dottie said. "And we're not leaving until we find out what you knew about Elizabeth's death."

I winced, thinking Dottie had seen way too many episodes of *Law and Order*. Her bedside manner with the dead was probably much better than with the living.

"Well, Deputies," Vanessa said, voice dripping with sarcasm, "I'm afraid I can't help you. Roy and I didn't get married until a year after Elizabeth was dumb enough to go swimming in the harbor at night. I didn't even know him while he was investigating that case."

Dottie's eyebrow shot up. "You lie like a rug, Vanessa. You were working in the county clerk's office the year Elizabeth died. Everyone knew you and Roy were already boinking. If I remember right there's video to prove it."

Vanessa's face flushed with anger. "You vicious—"

"Uh, uh, uh," Dottie said, wagging her finger. "Mabel and I don't tolerate that gutter language."

Vanessa straightened her shoulders and channeled the ice queen. "This is a place of business, not an interrogation room. Get out of my shop."

Dottie put her hands on her hips and stepped closer—her head only coming up to Vanessa's ample bosom. Her voice lowered and she half hissed, "We can continue this conversation here, or we can have a deputy pick you up for formal questioning. I'm sure your customers would love to see you escorted out in handcuffs."

I decided the best course of action was to stand perfectly still and hope no one remembered I was still in the room. I had no idea if we could follow through on that threat, and I didn't particularly want to find out. Vanessa looked like she'd be comfortable with resisting arrest.

"You wouldn't dare," Vanessa spat out.

"Try me," Dottie replied, reminding me of an old gunslinger. "I spent forty years cutting open dead bodies to find the truth. You think I'm squeamish about making a scene?"

For a moment, they stared each other down like two cats on a fence.

"Fine," Vanessa hissed, moving behind the counter. "What do you want to know?"

"Roy Milton is in prison," Dottie pointed out. "His power is gone. The men who protected him for years are either dead or desperately distancing themselves. He can't hurt you if you tell his secrets."

"You think I need protection from Roy?" Vanessa laughed, but there was an edge to it. "Roy was child's play. You think I got where I am today because I'm stupid? In the end I got more than half of everything Roy had, and he was happy to give it to me."

"Why?" I asked.

"Let's just say I learned early on to keep insurance policies," she replied.

"What do you know about Elizabeth Calvert's murder?" I asked.

"All I know is the night Elizabeth was supposedly killed Roy was with me," she said. "He got a call about ten o'clock and pulled on his pants faster than if his wife was standing in the room. Told me there was an emergency and he had to go. The next morning it was all over the news that Elizabeth's body had been found."

"You think he had something to do with her death?" I asked.

"Not Roy," Vanessa said. "He was a coward at heart. Wouldn't have the guts to kill anyone himself. Always had guys to do his dirty work for him."

"Who?" I asked.

"That's all the time I have today," she said.

"So it's someone besides Roy you're afraid of," Dottie said.

Vanessa mouth tightened stubbornly. "I have inventory to catalog."

Dottie grunted and we turned to leave the shop. But she stopped at the door and turned back. "You know what I find funny," she said. "Or maybe just coincidental. Is how you purchased this building from Lucinda for right at market value. It's prime real estate. Do the two of you stay in touch?"

Vanessa's composure cracked just slightly. "You're mistaken. I purchased this building through a brokerage firm."

Dottie just smiled knowingly and we left Vanessa standing rigid behind her counter, her face a carefully controlled mask that didn't quite hide the calculation behind her eyes.

"Well," I said once we were safely out of earshot, "That was pretty useless."

"We got more information than you realize," Dottie said. "She was lying about almost everything."

"How'd you know about her buying the boutique from Lucinda?" I asked.

"Hank told me," she said. "A friend of his was the presiding judge during Roy and Lucinda's divorce, and apparently Roy didn't want to divulge that he owned this whole strip of real estate. Had it buried under some bogus developer name. I'm sure Harrington helped him with that."

"Good grief," I said. "Commercial real estate on Grimm Island is worth millions."

"Exactly," Dottie said. "Makes you wonder how an elected sheriff could afford all that, doesn't it?"

"I take it the judge found out he was hiding assets?" I asked.

"And then some," Dottie said, grinning. "Turns out an investigative reporter had put together a nice little exposé on Milton's assets and published it in the *Gazette* with receipts. I believe you know the reporter."

"No," I said, mouth falling open. "Bea?"

"She's very gifted," Dottie said. "Probably one of the best investigative journalists in the country with the best sources. But she liked the gossip beat because it scandalized her family more."

Our walk back to the tea shop was slower than a snail race on a hot summer day. Dottie kept stopping to window-shop, claiming interest in everything from garden ornaments to fishing tackle. I wasn't born yesterday—she needed to rest but was too proud to admit it. All the Silver Sleuths were cut from the same stubborn cloth, acting like their Medicare cards were invitations to the Olympic trials.

"Want an ice cream?" I asked as we approached Lickety Split. "My treat."

Dottie's face brightened like she'd just spotted a perfectly preserved cadaver. "I wouldn't say no to one. I'm partial to the raspberry swirl."

We stepped into the parlor's cheerful interior, and Dottie made a beeline for one of those white wrought-iron chairs with the heart-shaped backs, lowering herself with the careful precision of someone whose knees had opinions about sudden movements. I ordered our ice creams and paid, but by the time I turned around, she'd already hauled herself back to her feet, clutching her purse like it contained state secrets.

"I can't dawdle today," she announced. "I want to be home in time for my afternoon soaps."

"So finish telling me about Lucinda and Vanessa. And Bea," I said, handing her the raspberry swirl.

Dottie's eyes sparkled with gossip as she took a lick. "Well, let's just say there's never been any love lost between Milton and Bea. That exposé sealed his fate—after the judge found out Milton had been hiding assets, he awarded Lucinda the majority of all their real estate holdings outright." She lowered her voice conspiratorially. "If Milton could've murdered Bea and gotten away with it, I think he would have. He was livid.

"But then Milton and Vanessa headed to divorce court," she continued, gesturing with her ice cream cone, "and Vanessa isn't nearly as smart as Lucinda was. Milton learned from his first mistake and got Vanessa and her attorney to agree to what they thought was a generous cash settlement."

"I'm assuming he didn't disclose everything again?" I asked, already knowing the answer.

"Bingo," she said, pointing her ice cream at me. "But Vanessa didn't know that, so she jumped at the cash offer and signed the papers. Went before the same judge too." Dottie's eyes narrowed. "From what I understand, the judge made a comment after he'd looked at the signed agreement that got Vanessa's wheels turning. You see, Lucinda's the one who reached out to Vanessa and offered to let her buy the boutique property."

"Good grief, why?" I asked, nearly dropping my cone. "I thought Lucinda hated her. She's a horrid woman."

"I don't know why," Dottie said, shrugging. "Maybe she felt sorry for her. Lucinda knew better than anyone what it was like to be married to Milton." She dabbed at her mouth with a napkin. "But it never set right with me. It'll be interesting to talk to Lucinda tomorrow."

"You think she and Vanessa are in contact now?"

"That would be a fascinating development, wouldn't it?" Dottie mused, a sly smile crossing her face. "Two women with every reason to hate each other, turning out to be partners?"

▭

The Perfect Steep was still buzzing into the dinner rush, and I was glad for Genevieve's help. Word of our investigation had spread through town with the efficiency of a Cat 5 hurricane, and it seemed like half of Grimm Island had suddenly developed an urgent need for tea and sandwiches. The usual after-dinner crowd had swelled to three times its normal size, with people lingering over their cups and craning their necks whenever the bell above the door jingled.

I moved between tables, fielding not-so-subtle questions with deliberate deflection. *No, I haven't heard anything about unmarked graves. Sorry, I don't know why the sheriff was looking at old harbor development records. Yes, these are new earrings. No, they weren't a gift from the sheriff.*

By closing time, my face hurt from maintaining a pleasant smile, and my ears were ringing from the constant hum of speculative conversation. As I flipped the sign to *CLOSED*, ushered Genevieve out the door and locked it behind her, I let out a sigh of relief that whistled between my teeth.

I didn't mind the extra business, but the barely concealed nosiness was exhausting. Still, I'd learned from the snippets of conversation that our investigation was stirring up old memories. I'd overheard Mrs. Townsend telling her bridge club that her late husband had mentioned irregularities with the harbor project permits. And Mr. Caldwell had reminisced about Elizabeth Calvert's unfortunate accident with a knowing look that suggested he'd never believed it was an accident at all.

People were talking. And where there was talk, there were slip-ups. Secrets couldn't stay buried forever.

As I wiped down the last table, my mind kept circling back to Vanessa and Lucinda. You couldn't be married to a man like Milton and not know some of his secrets.

I moved to the back of the shop to empty the dishwasher, the mundane task soothing after a day of high-tension conversations. The gentle rhythm of stacking cups and saucers grounded me, a reminder of the simple life I'd built here.

I was so lost in thought that at first, I didn't notice the cool draft from the back door. When it finally registered, I froze, cup in hand, the porcelain suddenly cold against my fingers. I knew I'd locked that door after taking out the trash earlier. I always locked it—island crime rates notwithstanding, ten years of living alone had made me meticulous about security.

Setting down the cup with a deliberately steady hand, I reached for my phone. But before I could dial, I noticed something else—a small white envelope on the floor just inside the door, as if it had been slipped underneath.

My name was written on it in block letters.

Common sense said to leave it alone, to call Dash immediately. But curiosity had always been my weakness, and before I could stop myself, I picked up the envelope and tore it open.

Inside was a single sheet of paper with eight words written in block letters that turned my blood to ice water.

*STOP DIGGING, OR YOU'LL END UP LIKE HER.*

The paper dropped from my fingers like it had suddenly caught fire. My heart hammered against my ribs with enough force to register on the Richter scale, and my lungs seemed to have forgotten their basic function. Every shadow in my usually cozy shop transformed into potential hiding places for whoever had invaded my space. The familiar squeak of the floorboard near the kitchen nearly sent me through the ceiling, until I realized it was just Chowder waddling in from his nap, blissfully unaware that his owner was two heartbeats away from a cardiac event.

I fumbled for my phone, dropping it once before managing to find Dash's number with fingers that felt like they belonged to someone else. I jabbed at the screen and held my breath.

"I was wondering when you'd call me," Dash answered, his voice warm and teasing.

"Someone was in my shop," I said, skipping the pleasantries. My voice came out surprisingly steady for someone whose internal organs were performing an Irish step dance. "They left a note. A threat."

The silence that followed was brief but loaded.

"Lock the door and don't touch anything else. I'm on my way." The dangerous edge in his voice made the hair on my arms stand at attention.

I stood frozen, staring at the eight words that had turned my quaint tea shop into a crime scene, when something warm pressed against my legs. Chowder looked up at me, his wrinkled face scrunched with what appeared to be genuine concern—a departure from his usual expressions of judgment or hunger.

"Someone's playing for keeps, buddy," I whispered, oddly comforted by twenty pounds of snorting, shedding bulldog. Chowder pawed at my ankle and whined, which in bulldog was practically a soliloquy of emotional support.

The initial shock began to fade, replaced by something unexpected —determination. Whoever left this note wasn't making a casual threat. They were scared. Scared of what we might uncover. Scared we were getting close.

I straightened my shoulders and took a deep breath. Elizabeth Calvert had been silenced permanently for seeking the truth. I'd be darned if a threatening note was going to stop me from finding it.

# CHAPTER
# TWELVE

Dash arrived in less than five minutes, blue lights flashing as his cruiser stopped outside The Perfect Steep. Deputy Harris was with him, the young officer looking simultaneously nervous and determined as he followed Dash's lead. Where Dash moved with the experience of someone who'd seen it all, Harris had the eager alertness of a rookie getting his first real taste of detective work.

"Where is it?" Dash asked, scanning the shop as if expecting to find the intruder still hiding behind the pastry case.

I pointed to the white paper on the floor, the block letters glaring up at us—*STOP DIGGING, OR YOU'LL END UP LIKE HER.*

Dash crouched beside it, careful not to touch the evidence. His expression darkened as he read the words, jaw tightening visibly. "Harris, get the kit. Dust for prints and when the next deputies arrive have them start looking for signs of break-in and doing door-to-doors. It's still daylight outside. Maybe someone saw something."

While Harris retrieved evidence-collection supplies from the cruiser, Dash gently guided me to a chair, his hand warm and reassuring against the small of my back. He handed me a bottle of water and then said, "Tell me exactly what happened."

I recounted the evening—closing up, washing dishes, discovering the unlocked back door and the note.

"You're sure you locked that door earlier?" he asked.

"Positive," I said. "I always double-check. Island habits."

Harris returned with an evidence kit, photographing the note from multiple angles before carefully lifting it with gloved hands and slipping it into a clear plastic bag. He moved to the back door, dusting the handle for fingerprints while Dash remained at my side. I took a drink of water to wet my parched throat and noticed my hands weren't shaking quite as bad as they were before.

"We're making someone nervous," Dash said, his voice low. "That's good. Means we're getting close."

"Close to what? Being the next body found in the harbor?" I replied, which earned me a look that was equal parts concern and admiration.

"With that kind of humor, you have the makings of being an excellent cop."

"No, thank you," I said. "Police uniforms are not at all flattering to the female body."

He laughed and squeezed my hand. "I want to station a patrol car outside your house tonight."

"Nope." I said. "Nothing screams come and get me like a police cruiser parked in the driveway. Haven't you ever seen a horror movie?"

"I don't really watch movies," he said.

"Good Lord," I said. "I let you kiss me without knowing a thing about you. How do you not watch movies?"

"Maybe you can convince me they're not all garbage on our next date," he said. "Then we'll kiss again and you'll know more about me. Now focus please. Someone threatened you. This isn't the time for stubborn independence. You've been followed and now this."

"I'll be fine," I insisted. "Chowder's a light sleeper. And I have excellent security. I'll even activate the alarm."

He closed his eyes. "You don't activate your alarm at night?"

"The panel is downstairs," I said. "By the time I get upstairs I don't want to walk back down to hit the button. But I'll remember tonight. I swear."

He closed his eyes and made a strangled sound somewhere between a groan and a laugh. "Fine," he said. "I'm following you home and checking every room myself. And then I'm going to wait outside the door and make sure you activate the alarm. Do you have cameras?"

"Top of the line," I said. "I don't really do technology though. I think the feed goes into the cloud somewhere. I don't know how to get it back out."

The look on his face was somewhere between pity and incredulity, and he leaned forward slightly.

"Don't kiss me," I said, narrowing my eyes.

He grinned and said, "I wasn't going to." And then he leaned a little closer and reached down. "You dropped the lid to your water bottle."

I grabbed it and screwed it on tight, my face flaming in embarrassment.

"Too bad you don't want me to kiss you," he said. "You're pretty cute when you're irritated."

An hour later, after a thorough investigation of the tea shop and an equally thorough search of my house, Dash finally seemed satisfied that no immediate danger lurked in my closets or under my bed. Chowder had followed him from room to room, supervising the security sweep with surprising attentiveness.

"Well, Mabel McCoy," he said. "You have a ridiculous amount of clothes. But no monsters in your closets."

"That's a relief," I said dryly. "Now stick a fork in me, because I'm done for the night. I've got Genevieve and Clarissa covering for me tomorrow. And if you show up and wake me up between the hours of midnight and eight tomorrow morning then I can't be responsible for what Chowder does to you."

Since Chowder was currently lying on his back at Dash's feet, it felt like an empty threat. But I needed sleep. And maybe another kiss. But I was trying not to think about that.

Dash looked down at Chowder and gave him another belly rub. "Lock the doors and turn on the alarm," Dash instructed. "Call me immediately if anything—and I mean anything—seems off."

"I've got you on speed dial," I said, herding him out the door.

He leaned in slowly and I tilted my head slightly, and then I felt his lips on my forehead.

"What's that about?" I asked.

"You're looking a little dangerous tonight. And somewhat unhinged. I'm playing it safe."

"Out," I said, narrowing my eyes. "Who kisses someone on the forehead?" I muttered under my breath and then closed the door in his face. He'd looked amused and on the verge of laughter.

"Not a word from you," I said to Chowder as I set the alarm. "You men are all the same. Do I look like a woman who wanted a kiss on the forehead?"

Chowder didn't answer. He bolted up the stairs and when I finally got into bed I realized he was already under the covers and snoring on his side.

"Just like a man."

<hr>

Despite telling myself I was going to sleep late come hell or high water, I'd been staring at the ceiling and replaying the note in my mind since five o'clock. *STOP DIGGING, OR YOU'LL END UP LIKE HER.*

Chowder snorted in his sleep, completely unbothered by existential dread or death threats. I envied him his canine simplicity.

I gave up on sleep and dragged myself into the shower where I sang "Que Sera, Sera" until my fingers were pruny and my attitude was sunny. Forty-five minutes later, I'd channeled my inner Doris Day and transformed from frazzled insomniac to something resembling a functioning human.

I chose a navy fit-and-flare dress with yellow lemons printed on it, trimmed with delicate white lace around a slightly lower neckline than I normally wore. I rarely took it out of the closet—the neckline had always felt a bit too daring for daytime on Grimm Island—but today I was feeling bold. Maybe it was the lack of sleep, or maybe it was a little revenge for Dash's patronizing forehead kiss. Conservative enough for lunch with a former sheriff's wife, but with just enough va-va-voom to make a point.

By nine, I'd consumed enough coffee to give a hummingbird heart palpitations and was pacing my kitchen, rehearsing questions for Lucinda.

"So, when exactly did you realize your husband was taking bribes? And by the way, did he ever mention murdering anyone? Just curious."

Chowder gave me a side-eye from his perch on the kitchen stool.

"What? Too direct?" I asked him. "Fine. You come up with something better."

The doorbell rang. I froze, suddenly remembering every horror movie I'd ever seen where the heroine answers the door only to meet her grisly end.

The bell rang again, followed by a familiar voice. "Mabel? It's Dottie. I'm early."

I exhaled and shuffled to the door, peering through the peephole to confirm it was indeed Dottie standing on my porch, with Bea right behind her. Dottie was wearing white pants and a moss-green sweater set that matched her glasses, while Bea was resplendent in a turquoise caftan with bold golden jewelry that probably weighed more than she did.

"Sorry," I said, opening the door. "After last night, I'm a bit jumpy."

"Understandable," Dottie replied, stepping inside with Bea close behind, leaving a cloud of expensive perfume in her wake. "I hope you don't mind I invited Bea along. Lucinda owes her big time for that exposé on Milton's hidden assets, and she might have looser lips with Bea there."

"Plus," Bea added with a sly smile, "Lucinda and I have what you might call a complicated relationship. She provided information for my stories, I helped destroy her ex-husband. The usual island dynamics." She gave my outfit an appraising once-over. "Look at you with that neckline. Someone's feeling frisky today." She winked. "I approve."

"Good Lord, Mabel," Dottie said. "You're wound tighter than a banjo string in a tornado. You need some chamomile. We've got time before lunch. Besides, Bea's got some inside information that might help us with Lucinda."

I followed them into the kitchen and watched as Dottie put on the kettle for tea. She pushed me down on a stool at the kitchen island and went about the business of getting things set up.

"I'm nervous," I confessed. "I'm not exactly experienced in extracting information from potential murder witnesses. Between being followed and the note left for me last night, I'm not sure I'm the best choice for a posse member."

"Nonsense," Dottie said. "I know you've seen *Tombstone* at least a dozen times. You're a perfect choice to be in this posse. You should get a gun. It'll make you feel more authentic."

"I've got one," I said. "It was Patrick's. I keep it in a shoebox in the hall closet."

"Fat lot of good it does you there," Dottie said, shaking her head.

"Relax," Bea said. "Just follow our lead. You'll be fine." She settled onto the stool next to me. "You know I was married to three of the biggest pathological liars in South Carolina. Trust me, I know when someone's hiding something."

"And I've spent forty years analyzing evidence," Dottie added, putting a teacup in front of me and pouring out from the pot. "People forget I used to get information out of bodies for a living. Living people are probably that much easier."

Bea waved a bejeweled hand as Dottie poured her tea. "I hate chamomile," she said, sniffing the cup. "Taste like weeds." She pulled out a flask from her purse and poured in a generous amount. "You know I wrote that exposé on Milton's hidden assets during his and Lucinda's divorce?"

"Dottie mentioned it," I nodded.

"What she probably didn't tell you," Bea continued, leaning forward conspiratorially, "is that Lucinda was my source."

Dottie's eyebrows shot up. "You never told me that!"

"Professional ethics, darling," Bea replied with a smirk. "A journalist never reveals her sources. But given the circumstances, I think the statute of limitations has expired." She took a sip of her tea and grimaced. "Still tastes like weeds."

"Get to the point, Beatrice," Dottie said.

"Anyway," Bea said, giving Dottie a narrow-eyed glare, "Lucinda brought me photocopies of bank statements, property deeds, all filed under shell companies. Milton had millions tucked away that she never knew about until she started digging."

"So Lucinda wasn't just going to let Milton get away with it," I said, thinking it through. "She fought back with the legal system."

"Honey, that woman had put up with decades of bad behavior—multiple affairs, being degraded in public—she turned victimhood into a revenge masterclass," Bea said admiringly. "Milton never knew what hit him. She didn't just want her fair share—she wanted justice. And she got it."

An hour later, armed with Bea's insights, we drove to The Blue Crab—a Lowcountry institution housed in a pristine Colonial-style building at the end of the municipal pier. With its crisp white columns, wraparound veranda, and panoramic harbor views, it was the kind of place where reservations were made months in advance and the maître d' knew which families had status. The interior featured polished heart pine floors, crystal chandeliers, and tables draped in starched white linens that were refreshed between courses. It was elegant without being stuffy, refined without being pretentious—exactly what you'd expect from one of the island's oldest establishments.

"Perfect choice for meeting Lucinda," Bea said as we were seated at a prime window table overlooking the water. "Public, but discreet. I have a standing reservation here. I did a little favor for the owner once upon a time."

I scanned the dining room nervously.

"Relax," Dottie advised. "No one's going to try anything in broad daylight with two dozen witnesses around."

"I've read enough murder mysteries to know that's exactly when they try something," I countered, adjusting the silverware that was already perfectly aligned. "Poison in the sweet tea, shellfish added to food when they know you're allergic…"

"You're starting to think like Walt," Bea laughed, arranging her napkin across her lap with theatrical precision. "Next thing you know, you'll be wearing a wire and speaking in code phrases. Bless him."

"Walt's paranoia is infectious," Dottie agreed. "But in this case, a little caution isn't the worst idea."

Before I could respond, a woman entered the restaurant, and Dottie straightened in her seat. "There she is," she murmured, raising a hand in greeting.

Lucinda Milton was nothing like I'd imagined. I'd expected a shriveled, bitter woman worn down by decades of Milton's shenanigans. Instead, the woman gliding toward our table looked like she'd just stepped off a yacht in Monaco. Tall, slender, with silver hair swept into a perfect chignon that probably hadn't moved since the Clinton administration. Her white linen pants and coral blouse screamed "I summer in Martha's Vineyard," and the chunky silver necklace around her neck could've doubled as a weapon in a pinch.

"Dorothy," she greeted, air-kissing Dottie. "It's been an age."

"Lucinda, you look marvelous," Dottie replied, gesturing to the empty chair.

"Beatrice," Lucinda acknowledged with a glacial smile that never quite reached her eyes. "Still spilling secrets, I see."

"Only the ones that deserve spilling," Bea shot back. "Your divorce exposé is still taught in journalism classes at Charleston College."

A smirk played at Lucinda's lips. "We both came out ahead in the Roy Milton stupidity sweepstakes."

"This is Mabel McCoy," Dottie interjected. "She owns The Perfect Steep tea shop on Harbor Street."

Lucinda's sharp green eyes sized me up like I was a racehorse she was considering buying. "Patrick's widow," she stated, no question mark required. "I sent flowers. I knew his grandmother. Terrible tragedy."

"Yes," I said automatically, the response worn smooth from a decade of repetition.

She settled into her chair with the grace of someone who'd never worried about making ends meet. A waitress materialized instantly—money still commanded that kind of service, even in a place like The Blue Crab.

"So," Lucinda said once drink orders were placed, "Dorothy tells me you're digging into my ex-husband's business. Can't imagine voluntarily spending time on Roy, but color me intrigued."

"The sheriff has reopened the Elizabeth Calvert case," I said, cutting to the chase.

Something dark flickered behind Lucinda's carefully maintained façade. "Well, isn't that a blast from the past." Her perfectly manicured fingers tapped the tablecloth. "Elizabeth Calvert. That poor girl."

"You knew her?" I asked.

"No. But everyone knew *of* her," Lucinda replied, twisting a diamond tennis bracelet. "When they pulled her from the harbor, you couldn't buy milk without hearing three different theories about what happened." Her eyes narrowed. "Roy was obsessed with the case—for about five minutes."

"Meaning?" Dottie pounced on the opening.

"One week he's Mr. Super Detective, interviewing witnesses at all hours, barely sleeping." Lucinda snapped her fingers. "The next? Accidental drowning, case closed, let's move on, nothing to see here."

"That didn't strike you as suspicious?" I asked.

"It wasn't my place to interfere in police work. Besides, I was busy cataloging his mistresses and figuring out which assets he was hiding." Her smile could've frozen Hell over. "Roy's extracurriculars kept me quite occupied."

"Like Vanessa," Bea said, cutting straight through the polite veneer.

"Among others," Lucinda confirmed with a dismissive wave. "Roy collected women like some men collect baseball cards. And there are certain types of women who are attracted to the power Roy wielded. Because we know they weren't attracted to his looks. Vanessa just happened to be the one who got the ring." She shrugged one elegant shoulder. "By then, I was focused on getting what was owed me. The Conroy name still opened doors, even if Daddy had gambled away the fortune behind them."

"So what finally pushed you out the door?" I asked. I'd never been much for small talk, especially when murder was on the menu.

Her perfectly shaped eyebrows rose slightly. "Direct approach. I approve." She gazed toward the harbor, where boats bobbed like toys in a bathtub. "It wasn't the affairs—women of my generation wrote the manual on looking the other way. It was the money."

"What money?" Dottie perked up like a bloodhound catching a scent.

"My daddy didn't raise a fool," she said. "I'd already decided to leave Roy once I found out he'd been hiding assets from me. I also knew he was involved in something with the Cromwells and the Harringtons, because we not only lived well, but Roy had secretly acquired a lot of assets. I'd been totally clueless. And that's just unacceptable.

"But after Elizabeth died, Roy stumbled home drunk—unusual for him. He was rambling about all kinds of things, incoherent really. But he mentioned blackmail and problems he didn't know how to solve. He said he didn't know who to go to. There was no one he could trust."

She took a delicate sip of tea. "When I asked Roy where all our money was coming from, he exploded like a cheap firecracker. Told me to shut up and to keep enjoying the lifestyle." Her voice dropped even lower. "Then I found a woman's watch hidden in his desk—expensive, with an inscription—*To Elizabeth—Seek Truth. Stay True.*"

The hairs on my arms stood at attention. I exchanged a look with Dottie, whose eyes had widened to cartoon proportions.

"From Elizabeth's body?" I asked, though we all knew the answer.

Lucinda nodded. "When I confronted him, Roy showed his true colors." She absently rubbed her wrist. "Grabbed me hard enough to leave fingerprints, demanding to know what else I'd found."

"So you left," Dottie said.

"Packed a bag, took his precious Cadillac, and drove straight through his award-winning azaleas on my way out." Satisfaction gleamed in her eyes. "Filed for divorce before the tire tracks had time to settle."

"The watch?" I pressed, not willing to let that thread drop.

"Kept it as insurance," Lucinda said with a smile that would've made a shark nervous. "If Roy fought the divorce or tried hiding more assets, that watch would've raised questions no one wanted answered."

"Do you still have it?" Dottie asked, practically vibrating with anticipation.

Lucinda shook her head. "After the divorce was final, I threw it into the harbor, right off this pier." She gestured toward the window. "Childish? Maybe. Satisfying? Absolutely."

"Also illegal," Bea said.

"What did I care?" she asked. "Roy was the sheriff. If he arrested me he'd implicate himself. And surely there's a statute of limitations on something like that."

My heart sank faster than that watch must have. "Did you tell anyone else about the watch?"

"Just my attorney. And now you three." She studied us with eyes that missed nothing. "Why dig all this up after so long?"

"Elizabeth's father is dying," I said simply. "His last wish is to know what happened to his daughter."

Something genuine flickered across Lucinda's carefully maintained façade and she nodded. "I remember Gerald Calvert. He came from generations of lighthouse keepers. Elizabeth was his only child if I remember right. He deserves to know the truth."

"We found financial records Elizabeth had hidden," I said. "About Harbor Development Corporation making irregular payments to officials."

"That makes sense," Lucinda nodded. "The harbor project faced serious opposition—environmental groups, historical preservation zealots, you name it." Her eyes met mine meaningfully. "Until suddenly, right after Elizabeth died, all that opposition magically disappeared."

"Who else besides Roy would have had a direct interest in Elizabeth's death if she'd brought her story about the harbor project to light?" I asked.

Lucinda considered this. "Paul Cromwell for certain—he was on the city council then and heavily invested in the development. Clinton Harrington, of course—it was his company handling the construction. And I don't know if this means anything, but it's bothered me for years."

"What did?" Bea asked.

Lucinda lowered her voice and said, "About a week before Elizabeth died, I was at the courthouse dropping off some paperwork for a charity event. I overheard an argument between Elizabeth and Jason Brooks in the stairwell. He was the assistant DA at the time."

My interest sharpened immediately. "What kind of argument?"

"Intense," Lucinda said, her gaze distant with memory. "It was obvious they didn't want to be overheard because they were doing that loud whispering that couples do, but it was very heated and both of them were upset. Elizabeth was saying something about needing to go public and people deserving to know. The more she talked the angrier Jason became. He was always so polished, you know. Made for the public spotlight and politics. He kept saying she didn't understand what she was getting involved in and that she needed to stop before she got hurt. He sounded desperate. Almost begging her."

"Did you hear them say anything else?" Dottie asked.

Lucinda shook her head. "I kept my distance, of course. One

doesn't survive in island society by being caught eavesdropping." She straightened slightly in her chair. "But I heard Elizabeth's parting words clearly—*I thought you were different from them*. There was such... disappointment in her voice." Lucinda's fingers traced the rim of her glass. "She went back down the stairs and let the parking garage door close rather definitively behind her. Jason remained where he was for several minutes and then started up the stairs. I slipped onto another floor before he spotted me."

"Brooks told us about an argument," I said, recalling our conversation with him. "But it was about Clint Harrington confronting them at Elizabeth's apartment after finding out about their relationship. He never mentioned arguing with Elizabeth."

"Men have selective memories," Bea remarked dryly. "Especially when it comes to fights with women they claim to care about."

"Their relationship was ongoing when she died," I said. "At least according to Jason."

"No reason to think otherwise," Lucinda said, shrugging. "They were definitely a main topic of conversation that summer. Jason and Clint were both from well-to-do families and Elizabeth was just the lighthouse keeper's daughter. And she was dallying with both those boys, so people on the island weren't exactly kind in what they had to say about her. But from what I witnessed in that stairwell, it wasn't all moonlight and roses."

"There's something else you should know," Lucinda continued, her voice dropping even lower. "After I left Roy, strange things started happening. My car was vandalized. Someone broke into my sister's house where I was staying. I received anonymous calls in the middle of the night."

"You think Roy was behind it?" I asked.

"I always assumed so," she said. "I told my attorney about it and I'd agreed to put a tap on my phone so they could trace the calls. But after the tap was installed the harassment stopped."

We finished our meal in relative silence, my mind whirling with new information and possibilities. As we were paying the bill, Lucinda placed her hand on my arm.

"Be careful," she said, her green eyes intense. "Elizabeth Calvert was bright, driven, and thought she was invincible. Roy once told me that the biggest mistake people make is underestimating what powerful men will do to protect themselves."

"I appreciate the warning," I said, "but I'm not backing down."

A smile ghosted across her lips. "I can see that. Just remember—on Grimm Island, nothing is ever quite what it seems." She released my arm and stood. "Now, if you'll excuse me, I promised my sister I'd be back by one."

We watched Lucinda glide through the restaurant, turning heads even at her age with her confidence and grace.

"How in the world did a man like Roy Milton snag a woman like that?" I asked, shaking my head in disbelief.

"Oh, easy," Dottie said. "Before she got all of Roy's money Lucinda was as ugly as homemade sin. But she had that family pedigree on the island, and rumor was her talents in the bedroom more than made up for her lack of beauty."

"She must have a heck of a plastic surgeon," I said.

"Oh, she did," Bea said. "My Randolph was excellent at his craft, rest his soul." Bea ran a finger down her firm jaw and down her smooth neck. "Too bad he couldn't keep it in his pants. He had a heart attack right in the throes of passion with one of his patients. I always figured justice was served to all parties involved in that little scenario. And that's when I decided never to marry again. Third time was definitely the charm."

My eyes widened as she told the story. It was impossible not to have heard gossip about Bea if you were from the island, but apparently my mother had left out some important details for my little ears when it had occurred.

"Well," Dottie said, moving on. "I'd say that was illuminating. Especially the part about Brooks arguing with Elizabeth. You should follow up with him about that, Mabel."

My smile turned into a wince. I was sure Jason Brooks would be ecstatic to have me call him up and ask him personal questions.

"Don't forget the watch," Dottie added. "Even if it's at the bottom of the harbor, its existence tells us something important."

"That Milton took evidence from the scene," I nodded. "The inscription is curious though—*Seek Truth. Stay True.* Makes you wonder who gave it to her."

"Could have been Brooks, could have been anyone if she was as loose with her lips as Lucinda said," Bea said thoughtfully. "She wasn't on my radar back then. I had bigger fish to fry and she was just a college girl with no family name. But whoever gave her the watch, Elizabeth considered it important enough to wear. And Milton considered it important enough to steal."

As we left the restaurant, I couldn't shake the feeling we were being watched. I scanned the pier, seeing nothing obviously suspicious —just tourists with ice-cream cones, fishermen with their gear, and locals going about their business.

"Something wrong?" Bea asked, noticing my scrutiny.

"Probably just paranoid after that note," I replied, forcing a smile.

We were halfway down the pier when my phone rang. I didn't recognize the number but answered anyway.

"Hello?"

"Mrs. McCoy? This is Deputy Harris." His breathing came in labored pants. "Sheriff Beckett asked me to call you. There's been an incident."

My heart seemed to stutter in my chest. "What kind of incident? Is he okay?"

"He's fine," Harris assured me quickly. "But there's been a homicide. Vanessa Garfield was found in her home about twenty minutes ago. Sheriff thought you should know right away."

The world seemed to tilt beneath my feet. "Vanessa? How—"

"Looks like she was strangled," Harris replied, his voice dropping. "She didn't show up to open her boutique this morning. When her assistant couldn't reach her, she called the department for a welfare check." He paused. "And Mrs. McCoy? There was a note pinned to her nightgown. All it said was your name."

The phone nearly slipped from my suddenly numb fingers and little black spots danced in front of my eyes.

"We're sending a patrol car to pick you up," Harris continued. "Sheriff wants you somewhere safe until we figure this out."

"I'm at The Blue Crab with Dottie and Bea," I managed, my voice sounding distant and hollow. "On the pier."

"Go back inside," Harris ordered. "Deputy Reynolds is already en route."

I ended the call, my hand shaking so badly I nearly dropped the phone.

"Mabel?" Bea's perfectly penciled eyebrows drew together in concern. "What is it? You're white as a sheet."

"Vanessa's dead," I managed. "Strangled. There was a note. With my name on it."

"Good Lord," Dottie whispered.

Bea's eyes narrowed dangerously. "Then we need to get somewhere safe. Now."

I tried to keep my voice steady. "I have that feeling like someone's watching."

"That means you have good instincts," Dottie said. "Follow them. Someone is obviously trying to send you a very clear message."

"Why Mabel and not us?" Bea asked.

"They must think Mabel is the threat," Dottie said.

I would have laughed if I could have gotten the sound past the sawdust in my throat. I was Mabel McCoy, tea shop owner. I wasn't a threat to anyone.

# CHAPTER
# THIRTEEN

DASH WAS WAITING FOR US AT THE PERFECT STEEP WHEN
we got back, pacing the length of the shop like a caged panther. The
Silver Sleuths had already assembled, looking like the geriatric Justice
League—Walt studying cars and passersby on the street, Hank scribbling notes on a legal pad, and Deidre color-coding something with
three different highlighters.

Chowder, who'd been left in Genevieve's care during our lunch
with Lucinda, waddled over to greet me with slightly more enthusiasm than usual, as if sensing I needed the emotional support of his
wrinkled face and doggy breath.

"Everybody okay?" Dash asked, scanning us for visible damage.

"Uninjured but thoroughly freaked out," I replied.

"I need bourbon," Bea announced, sailing past Dash. At my raised
eyebrow, she simply said, "Emergencies call for emergency measures,
darling. And it's after noon. Don't look so judgmental."

Dash guided me to a chair, his hand warm at my elbow. "I told
Genevieve to close up early and go home."

"Good. She doesn't need to be mixed up in this." I sank into the
chair, suddenly exhausted. "What happened to Vanessa?"

Dash ran a hand through his hair, mussing it in a way that would have been distracting under other circumstances. "Her assistant called when she didn't show up to open the boutique. No answer on her cell. Harris and Reynolds did a welfare check." His jaw tightened. "They found her in the living room."

"Harris said she was strangled," I said, the word heavy on my tongue.

"With what looks like one of her own scarves. Silk. High-end."

"What was my name doing on a note pinned to her nightgown?" I asked, getting to the part that had been making my stomach churn since Harris's call.

"It was the only thing written." Dash's eyes were troubled. "Typed, not handwritten. Pinned with a decorative brooch."

"No signs of forced entry?" Walt asked.

"None," Dash confirmed. "Signs point to her knowing her killer. We found wine glasses. Two on the coffee table. One with lipstick, one clean."

"Romantic?" I asked.

"Maybe," Dash said. "We also found this clutched in her hand." He showed me a photo on his phone of a crumpled document. Even from the small screen, I could make out the Harbor Development Corporation letterhead.

"Convenient," I said, looking at Dash.

"My thoughts too," he said.

"It's a bit too perfect, isn't it?" I said. "My name on a note, a Harbor Development document conspicuously placed…it's like someone's trying to create a narrative."

"A narrative that connects Elizabeth's death to Vanessa's through corruption," Dash nodded.

"Which means either the same person killed both women—" Bea started.

"Or someone's trying to make it look that way," I finished.

"This changes everything," Dash said, his expression grim. "We need to establish proper security protocols."

"The Silver Sleuths are at your service," Dottie announced,

straightening in her chair like she was accepting a mission from the Pentagon. "We can set up a rotation system."

"That's actually not a bad idea," Dash agreed, surprising me. "Mabel shouldn't be alone until we know who's behind these threats."

I opened my mouth to protest, but Walt was already pulling a small notebook from his pocket. "I'll take night watch—insomnia has its advantages. We'll need a comprehensive perimeter check every hour, communication protocols, and contingency plans for various scenarios."

"My house isn't a military installation," I said, but no one seemed to be listening.

"I can do afternoon shifts," Dottie volunteered. "My knees won't handle those stairs after dark."

"Morning duty for me," Deidre chimed in. "I'm up with the birds anyway."

"Count me out for overnights," Bea declared, swirling her drink. "Beauty sleep is nonnegotiable, darlings. I can only sleep in my own bed. But I'll handle day shifts and bring the sidecars."

I looked at Dash, expecting him to shut down this geriatric security detail, but he was nodding thoughtfully. I narrowed my eyes at him and he winked at me. Ridiculous man.

"Fine," I sighed, recognizing defeat when it was staring me in the face. "But house rules apply—you're welcome to the guest rooms, don't feed Chowder too many snacks, and my kitchen stays exactly as is." I smiled at Deidre. "Even if my organization system defies all logic."

"A small price to pay for your safety," Deidre replied with a good-natured wink.

"It's been years since I had a good sleepover," Dottie said.

While the Silver Sleuths worked out their rotating security schedule, I slipped away to my office, muttering something about checking messages. The truth was, I needed a moment to process everything—and to make a call.

Once alone, I pulled out my phone and dialed Jason Brooks.

He answered on the third ring. "Brooks."

"Mr. Brooks?" I questioned. "This is Mabel McCoy."

"I was hoping you'd call me," he said, and I could hear the smile in his voice. "I was about twenty-four hours from getting in touch with Hank and asking for your number."

"You were?" I asked. "But why?"

He laughed and I imagined him sitting behind his massive desk, looking out over the Charleston skyline. "Because I wanted to hear your voice again. And I wanted to see if you'd like to have dinner with me."

I had one of those out-of-body experiences that you read about in *Cosmo* magazine. A thousand thoughts drifted through my head at once and jumbled all together somewhere before the thoughts reached my tongue.

"Did you want to talk about the case?" I asked. "That's actually why I was calling. No need for dinner."

He laughed again and said, "That sound you hear is my ego crumbling. And no, I didn't want to have dinner to talk about the case. I wanted to have dinner because I think you're a beautiful woman and I'd like to get to know you better."

"Oh," I said, and my mouth froze in a perfectly formed *O*.

What was happening? I'd gone ten years as a widow and hadn't even noticed that other men existed. And in the span of a week I'd had two very attractive men want to take me to dinner. Of course, Jason Brooks was a good twenty years older than I was, but Patrick had been twelve years older. And then there was Dash—I couldn't begin to guess how old he was, and I hadn't asked.

"Oh," I said again. "Umm, sure. It's just I'm not used to—"

"Surely you're not going to tell me that the men in this state are too stupid to see you and not immediately be intrigued?"

I felt the blush heat my cheeks before I could control it and I glanced at the door, hoping no one picked this particular moment to barge in. Apparently I wasn't immune to flattery. "No," I said. "It's just I've not really dated since my husband died."

"Forgive me," he said and I could hear the sincerity in his voice. "I didn't realize. I'll tell you what. You have my number. The offer still stands. And when I've occupied your every waking moment because of my wit and charm you can call me back and accept my offer. Deal?"

I found myself laughing before I could help it. He was outrageous and very charming. "Deal," I said.

"Now if you didn't call me to flirt," he said. "Why did you call?"

"Oh, right," I said. "I had a question about the Elizabeth Calvert case."

A beat of silence. "I had a feeling."

"We've been tracking down those who would've been questioned previously, and we spoke with a woman who overheard an argument you had with Elizabeth in the courthouse stairwell, about a week before she died. She said it was quite heated. Do you remember?"

"Of course," he said. "It's impossible to forget. We argued about the research she was doing for the *Observer*. She was just a student and an intern. And she'd sunk her teeth into something even seasoned investigative reporters would shy away from. Elizabeth had found evidence proving the Harbor Development was full of corruption and money laundering. I was trying to convince her to be cautious, to let me help her and handle it through proper legal channels. She wanted to confront the involved parties directly."

"So you were arguing about her approach, not the findings themselves?"

"She was angry because I insisted on following protocol rather than charging ahead," he said. "Elizabeth was...passionate. And impulsive. She saw injustice and wanted immediate action. Taking on the Harringtons and their allies wasn't something to do without a plan. They're powerful people. I was worried for her safety."

"With good reason, apparently," I noted. "Did you tell Sheriff Milton about this argument?"

He paused. "Unfortunately Milton wasn't interested in anything that didn't support his accidental drowning theory. And he didn't want to hear from anyone who said otherwise."

"You're not the first person to say that," I said. "Did you ever share the information that Elizabeth gave you with anyone else over the years?"

"No," Brooks said. "Until your visit the other day, nobody's asked me about Elizabeth in decades. It didn't seem relevant after all this time." He paused and then said, "My sister called from the island about twenty minutes ago. My family still lives there, you know. She said Vanessa Garfield was found dead this morning. Murdered. Is that true?"

"News travels fast," I said.

"It always has," he said. "I remember Vanessa. She worked at the county clerk's office. Made her way through several of the higher-ups before she landed on Milton and decided he was her meal ticket. She was an ambitious woman."

"And now she's dead," I said. "It's hitting pretty close to home."

"Which means you need to be careful. If there's anything I know about the people on Grimm Island it's that there are certain parts of history best left forgotten. I was told more than once when I worked for the DA's office that it's best to let sleeping dogs lie. You don't want to end up as collateral damage."

"That's becoming a popular sentiment," I said dryly. I hesitated, then decided to push my luck. "One more thing—someone mentioned a watch that Elizabeth wore. Expensive, gold, with diamonds around the face. An inscription on the back that said *Seek Truth. Stay True.* Did you give it to her?"

"If it was expensive it didn't come from me," he said with a laugh. "Not back then. I was just a lowly assistant DA. But I remember the watch. She rarely took it off."

"I appreciate your time," I said.

"The pleasure was all mine," he said. "I'll be looking forward to that phone call." And then he disconnected.

Walt poked his head into the office and I startled guiltily. I'd been daydreaming about being flirted with instead of thinking about the case.

"There you are," Walt said. "Got us a meeting with Clint Harrington Jr. in a half an hour. On the mainland. We need to move out."

I blinked in surprise. "How did you manage that?"

Walt tapped the side of his nose mysteriously. "I've got connections."

"Should I be impressed or terrified?"

"Both," Walt replied with a wink. "You don't spend three decades in Naval Intelligence without learning how to collect leverage. Now grab your purse. Ticktock."

I snatched my bag and followed him out to the main room where Dash was reviewing reports with Harris.

"Where are y'all headed?" he asked.

"Field trip," I replied brightly. "Walt got us a meeting with Clint Harrington."

"Don't worry," Walt said. "I'm carrying. She's perfectly safe."

Bea went into a coughing fit and Dash looked incredulous. I was starting to think maybe I should take Patrick's gun out of the shoebox and keep it with me. No knock to Walt, but his reflexes weren't exactly what they used to be.

"And it's broad daylight," I said, trying to ease Dash's mind. "We're perfectly safe. This is our best chance to talk to Harrington while he's willing."

Dash looked back and forth between me and Walt, obviously trying to work through every possible scenario. Finally, he sighed. "Check in every hour. And take a radio. Cell service can be spotty on the causeway."

"Done," Walt agreed, looking smug.

"And Reynolds will follow at a discreet distance," Dash added, signaling to the deputy. "Just as a precaution."

"Noted," Walt said, adding under his breath as we headed out, "Amateur. Man couldn't follow a parade if he was standing on the float."

▭

Walt drove a pristine black Volvo that probably had bulletproof glass and an ejector seat hidden somewhere. The man might be pushing eighty, but his car was a fortress on wheels.

"Nice ride," I said, running my hand over the immaculate leather interior. "I expected you to drive a tank."

"Considered it," Walt replied without a hint of humor. "But the gas mileage is terrible. And Margaret would never let me have one anyway."

As we crossed the causeway, I noticed his military posture relax slightly. For the first time since I'd known him, Walt looked almost… normal.

"I've never heard you talk about Margaret much."

"Fifty-two years, three months, and seventeen days we were married," he replied without hesitation. "Not all smooth sailing, mind you. Marriage never is when you spend half your life deployed. But we weathered the storms together."

"That's lovely, Walt," I said, genuinely touched by this glimpse of the man beneath the hypervigilant exterior.

"Now," he said, obviously deciding that was enough personal talk, "When we get there, watch his eyes, not his mouth. The mouth can lie, but the eyes always tell the truth."

"Right," I said, and settled in for the rest of the drive, singing "Little White Lies" to myself.

The Harrington Construction headquarters surprised me. Instead of the cold glass and steel monument I expected, the lobby was all reclaimed wood and worn leather furniture. Photos of construction sites and workers in hard hats lined the walls, not the typical corporate bragging gallery of handshakes with politicians.

Inside, the receptionist wore jeans and a polo with the company logo. "Mr. Harrington's expecting you," she said with a warm smile. "Head on up."

Clint Harrington Jr. was nothing like I'd imagined. Where Brooks was polished corporate slick, Harrington was job-site rugged. He wore dark jeans, work boots with construction dust still on them, and a sport coat that looked like it had been tossed on as an afterthought. His hands were calloused and his tan came from actual time outdoors, not some salon.

His office had a working drafting table covered with blueprints and a wall of hard hats from different projects. Only the spectacular harbor view revealed this was the office of someone important.

Harrington looked up from his blueprints, eyeing me with curiosity before turning to Walt. "Mr. Garrison. It's been a while." He shook Walt's hand and then extended a hand to me. "Clint Harrington. You must be Mabel McCoy. I was a friend of Patrick's. I was sorry I was out of the country when he died. Scared the daylights out of me. I get a physical every year like clockwork."

"You knew Patrick?" I asked, surprised because I couldn't recall if Patrick had ever mentioned Clint Harrington. But to be fair, we didn't do a lot of socializing back then. We'd only had eyes for each other the two short years we were married.

"Sure, our families go way back," he said, clearing a stack of permits from some chairs. "I've probably got some pictures around somewhere if you'd ever like to see them. Please, sit. Though I trust this won't take long. I've got some problems on a site and I need to drive out and remind my foreman what I'm paying him for." His polite words didn't match the tension radiating from him.

"We'll be quick," Walt said. "Appreciate you seeing us on short notice. You see, Mabel and I have recently been deputized to clean up some of Milton's messes."

Clint's eyes widened in surprise as he looked back and forth between us. "I can see why you'd be an asset, Walt."

I decided not to take offense that he didn't include my name as an asset.

"We have some questions about Elizabeth Calvert," Walt said.

Harrington's jaw tightened like someone had cranked it with a wrench. "That's one of the messes Milton left behind? I thought he closed the case. Accidental drowning."

"You believe that?" Walt asked.

"Never did," Clint said. "But there was no proof otherwise."

"Her father's dying," I said. "His last wish is to know what really happened to his daughter."

Something flickered across Harrington's face. "But I'm not sure how I can help. It was almost thirty years ago. Elizabeth and I were close once, were lovers, talked about our futures and dreams together. But Elizabeth had big ambitions. She was never quite satisfied with just being the lighthouse keeper's daughter."

"Elizabeth was researching the Harbor Development Corporation the summer she died," I said. "Your father's company—this company—was the primary developer."

A dull flush rose from his neck to his cheeks and his gaze hardened. "Elizabeth was naïve about business," he said, a muscle twitching in his jaw. "You'd have thought she was looking for a Pulitzer the way she dug her teeth into that story. She saw conspiracy where there was just standard practice. The environmental adjustments, the zoning modifications—that's how projects get done in the real world."

"It's also how laws get broken," Walt pointed out mildly.

"You want to talk about breaking laws?" Harrington's composure shattered like cheap glass. "Let's talk about Jason Brooks."

The venom in his voice when he said the name practically blistered the paint on the walls.

"What about him?" I asked, fighting the urge to take a step back.

"Brooks," he spat, pacing now like a caged animal. "That manipulative bastard seduced her with his fancy law degree and worldly sophistication. Elizabeth was brilliant but sheltered. She'd never dealt with someone like him before. Where do you think she came up with the idea for that story? He was feeding her nothing but conspiracies."

Walt gave me an almost imperceptible nod to continue. "You've got a lot of anger there, son."

Harrington stopped pacing, his hands white-knuckling the back of his chair. "You know what no one understands? I loved her. Really loved her." His voice cracked. "We were talking again those last few days before she died. About reconciliation."

He swallowed hard. "I went to her apartment. I thought we were meeting alone. Then I find Brooks there with all those papers spread out, and I thought they were playing me for a fool."

"Brooks mentioned that confrontation," I said carefully. "But not that you and Elizabeth were discussing getting back together."

"Of course he didn't," Harrington scoffed. "It wouldn't fit his narrative of the jealous ex-boyfriend."

I took a calculated risk. "Do you recall a watch that belonged to Elizabeth? It had tiny diamonds around the face, supposedly with an inscription on the back?"

Harrington's expression shifted, his eyes narrowing slightly. "The watch? Sure. She never took it off."

"You know who gave it to her?" I asked.

He studied me for a moment and swallowed once. "No. I don't. She called me the day she died you know. Wanted to meet at the docks that night at ten. Somewhere private we could talk. Said she needed to explain what Brooks had been doing at her apartment. She said she needed my help."

He stopped abruptly, staring out at the distant silhouette of Grimm Island. "When I got to the docks, she wasn't there. Her car wasn't there either. I figured she'd changed her mind." His voice dropped to a whisper. "I didn't know she was already dead."

"Did you tell Sheriff Milton about your meeting at the docks?" Walt asked.

Harrington laughed—a harsh, empty sound. "I tried. He wasn't interested in anything that didn't support his accidental drowning theory."

A chill ran down my spine. Brooks had said almost exactly the same thing.

"It's been almost thirty years," I said. "I've seen the ledgers and some of the paperwork. Her research didn't come up with nothing. Something was going on between your dad, Milton and Paul Cromwell."

He sighed, looking defeated. "I know. Dad left me with a heck of a mess when he died and I took over the company. It almost broke us for me to get everything back on the up-and-up. There were financial irregularities in the Harbor Development Corporation records. Money through shell companies, kickbacks to officials. She was particularly obsessed with environmental violations—protected wetlands being developed despite conservation laws."

"Your father's company was responsible for that development," Walt pointed out.

"Along with Milton, Cromwell and most of the city council and other high-ranking officials. Even our state reps and a senator." He turned back to the window. "The Harbor Development was clean compared to some of the other projects happening back then. Elizabeth wasn't wrong. But she didn't have the resources or the street smarts to stay out of the kind of trouble that story was bringing her. It was hundreds of millions of dollars on the line. People will do a lot of unscrupulous things for that kind of money."

"You think someone in that circle killed her?" I asked.

"I think it's more than possible," he said. "And Milton would hold all the power to cover it up. It doesn't matter much now. It's ancient history. Elizabeth is dead. Milton is in jail. Dad and Cromwell are both gone. I don't know what else I can tell you. I hope Gerald Calvert finds peace before he passes. I always liked him."

"Just one more question," I said as he was clearly preparing to usher us out. "There were very few statements in the case file. Where were you the night she died?"

His expression didn't even flicker. "At a fundraiser for the Charleston Symphony with my parents until about nine. About two hundred witnesses can place me there. I left early, drove to the docks to meet Elizabeth as we planned, but she never showed. When I didn't find her there, I went back to the fundraiser after-party. Plenty of people saw me there after eleven." He glanced at his watch pointedly. "Now if you'll excuse me, I have a meeting in five minutes."

"You realize that means you don't have an alibi during the time the medical examiner said Elizabeth was murdered," I pointed out.

"Not much else I can say," he said. "All I can tell you is the truth."

▭

"What do you think?" I asked Walt as we rode the elevator down.

"He was telling the truth about loving her," Walt said, checking his watch with military precision. "The anger was real too. But he didn't tell us the whole truth. Now we just have to figure out what's missing."

As we walked to the car, I spotted Reynolds across the street in his cruiser, and I gave a quick wave.

"He's not even trying," Walt said, unlocking his Volvo and opening the door for me. "A good tail doesn't let you spot them. That's just sloppy work."

I slid into the passenger seat, glancing back at Reynolds. "At least Dash is being thorough. I appreciate the extra eyes after that note."

Walt harrumphed as he started the engine. "True. Can't be too careful these days."

I pondered this as we crossed back over the causeway to Grimm Island, the late afternoon sun glinting off the water. Reynolds maintained his distance behind us, a reassuring presence despite Walt's critique of his surveillance technique.

▭

My house had transformed into FBI headquarters—minus the efficiency but with a lot more bourbon. The Silver Sleuths had taken over every available surface, spreading evidence photos, timeline charts, and suspect lists across my once-pristine dining room.

"Mrs. Whitaker just dropped off her famous chicken and rice," Dottie announced, emerging from the kitchen with a casserole dish that could have doubled as a small bathtub. "That makes four casseroles since we got here. Word's spreading faster than kudzu that your house is the new crime-solving central."

"At this rate, we could feed the entire sheriff's department," I said, navigating around Walt's meticulously arranged floor files. My vintage heels clicked against the hardwood as I dodged case notes and color-coded index cards.

Every few minutes, blue and red lights swept across my front windows as another patrol car drove by, Dash's security measures in full effect. In the living room, Bea had commandeered my record player for her Ella Fitzgerald collection, while the television in the den broadcast the local news covering developments in the Vanessa Garfield investigation.

"They're calling it the Grimm Island Conspiracy now," Hank reported, looking up from the Charleston paper. "Your name's mentioned three times."

"Wonderful," I muttered. "Just what I need."

"Mabel!" Bea's voice carried above Ella's smooth contralto. "Get in here! I've got something juicy!"

I found her at my dining table, a half-empty sidecar beside her and an expression that meant somebody's secrets were about to become public knowledge.

"My contact at First Island Bank just called," she said, lowering her voice to a conspiratorial whisper despite the fact that we were alone. "Vanessa Garfield deposited ten thousand dollars in cash the day before she died."

"Blackmail money?" I asked, sliding into the chair opposite her.

"Or she sold information," she replied, tapping red-tipped nails against her glass.

Dash appeared in the doorway. He'd changed out of his uniform and wore jeans and a navy-blue henley that had the top couple of buttons unbuttoned. My lungs started to ache and I realized I was holding my breath. I fought the urge to slap some sense into myself.

The doorbell chimed for what felt like the hundredth time today.

"It's Meredith Johnson with a peach cobbler," Deidre called from the hallway. "She's asking if she can use the powder room—claims it's an emergency."

"Tell her the plumbing's acting up," I called back. "Last thing we need is the island rumor mill getting a firsthand look at our evidence board."

"You're learning," Dash said with approval. "I might make a detective out of you yet."

"Only if I can pick my uniform," I said. "I'm not wearing those ugly pants."

"We should check Vanessa's phone records," Dottie suggested, joining us with a steaming mug of what smelled like her special ginger tea. "See who she was talking to before she died."

"I've already got the warrant and sent in a request," Dash said. "Should have them at any time."

The discussion continued as theories bounced around the room like pinballs, each one setting off new possibilities. My eyes grew heavier with each passing minute, the adrenaline that had kept me going finally ebbing away.

"I need to step away from this for a bit," I announced, interrupting Hank's detailed analysis of offshore banking laws. "My brain feels like it's been through a blender."

"Take all the time you need," Deidre said kindly. "The others will get settled and things will quieten down. Don't worry. I'm going to make myself comfortable in the living room with my tea and book."

I knew better than to argue about my unwanted security detail. At least Deidre would be quiet company.

"Before you go," I said to Dash.

"Here's your hat, what's your hurry?" he asked, smiling.

"Sorry," I said. "My manners disappeared with the last casserole. I was just going to say that Clint Harrington admitted that there was impropriety with the development deal. And he named Milton, Cromwell, and his dad as being involved, along with a handful of other prominent citizens."

"It's motive," Dash said. "Just because he confessed to his father's crimes doesn't mean he didn't commit murder. That company was his legacy. He'd have as much of a reason for Elizabeth to be dead as anyone." He gave me a long stare and then moved in closer, bringing his hand to the side of my face. "You're asleep on your feet."

"Don't kiss my forehead," I said, slightly dazed by his touch.

He grinned. "What should I kiss instead?"

The thought scrambled my brains and something incoherent came out of my mouth.

"A question for another night," he said, taking a step back. "Go get some sleep, Mabel."

I'd thought about taking a cold shower, but I couldn't put myself through that kind of torture. I'd spent forty-five luxurious minutes under the hot spray, and I'd thanked my lucky stars for the invention of the tankless water heater.

By the time I emerged from the shower, the house had quieted considerably—Bea's records replaced by the gentle ticking of the grandfather clock in the hallway. Wrapped in my vintage silk robe, I padded downstairs to the kitchen in search of something to eat that wasn't encased in cream-of-mushroom soup.

I flipped on the light, already mentally inventorying the contents of my refrigerator—and stopped dead in my tracks.

There, on my pristine counter, sat an elegant woman's watch—gold and encased with diamonds.

# CHAPTER
# FOURTEEN

I didn't scream. Fear had a way of freezing your vocal cords when you needed them most.

"Deidre," I called out, surprised by the steadiness in my voice. "Could you come here a moment?"

I heard her book close in the living room, followed by the soft shuffle of her slippered footsteps approaching. When she appeared in the kitchen doorway, her brows shot up toward her hairline.

"Good heavens," she breathed, staring at the gleaming watch lying ominously on my countertop.

I grabbed a clean tea towel from the drawer, carefully wrapped it around my fingers, and gingerly turned the watch over to see the back. Sure enough, engraved in elegant script were the words: *To Elizabeth— Seek Truth. Stay True.*

"Someone's been in the house," I said, setting the watch down on the towel. The gold gleamed under the kitchen lights, far too pristine to have spent decades underwater as Lucinda had claimed. Tiny diamonds winked around the face, catching the sunlight like miniature stars.

A low growl from the corner made us both jump. Chowder stood alert, wrinkled face scrunched in an expression I'd never seen before. The fur along his back stood on end.

"What is it, boy?" I whispered.

He waddled past me with surprising speed, growling deeper as he reached the mudroom door. When I followed and tested the knob, it turned easily in my hand.

"Unlocked," I said, snatching my hand back. "I always lock it."

Deidre was already dialing her phone. "With the Silver Sleuths coming and going all day, it's no wonder. Half of us probably forgot to check it. I'm calling the sheriff."

"Where are the others?" I asked, suddenly aware of the quiet house.

"Dottie's watching the news in the den, Walt's on patrol outside, and Hank's in the study making calls to his courthouse contacts," Deidre explained. "Bea called about twenty minutes ago. Said she's got her grandson digging through some financial records and will head over as soon as she has something concrete."

"Check the rest of the house," I said, moving carefully toward the hallway. "Make sure nothing else has been disturbed."

My skin prickled with the realization that someone had been in my home while all of us were here, vulnerable, unaware. With Deidre, Dottie, Hank, and Walt staying with me as my self-appointed security detail, we should have noticed something. Clearly we hadn't.

I hurried upstairs to change out of my housedress. No way was I greeting Dash in my vintage floral housecoat and fuzzy slippers, not when someone had just invaded my home. I grabbed a pair of high-waisted tan trousers and a short-sleeved blouse with mother-of-pearl buttons—my Katherine Hepburn, tough-girl-inspired outfit. My hands trembled slightly as I tucked in the blouse and fastened the trousers at my waist.

Dash's SUV screeched to a halt outside my house less than ten minutes later. I hurried to unlock the front door for him, pulling it open just as he reached the porch. His hand hovered near his weapon as he stepped inside, Deputy Harris following close behind with an evidence kit.

"Are you hurt?" Dash demanded, his eyes scanning me from head to toe.

"Not physically," I replied, smoothing a hand over my trousers. "But I'm mad enough to spit nails about someone letting themselves into my home without an invitation."

His attention shifted to the gold timepiece on my counter, his expression hardening. "Is that what I think it is?"

"Elizabeth Calvert's watch," I said. "Maybe. More than likely a remarkably good copy. I used a tea towel to handle it." I gestured to the cloth beneath the watch. "Didn't want to contaminate any evidence. The engraving is on the back."

Dash nodded, looking impressed despite the gravity of the situation. "Smart thinking."

He moved to examine the mudroom door, crouching to study the frame. He ran his fingers along the edge, brow furrowed. "Lock's intact. No signs of forced entry." He stood and examined the door handle more closely. "Most likely someone simply left it unlocked with all the traffic in and out today. Though whoever broke in could have had a key or picked the lock."

"With all the traffic coming and going all day, I wouldn't be surprised if someone forgot to lock it," I said, sighing. "Dottie went out to get the mail, Walt's been doing his perimeter checks, and neighbors keep bringing casseroles. Anyone could have forgotten to lock up."

"Whoever did this is good," Dash replied, his expression grim. "And they weren't concerned about being caught, which means they knew exactly when to slip in and out."

A chill skittered down my spine like a spider. The thought of being watched so closely made me want to retch.

"Mrs. Pembroke," I said suddenly. "If anyone saw something, it would be her. The woman spends more time watching this street than she does sleeping."

Dash was already moving toward the door. "Let's ask her."

Mrs. Pembroke answered her door before we were on her porch, wearing a floral caftan and house slippers. Her hair was in tight rollers lined up like soldiers, and I could see the local news playing behind, the weatherman gesturing at a map while the *Evening Report* banner scrolled across the bottom of the screen.

"Well, well," she said, eyes darting between us. "What brings Grimm Island's finest to my door?"

"There's been a break-in at Mrs. McCoy's house," Dash explained. "Did you happen to notice anyone unusual in the area today?"

"With all the comings and goings at your place today, it's been like Grand Central Station over there. Looks like a retirement home with all the old people coming in and out, that delivery boy from the bakery, cops driving by, and those ladies from your church bringing enough casseroles to feed a small army." She paused, leaning in conspiratorially. "But there was someone who caught my attention specifically."

"Who?" I asked, already dreading the answer.

"A police officer," she said, her voice dropping to a dramatic whisper. "About an hour ago. I noticed because he parked at the side of Norma and George's house and then walked to your side door bold as can be and let himself in."

Dash went rigid beside me. "An officer? You're certain?"

"I know a uniform when I see one," she replied with a sniff. "Though I couldn't see his face. Kept his head down. Given all the police activity around here lately, I didn't think much of it at the time. He was in and out in just a minute or so. But it struck me as strange, especially when I called out a hello and he didn't answer."

"Can you describe him at all?" Dash pressed. "Height? Build?"

"Tall," she said, eyes narrowing in concentration. "Broad shouldered. Moved quickly. Actually, now that you mention it I couldn't see his hair color. He was wearing one of those police jackets and had the hood up."

Dash handed her his card, instructing her to call him directly if she saw anyone else around my property. The muscle in his jaw worked overtime as we walked back across the street.

"Someone in uniform," he said, voice deadly quiet. "Used their position to access your home. I can't stand dirty cops."

I shivered, but not from the evening breeze.

Deidre, Hank, and Walt were staring out the window, watching us walk back across the street, and Dottie was on the front porch, standing like a sentinel with her hands on her hips.

"What happened?" Dottie demanded as we approached. "Emma Jean Pembroke has the biggest mouth this side of the Mason-Dixon."

"She saw someone in a police uniform sneaking around the house," I explained as we moved inside. The aroma of cinnamon and vanilla wafted from the kitchen where Deidre had apparently decided stress-baking was the appropriate response to our situation. I spotted a fresh batch of snickerdoodles cooling on the counter.

"A police officer?" Walt's eyes narrowed with suspicion. "I told you we should have taken more precautions with security around here."

"Not now, Walt," Dottie said, patting his arm. "Let's hear what the sheriff has to say."

Dash quickly brought them up to speed while I sank into a kitchen chair, the reality of the situation finally hitting me. Someone had been in my house—walking through rooms where I slept, ate, and lived— without invitation or warning. The violation of privacy made my skin crawl.

"Here," Deidre said, putting a steaming cup of something that smelled suspiciously like alcohol and honey in front of me. "It's a hot toddy. For your nerves. And it's good for a sore throat. Just in case you have one."

I took a sip and coughed as liquid fire blazed a trail down my throat. "Any word from Bea?" I asked, my eyes watering.

As if summoned by her name, the front door burst open and Bea's voice echoed through the foyer. "You won't believe what I've found."

She swept into the kitchen moments later, bearing an enormous stack of file folders and trailing a cloud of Opium perfume that could knock a man unconscious at twenty paces. She wore a turquoise silk caftan and a matching turban on her head.

"These old bones may be slow, but my brain still works at full speed," Bea announced, dropping her stack onto my kitchen table with a hefty *thump*.

"Did you just come from telling fortunes at the fair?" Deidre asked.

"Hush, Deidre," Bea said. "My grandson—"

"Which one?" Deidre interrupted.

"Steven," Bea said. "He's the computer genius. Dresses like those emaciated models in *Vogue*. Never wears socks."

"Gotcha," Deirdre said.

"Anyway," Bea continued, "He dug up something juicy on Harrington Construction circa 1996."

She spread financial statements across the table like a dealer at a high-stakes poker game. "They were practically bankrupt. Falsifying statements to banks, juggling creditors, borrowing from Peter to pay Paul—the works."

"And if Elizabeth exposed their fraudulent Harbor Development deal…" I began.

"Junior would have lost everything," Bea finished with a flourish. "Inheritance, position, future—poof!"

"That's a powerful motive," Walt observed, studying the documents.

"But it doesn't explain the police connection," Hank noted, adjusting his glasses. "And it doesn't connect the past to the present of why someone dressed as a cop would break into Mabel's home and leave Elizabeth's watch."

"The Harbor Development wasn't just about money," Dottie added. "It was about power. Harrington, Cromwell, and Milton formed an unholy trinity. Anyone who threatened that balance was swiftly dealt with."

"This has to be a replica of the watch," I said, studying it more carefully. "Look at the condition—it's practically brand new. No tarnish, no scratches. If the original had been at the bottom of the harbor for years like Lucinda claimed, or even stored away for decades, it wouldn't look this pristine."

Dash nodded. "Someone went to considerable trouble to have this made. All we have is a couple of photographs of her wearing it. Since it wasn't logged into evidence and there's no mention of it in the case file, we don't know if she was wearing it when she died or not. But someone knew about the watch. Either that Milton had deliberately left it out of the case file or that Lucinda was keeping it as an insurance policy. But either way, someone had enough knowledge of the watch to be able to make a replica."

"We need to track down where this particular watch came from," Deidre declared, tapping her fingers against the tabletop. "Dottie and I can start calling jewelry stores first thing tomorrow. A salesman is likely to remember a custom order."

"I'll call Lucinda in the morning," I added. "I think she has some explaining to do about this watch."

"They would have needed someone inside the department back then," Hank said, the former judge's mind clearly putting the pieces together. "Someone who could alter evidence, control the investigation."

"And with Milton in prison, they'd need someone else on the inside now," Walt added grimly. "Someone who's been there long enough to know where all the bodies are buried. The evidence room break-in, someone familiar with the security codes, the officer Mrs. Pembroke saw...it all points to police involvement, past and present."

As the others continued their discussion, I found myself distracted by a persistent thought that had nothing to do with Reynolds or the evidence. The memory of Dash's kiss and the growing connection between us made any secrets I was keeping from him feel like sandpaper against my subconscious. The Baptist in me wasn't really comfortable with guilt.

I caught Dash's eye across the table and gave a slight nod toward the kitchen. He followed me a moment later while the Silver Sleuths remained engrossed in debate about which officers had been with the department long enough to be suspects.

"I've got a confession to make," I said, keeping my voice low as I busied myself making a fresh pot of tea. "It's about Jason Brooks."

Dash's attention sharpened immediately. "What about him?"

"Well, you see, when I called him about the case the other day..." I hesitated, my fingers tracing the rim of an empty teacup. "He asked me out to dinner. Said he thought I was beautiful and wanted to get to know me better."

Dash's expression shifted subtly, something darkening in his eyes. "Really," he said. There was no emotion in his expression, and I fought the urge to squirm under his gaze.

"It caught me off guard," I said. "I'm not really used to having attention from men. Other than you, I mean. But he was very charming about it—said when I'd been won over by his wit and charm I could call him back and accept his offer." I shook my head. "I was flattered, but I had no intention of calling him back. I just wanted to tell you."

"I appreciate the honesty," he said.

"You don't seem surprised," I observed.

"Brooks has a reputation," he said simply. "And Mabel, just so you're aware, men give you attention. I've worked in this town a little over a month, and I've seen it time and time again and always been in awe of your naïvety. You're a beautiful and successful woman—independent—a little intimidating." He grinned and moved a little closer, so our bodies almost touched. "It's just that you've only recently taken notice that there are men out there."

My mouth dropped open in surprise.

"And just for the record," he said, his voice going so quiet I had to lean forward to hear him. "I'm interested. And I don't share."

I inhaled a sharp breath at the promise in his eyes, and all thoughts of Brooks and guilt drained right out of my brain. His breath hovered over my lips and just before I got the chance to see stars explode behind my eyelids a loud crash came from the dining room, followed by a muffled curse in Dottie's distinctive voice.

Dash and I exchanged looks, then moved to the doorway to find all five Silver Sleuths in various unconvincing poses of innocence. Dottie was picking up pieces of a shattered teacup, Bea was suddenly fascinated by her fingernails, Walt was pretending to study his notepad, and Deidre had mysteriously appeared right beside the kitchen door.

Only Hank was facing us directly with his arms crossed over his chest. I felt like a teenager who was about to get scolded.

"The acoustics in this old house are remarkable," Deidre said, adjusting her glasses. "Sound travels so clearly from room to room. It's the way these old places were built."

"We weren't eavesdropping," Bea said, abandoning all pretense. "We were conducting auditory surveillance. That's the proper terminology, isn't it, Walt?"

Walt nodded solemnly. "Standard reconnaissance procedure."

"Honestly," I sighed, hands on my hips. "You five are impossible."

"So Jason Brooks asked you to dinner?" Dottie asked, not even trying to hide her interest as she dumped broken china into her palm. "My, my. He always did have an eye for the pretty ones. And you are partial to older men, aren't you dear?"

"I have no interest in Jason Brooks," I said firmly.

"Men like that are always trouble," Bea said, adjusting her turban. "All charm on the outside, something else entirely underneath." She waggled her penciled eyebrows. "Though the charming ones do know their way around a—"

"Thank you, Bea," I cut her off before she could finish whatever inappropriate observation was coming. "That's quite enough."

"Just saying." Bea shrugged, her bangles jingling with the movement. "A woman should keep her options open. Though I do think the sheriff here is much more your type. More substance, less polish. How old are you, Sheriff? Our Mabel does tend to go for more mature men."

"You don't have to answer that," I told Dash. I felt heat creeping up my neck.

He looked at me and smiled, and I felt the shiver of anticipation race down my spine.

"I'll answer the question," he said. "I'm thirty-eight."

"There you go, Mabel," Bea said. "Old enough to know a thing or two about what women like. Why all these celebrity women who need daily doses of collagen are trotting around with twenty-year-olds is a mystery to me. I'd take an experienced lover over an enthusiastic lover any day of the week."

My face was on fire and I felt the growl rumble in my throat before I could help it. "Don't you all have something better to do?"

"Not really, dear," Deidre said, adjusting her glasses. "This is the most excitement we've had since Walt thought he spotted a Russian spy at the Piggly Wiggly last summer."

"That woman was speaking in code," Walt insisted. "No one legitimately needs seventeen cans of creamed corn."

Before anyone could respond, Dash's phone rang. He checked the screen. "Saved by the bell," he told me. "We'll finish this conversation later." He stepped into the hall and said, "Harris," into the phone.

No sooner had the door closed behind him than Dottie's phone began to buzz. She glanced at the screen and her eyebrows shot up toward her hairline.

"Well I'll be," she muttered, answering with a brisk, "Simmons."

We all fell silent, watching as Dottie's expression transformed from mild interest to intense concentration. She reached for a pen and began scribbling furiously on the back of an envelope, nodding and occasionally interjecting with "Yes," or "I suspected as much."

"Send me the full report," she finally said. "And Janet? I owe you a bottle of that Kentucky bourbon you like." She hung up, her eyes gleaming with the fevered excitement I'd only seen in Walt when he talked about Soviet espionage.

"What is it?" I asked.

"That," Dottie announced triumphantly, "was Dr. Janet Friedman. She's been the senior medical examiner in Charleston since I retired. She owes me a couple of big favors, so I had the sheriff get a warrant so she could look at the autopsy files of Elizabeth Calvert and retest samples that were taken."

"You're a genius," I said, feeling a surge of excitement from whatever news was to come.

"Thank you, dear," she said. "I actually am a genius."

"Goodness gravy, Dottie," Walt said, exasperated. "We'll all die before you tell us. What'd the woman say?"

"What I suspected all along," she said. "Elizabeth Calvert didn't drown in the harbor. In fact, she didn't drown at all. Cause of death was strangulation, which should have been very easy for the original medical examiner to determine. But the interesting thing is she had particulates of water and spores on her skin and clothing that can only be found in Osprey Cove."

"Osprey Cove?" Bea asked, looking puzzled. "That's miles from where her body was found."

"Exactly," Dottie said, slapping the table for emphasis. "She was killed somewhere else, then transported to the marina. And here's the real kicker—Janet found epithelial cells under Elizabeth's fingernails. DNA. She fought back, scratched her attacker."

"That's incredible," I said, "But DNA testing wasn't common back then, was it?"

"Enough to where it was standard operating procedure to preserve samples," Dottie explained. "And here's what's really interesting," she said, lowering her voice as if sharing state secrets. "Janet's team just completed Vanessa Garfield's autopsy. Cause of death confirmed as manual strangulation, with hyoid bone fracture and petechial hemorrhaging consistent with significant force applied for at least two minutes. But the bombshell?"

She paused for dramatic effect and I thought Walt was going to come across the table for her if she didn't speed things up.

Dottie smiled before she continued. "The DNA recovered from beneath Vanessa's fingernails is an exact match to epithelials preserved from under Elizabeth's nails. Thirty years apart, both women fought the same killer in their final moments."

A collective gasp went around the table.

"Well, I'll be," Walt said, his expression grim. "Same killer."

"Without a doubt," Dottie nodded. "Both women scratched the same person while fighting for their lives."

"Do we have a match to anyone in the system?" Deidre asked.

"Not yet," Dottie said. "But we've got a DNA profile now. All we need is a sample from a suspect to compare it to."

The hallway door opened and Dash returned, his expression serious. "Harris found something on the security footage— "He stopped, noticing our intense expressions. "What did I miss?"

"Evidence," Dottie said with satisfaction. "Definitive evidence linking both murders to the same killer." She filled him in quickly.

"We're closing in," Dash said. "That's good work."

Dottie beamed at the compliment.

"What did Harris want?" I asked.

"I need to get back to the station," he said. "Harris discovered something on the security cameras I had installed last week. Cameras the rest of the department doesn't know about."

"What did he find?" Dottie asked.

"He wouldn't say over the phone," Dash replied, already heading for the door. "But it sounds like we might have caught our evidence room intruder on tape. I need to see the footage for myself."

"I'll go with you," I said, starting to rise.

Dash shook his head. "Stay here where it's safe. I've got half the department out looking for whoever left that watch. The Silver Sleuths will keep you company, and I'll have a patrol car drive by every fifteen minutes." He looked at Walt and Hank. "Don't let anyone in you don't know personally."

"You got it, Sheriff," Walt said, straightening to military attention. "We'll keep her safe."

"I'll be back as soon as I can," Dash promised, his gaze lingering on me for a moment before he headed out the door.

We watched from the window as his SUV pulled away, the tension in the room thick enough to cut with a knife.

"Well," Bea said, breaking the silence, "That's my cue to go home. I'm up past my bedtime and I'm going to have to give myself an eye treatment to get rid of the puffiness."

"I'll walk you to your car," Walt said. "I've got to do another perimeter check anyway."

We said our goodbyes and Bea promised to be back before lunchtime the next day. Bea didn't really get going until around brunch time, and usually only if she had a mimosa. Bea had lived by her own set of rules for most of her life—she drank too much, smoked when she thought no one was looking, read sordid romance novels and lived on gossip and other people's misfortune. But I figured once a person made it past their eightieth birthday, they weren't too likely to take advice about anything having to do with living a healthy lifestyle.

"I'm tuckered out," Dottie said. "If y'all don't mind I'm going to head upstairs and get ready for bed. Especially if I'm taking the early morning shift to watch Mabel."

"I don't need a babysitter," I reminded them. "I'm a grown woman who's lived alone a long time."

"Sheriff's orders," Dottie said, patting me on the shoulder. "It's so attractive when a man takes charge, don't you think?"

"He's cut from a different cloth," Deidre agreed. "They don't make men like the sheriff much anymore. Did you see those muscles in his arms and shoulders? I've always been partial to shoulders."

"You've always been partial to a man that breathes," Dottie said. "But the sheriff does have that take-charge way about him. Very manly. I think he's got a tattoo he hides under his sleeves. I've been trying to catch a glimpse ever since we started working on this case."

"Why don't you just ask him?" I asked.

"I'll wait," she said. "You're bound to see him with his shirt off sooner or later."

My mouth opened, but no words came out. I really wished Dottie hadn't planted that seed in my head.

"Sweet dreams," Dottie said, grinning, and then headed up the stairs.

Hank had gone up to bed not long after Dottie, and Deidre gave me a knowing look as he headed up the stairs.

"Those two aren't fooling anyone," she said, shaking her head and curling up in an overstuffed chair in the living room. "Been carrying on for more than a year now."

"What?" I asked. I was still recovering from the comment about seeing Dash without his shirt. My brain wasn't processing the thought of Hank and Dottie sleeping in sin in my upstairs guest room.

"Girl, that widow's veil has made you blind as a bat," she said.

"You need to yank that thing off and burn it to ashes. You're missing out on a lot of life."

Deidre's words felt like a little dart to my chest. There was nothing in her tone that was malicious, but maybe there was a little too much truth in what she'd said that made me feel like squirming under her scrutiny.

Walt chose that moment to come back inside, but it was short lived because he grabbed a flashlight from the mudroom and said, "I'm going to check the shed and the alleyway. Your property is much too easy to access, Mabel. Maybe you should consider moving."

I just sighed and went back to the dining room to sift through the papers Bea had brought over from her grandson. But not long after I'd sat down, a knock sounded at the front door. Deidre peered through the curtains and said, "It's Mark Reynolds. I hope nothing has happened. It's never good when the police knock on your door at night."

"Or in the daytime," I said, remembering the officer who'd come to tell me that Patrick had an accident on the golf course and I needed to go to the hospital. What they hadn't told me was that he was already dead. They waited until I arrived at University Medical Center before they told me he was gone.

"Mabel?" Deidre asked. "Aren't you going to answer the door?"

"Right," I said, shaking myself from the memory.

"Who is it?" Deidre asked.

"It's Deputy Reynolds," I said, already unlocking the door. His was a face I'd grown used to seeing almost daily at the tea shop, his afternoon visits as regular as the tides.

I pulled open the door to find him in full uniform, his expression serious but kind, those pale blue eyes crinkling at the corners the way they always did.

"Deputy Reynolds," I greeted, relief evident in my voice. After the threat and everything else that had happened, seeing a trusted face was exactly what I needed. "Is everything okay?"

"You know you can call me Mark," he said. "Evening, Ms. Deidre."

"Are you softening us up?" Deidre asked. "Is somebody dead? If so, you should just come out and say it. We can take it."

Deidre came up behind me and grabbed my hand, squeezing it as hard as she could.

"Oh, no ma'am," he said. "Nothing like that. Sheriff Beckett sent me to bring Mabel to the station." He looked at me and said, "He needs your help identifying someone on the security footage."

"Did he catch who broke into the evidence room?" I asked, excitement building. After all this investigation, we might finally have a break.

Reynolds nodded. "Looks that way. He figured you'd want to know."

"He's right about that," I said, already reaching for my purse. This could be the breakthrough we'd been waiting for.

"I'll go too," Deidre said, appearing behind me in her nightclothes, her silver hair slightly mussed from leaning against the chair.

Reynolds winced and said, "Sorry, Ms. Deidre. You're in your nightclothes and the sheriff said to make it quick."

Deidre looked down at her pajamas and grimaced. "I guess you're right. What about Walt?"

"I saw him when I pulled up," Reynolds said. "Had a flashlight and what looked like a pitchfork."

"That sounds like Walt," I said, sharing a knowing smile with Reynolds. We'd both known Walt long enough to expect nothing less. "I won't be long. I'll catch a ride back with Dash so you won't have anything to worry about."

"We'll wait up until you get back," Deidre said.

"She'll be asleep before we get down the street," I whispered to Reynolds, making him chuckle with the familiar observation.

"I apologize for the mess," he said as we made our way to his cruiser. "The sheriff's got me going through all kinds of files. I've got boxes in the front seat. Do you mind sitting in the back?" He opened the rear door of his cruiser for me.

"Oh," I said. "Not a problem." I slid onto the vinyl seat. The door closed with a solid *thunk* behind me.

As Reynolds pulled away from the curb, I noticed something odd—there were no door handles on the inside of the back seat. Of course not, I realized. This was where they transported suspects.

A cold knot of dread began to form in my stomach as I remembered Walt's words from earlier: *Someone who's been there long enough to know where all the bodies are buried.*

"Don't worry, Mabel," he said, his cold gaze meeting mine in the rearview mirror. "This won't take long at all."

# CHAPTER
# FIFTEEN

I knew I was in trouble the moment Reynolds made the wrong turn.

"Isn't the sheriff's office the other way?" I asked, keeping my voice light even as my stomach plummeted faster than an express elevator in a horror movie. The vinyl seat beneath my thighs suddenly felt slick and cold, and I shifted uncomfortably.

"Taking a shortcut," Reynolds replied, his eyes flicking to the rearview mirror to meet mine. The kindly deputy who'd been a constant in our community since my childhood was gone, replaced by something cold and reptilian that sent ice water cascading down my spine.

*Bad, bad, very bad.*

My hand slid toward my purse, still clutched in my lap like a life preserver. My phone. If I could just text Dash...

"I'll take that," Reynolds said, his tone casual as he reached his hand back through the partition. "Can't have you calling for help."

"Now why would I need help? Aren't you supposed to be the one giving help? Protect and serve, right?" I asked, my voice emerging unnaturally high as I surrendered my purse, fingers trembling. My mouth had gone desert dry, tongue sticking to the roof of my mouth like I'd been chewing saltwater taffy.

Reynolds chuckled, the sound as warm and comforting as a shark's smile. "You know, this is your own fault. I've been coming to your shop for years, watching you serve tea with that perfect smile, pretending you're some kind of genteel Southern lady. All those conversations, and you never once suspected anything was wrong. And now you're diving into things you don't understand, playing detective with those old busybodies."

"What?" I asked, his words barely penetrating. I was paralyzed as icy fingers of fear traced down my spine. This man who'd come into my shop almost daily for years, who'd shared his tea preferences and island gossip, who'd seemed like one of the good ones—he'd been lying all along. "What are you talking about?"

"And then I'd see you around town," he continued, lost in his own thoughts now. "I'd stop in for tea, do my job to make sure the community knew they could trust me. That I was one of the good guys. Not like that idiot Milton.

"You'd give me free scones and coffee, living your perfect life with your tea shop and vintage dresses and old music." He shook his head. "And then the new guy comes to town and suddenly you take notice. You remind me of my ex-wife. Swayed by the idea of a bad boy giving a little adventure to your boring life. What were you thinking? That you were going to become some Mata Hari spy? You make tea, for God's sake. But here you are, right in the middle of a past that never should have resurfaced."

I swallowed hard as we turned onto the outskirts of downtown Grimm Island. The familiar route was now transformed into something sinister. Streetlights cast golden pools across the empty road, but instead of finding them comforting, I felt as if each illuminated circle seemed to emphasize the darkness between.

"I don't know what you're talking about," I said. "What am I right in the middle of?" I tried to buy time while my mind raced frantically for escape options. The door handles were nonexistent, the partition secure. I was literally in a moving cage with a man I thought I'd known.

"You know exactly what trouble," he replied, slowing the cruiser as we approached the harbor area. The usual tourist spots were closed for the night, leaving only empty parking lots and dark storefronts. "Should've left well enough alone, Mabel. Some secrets are meant to stay buried."

*Just like Elizabeth*, I thought, a fresh wave of fear crashing over me.

The cruiser bumped onto a gravel road that led toward a cluster of old boathouses—weathered wooden structures that looked even more ominous in the darkness. My grandmother would have called this a come-to-Jesus moment.

For some reason, "Nearer, My God, to Thee" popped into my head and I had to slap my hand over my mouth to keep a nervous giggle from escaping my lips.

"What are you doing?" Reynolds asked. "Are you laughing? Are you one of those crazy women? My ex-wife was crazy. Said it was menopause, but she was crazy long before that came along."

"I'm not crazy," I said indignantly. "And probably your wife wasn't either. You're a terrible person. You're kidnapping me. I thought you were a good cop. A nice man."

"I am a nice man," he said. "Just ask anyone. I've served this community for almost thirty-five years."

"You're not a nice man!" I said, exasperated. "Nice people don't do things like this. Especially not cops."

He snorted. "Lady, if you've been on this island more than five minutes you know the cops here have never been nice."

"Well, you're a good actor then," I said, crossing my arms over my chest. "Maybe you should've gone to Hollywood. You should be ashamed of yourself."

"Ahh, the high and mighty Mabel McCoy," he said, chuckling.

"It's called manners. You should get some. Your mother would be rolling in her grave if she could see you now."

I didn't know Deputy Reynolds' mother. Had never met her, and had no idea if she was dead or alive. But it was the only thing I could think of to say. And it must have hit, because he looked like he was on the verge of apologizing just before he pulled the cruiser down a graveled road and parked to the side of a boathouse that had seen better days. It looked like it was held together with splinters and stubborn seagrass. And then I realized with a horrifying jolt that we weren't far from where Elizabeth's body had been found all those years ago.

He got out of the car and then opened my door. "Out," he ordered.

It was then I realized his service weapon was in his hand. The metal glinted dully in the moonlight, and my heart thundered so loudly in my chest I was surprised it didn't set off car alarms.

The night air hit me with a wall of sensations—briny seawater, rotting wood, the distant drone of a motorboat somewhere out in the darkness. Waves lapped gently against the pilings, a peaceful sound that felt obscene against the backdrop of danger.

I stumbled slightly as he guided me into the boathouse, my low heels not designed for navigating weathered dock planks. The structure smelled of mildew and salt water, decades of humidity trapped in the wooden beams. A single bulb hung from the ceiling, casting sickly yellow light over what appeared to be an abandoned fishing operation —nets hung like ghostly curtains along one wall, and ancient tackle boxes were stacked haphazardly in a corner.

"Go," he said, and I felt his gun against the middle of my back.

How had things gone so wrong so quickly? This was not how I'd imagined the end of my life. Who was going to remember me? I owned a tea shop and entertained myself with jigsaw puzzles and by buying clothes for my overweight dog. I'd never done anything earth shattering or exciting. I hadn't travelled except for the few places Patrick had taken me. How pathetic was my life? I was going to die here and I was so isolated and boring that no one would give two flips.

"Are you deaf or something?" he asked. "I said go."

Reynolds pushed me into a wooden chair that creaked ominously beneath my weight, and then he produced zip ties from his pocket and secured my wrists to the chair arms. The plastic bit into my skin, and I bit my lip to keep from crying out.

"Are you crying?" he asked, looking slightly alarmed.

"I'm fine," I said. "I'm just having a bit of an existential crisis."

"I don't even know what that means," he said. "I guess I should've gone to college."

"Maybe you would've learned not to kidnap people if you had!" I yelled, sounding slightly hysterical.

"Get a grip lady."

"Let me guess," I said, not bothering to hide my disgust. "I sound like your ex-wife."

"Geez," he said, rubbing the top of his head. He paced the small space, his boots leaving imprints in the dust that covered the floorboards. He seemed agitated, glancing repeatedly at his watch.

"You might as well tell me what you had to do with Elizabeth Calvert's death," I said. "Did you kill her?"

"No," he said, looking much too offended considering my current condition. "I've never killed anyone."

"Good to know," I said dryly.

"What are the chances?" he asked, almost to himself. "What are the chances the new sheriff would come into town and immediately start going through the cold case files? Took me off guard, otherwise I would've made them disappear. But he took them and locked them away. And then all of a sudden I find out he's deputized you and a group of people old enough to be on the ark. What sense does that make?"

"Considering you're worried enough to kidnap me," I said, "It makes a lot of sense to me."

"I don't remember you being such a smart-mouth," he said.

"I think it's a newly acquired skill."

"Lucky me," he said. "Thirty years." He paced some more. "Thirty years of keeping my mouth shut, of looking the other way. I hadn't been on the job long back when it happened—and I had a baby on the way and a mortgage I could barely afford."

My mind flashed to the family photos I'd seen on his desk at the station—grown children now, grandkids. A life built on the foundation of a terrible secret.

"So yeah," he said. "I went on the take. I don't regret it either. A man's got to do what a man's got to do. And I was providing for my family. I was a good cop."

I decided it was prudent I keep my mouth shut at this point.

"But someone found out what I was doing, and that's when things went sideways," he continued. "Now I belong to someone else, and I haven't been free since."

"That's why you helped whoever killed Elizabeth?" I asked.

"It wasn't me that killed her," he said. "I swear. But yeah. I didn't have a choice."

"You helped dispose of her body," I whispered, the pieces clicking into place. "You helped cover it up."

He nodded, a muscle working in his jaw. "Like I said, I didn't have a choice. I'd taken a lot of money from Harrington Construction to look the other way on some permit violations. Did some other jobs for them too. Enough to end my career before it began. He found out about it. I don't know how, but he did."

"He?" I asked, immediately thinking of Clint Harrington and the conversation we'd had.

"Doesn't matter who," Reynolds snapped. "What matters is, it happened. And when Sheriff Beckett started digging it all up again, I had to take action. Break into the evidence room, get rid of anything that might lead back to me." His laugh was bitter. "Never expected you to find that diary. Or that ledger in the lighthouse."

"How'd you know about that?" I asked.

"I got a call," he said. "Nothing stays secret long on Grimm Island."

"You planted the watch in my house," I said. It wasn't a question.

"Had to keep you off balance. Figured if you were scared enough, you'd back off." He shrugged. "Should have known that wouldn't work. You're as stubborn as those old fossils you run around with."

"Was that you following me too?" I asked.

He looked confused at that. "I followed you because the sheriff told me to."

"That wasn't you in the dark sedan?" I asked.

"Stop trying to confuse me with your nonsense," he said. "I've got a pounding headache."

"Maybe it's a brain tumor," I said.

"You're a real pain in the behind."

"So what now?" I asked, working my wrists against the zip ties as subtly as possible. The plastic was unyielding, but I'd noticed a rusty nail protruding from the arm of the chair. If I could position my hand just right…

"Now we wait," Reynolds said, checking his watch again. "He'll be here soon and then he can handle the situation."

My blood ran cold. "You mean kill me."

"Not my problem what he decides to do with you," Reynolds said. "I'm washing my hands of the whole thing. You're the one who kept pushing, kept digging. Some secrets are worth killing for."

"Like Elizabeth's secret? What did she know that was worth dying for?" I pressed, my fingertips inching toward the nail.

"Wrong question," Reynolds replied. "It's not what she knew. It's who she threatened." He moved to the boathouse door, peering out into the darkness. "She would've ruined everything."

Before I could press further, his phone rang, the shrill tone slicing through the tense atmosphere. Reynolds pulled it from his pocket, glancing at the screen. His face paled visibly.

When he answered I couldn't hear the anger in his voice, but I could see it on his face. "Yes, she's here. No one followed us. I made sure of it."

I strained to hear the voice on the other end, but could make out nothing beyond a muffled baritone.

"Understood," he said. "Twenty minutes." He hung up, shoving the phone back into his pocket. "Arrogant jerk."

"Who was that?" I asked, though I was pretty sure I didn't want to know the answer.

"You'll find out soon enough," he said. "Then you're his problem."

My heart rate kicked up several more notches, jackhammering against my ribs with such force I felt light-headed. I forced down the hysteria that wanted to bubble up and focused instead on the nail that was now pressing against my zip tie. If I could just get the right angle…

A flash of headlights swept across the boathouse window, illuminating Reynolds' face in a ghastly white glow.

"He's here," Reynolds said, and I felt fear like I never had before. Something in his voice made me realize that Reynolds was afraid too. We were both expendable. Loose ends to be tied up.

"False alarm," he said. "It was just a boat cutting across the water."

The zip tie at my wrist snapped, and I felt the bite of the nail as it penetrated my skin. I'd worry about tetanus later. For now, I was worried about survival.

# CHAPTER
# SIXTEEN

I stared at Reynolds, who still had his back to me, his attention focused on the window. Blood trickled down my palm, warm and sticky, but I was free—or at least my right hand was. My left wrist was still secured to the chair arm, but with one hand free, I had options. The question was, what now? My phone was in Reynolds' possession, and I had no weapon except possibly the chair I was still technically sitting in, trying not to give away that I'd freed myself.

I glanced around the boathouse, looking for anything that might help me. The place was a graveyard of forgotten fishing equipment—frayed nets, corroded hooks, ancient tackle boxes. Nothing immediately useful, except maybe as a distraction.

"Whoever's coming," I said, trying to keep my voice steady, "they'll have to get rid of you too. You know that, right? You're as much of a liability as I am."

Reynolds spun around, his face twisted with anger. "Shut up. You don't know what you're talking about."

"Don't I?" I countered, shifting slightly to conceal my freed hand. "Whoever this person is, they've already killed twice. What makes you think you're not next on the list?"

"Because I've kept his secret for thirty years," Reynolds snapped. "I'm the one who's been loyal."

"And now you've led me straight to him," I pointed out. "You don't think he'll be a little concerned about that? The only witness you were supposed to eliminate?"

Doubt flickered across Reynolds' face, and I knew I'd hit a nerve. He glanced at his watch again, then back at the window. "He's late. He's never late."

"Maybe he decided you're too much of a risk after all," I suggested, inching forward on the chair. If I could just get him to turn away again, I might be able to work on freeing my other wrist.

Reynolds pulled out his phone, checking the screen before shoving it back in his pocket with a curse. "No signal out here. Perfect."

"Why don't you go outside and check?" I suggested, gesturing toward the door with my chin. "Maybe he's waiting for a signal from you."

"And leave you alone? How stupid do you think I am?"

*Pretty stupid, considering you kidnapped me in the first place*, I thought, but kept that particular observation to myself.

"At least loosen these zip ties," I said instead, putting a whine in my voice that even annoyed me. "It's cutting off my circulation."

Reynolds hesitated, then approached, squinting at my left wrist in the dim light. "It looks fine to me—"

I struck with all the force I could muster, driving my still-bound wrist upward while simultaneously bringing my freed hand around in a wild swing that connected with his temple. Reynolds staggered backward, and I took advantage of his momentary disorientation to grab a rusty fishing weight from the tackle box with my free hand. I swung again, catching him on the jaw.

He dropped to one knee, blood trickling from a cut on his face, but he wasn't out. I scrambled to get the chair between us, my left arm awkwardly angled due to the zip tie still connecting me to it.

"You little—" Reynolds growled, lunging for me.

I sidestepped, dragging the chair with me, and swung the fishing weight again. This time it connected with the back of his head, and he went down hard, sprawling face-first on the dusty floorboards.

For a moment, I just stood there, panting, the fishing weight still clutched in my trembling hand. Reynolds lay motionless, and panic surged through me. Had I killed him? I wasn't going to stop and check.

Working quickly, I used the rusty nail to free my left wrist from the chair, wincing as the jagged metal scraped my already tender skin. I searched Reynolds' pockets, finding my phone and his keys. I tried my phone first, but there was no signal. Reynolds' department-issued phone showed the same.

"Of course," I muttered. "Because it's only the modern age of technology. Why would I expect to have cell service in America?"

Reynolds groaned and began to stir. I backed away, heart hammering, and made a split-second decision. The boathouse door creaked as I pushed it open, and I plunged into the darkness, leaving Reynolds and his weapon behind.

The night air felt thick with humidity as I navigated the maze of weathered docks, my low heels clicking against the boards and occasionally catching in the gaps. The moonlight provided just enough illumination to avoid falling into the harbor, but not enough to clearly see what lay ahead.

*"At first I was afraid, I was petrified,"* I sang under my breath, the lyrics a talisman against the fear threatening to overwhelm me.

Behind me, I heard Reynolds cursing as he regained consciousness. A flashlight beam cut through the darkness, sweeping across the wooden walkways like a searchlight.

"Mabel!" he called, his voice echoing across the water. "You're only making this worse for yourself! Come back now, and maybe I can still help you!"

"Help me right into an early grave," I muttered and then sang, *"But I will survive. I will survive.* Come on Mabel. Get it together."

I moved as silently as possible, making my way toward what looked like a cluster of small buildings farther along the marina. One had a light on—a small, shabby structure with a sign identifying it as the harbormaster's office.

The beam of Reynolds' flashlight swept dangerously close, and I dropped to my hands and knees, crawling beneath a pier. The water lapped at the wood just inches below me, and something slimy—I refused to think about what—pressed against my cheek as I flattened myself against a piling.

Reynolds' footsteps thudded overhead, boards creaking under his weight. Through gaps in the planks, I could see the flashlight beam playing across the water, so close I could see the particles of dust dancing in its glow. I held my breath, counting the seconds, certain he could hear my heart trying to pound its way out of my chest.

"Stupid woman," he muttered above me. "Where did she go?"

I remained frozen until his footsteps receded, then counted to thirty before daring to move. My muscles screamed in protest as I uncurled from my hiding spot, knees and palms scraped raw from the rough wood.

I emerged onto the walkway, orienting myself toward the harbormaster's office, then made a desperate dash for it. My heel caught on a loose board, sending me sprawling forward with a startled cry. I landed hard, the impact driving the air from my lungs. For a terrible moment, I couldn't move, couldn't breathe.

When I managed to get up, I realized my left shoe had broken beyond repair. I quickly slipped off both shoes—better to run in bare feet than with one heel missing—and continued toward the harbormaster's office, splinters immediately pricking the tender soles of my feet as I ran across the rough wood.

The door was locked, but through the window I could see an elderly man with a shock of white hair dozing in a chair, a portable TV flickering silently on the desk before him.

I knocked frantically, startling the poor man so badly he nearly fell from his chair. He squinted at me through the glass, clearly trying to make sense of a bedraggled woman appearing at his door in the middle of the night.

"Please," I mouthed, gesturing urgently. "Help."

He hesitated, then shuffled to the door, opening it just enough to peer out. "Marina's closed," he said, his voice gravelly with age and cigarettes. "Come back in the morning."

"I've been kidnapped," I said, the words tumbling out in a rush. "By a police officer. He's after me right now. Please, I need to use your phone. Please."

The man's eyes widened, taking in my disheveled appearance, the blood on my wrist, the wild panic I knew must be written across my face. He stepped back, opening the door wider.

"Come in, come in," he said, locking the door behind me. "Phone's on the desk. You want me to call 911?"

"No," I said quickly, lunging for the phone. "I need to call the sheriff directly. The one who's after me, he's with the department. I don't know who to trust."

The old man nodded, understanding darkening his weathered face. "Not the first time Grimm Island's had trouble with its lawmen," he said. "Make your call. I'll keep an eye out."

My mind went blank as I tried to remember Dash's number. I visualized it in my mind, a trick I'd learned in college, and dialed. My hands shook so badly I misdialed twice before finally getting the number right. He answered on the first ring.

"Beckett."

"Dash," I gasped, relief flooding me at the sound of his voice. "It's Mabel. I'm—"

"Mabel!" he interrupted, tension vibrating through the connection. "Where are you? Are you hurt? We've been searching everywhere."

"I'm at the harbormaster's office at the marina," I said, words tripping over themselves. "Reynolds kidnapped me. He was going to hand me over to whoever killed Elizabeth. Dash, I think he's still out there looking for me."

"Stay where you are," Dash ordered, and I could hear the sound of a car engine revving in the background. "I'm five minutes out. Harris and Jackson are closer. I've given them the address. Do not leave that building, you understand?"

"Understood," I said, peering anxiously through the window. "How did you know I was missing?"

"The Silver Sleuths," Dash replied. "Deidre got worried when you didn't come back with Reynolds. When they couldn't reach you they called me and we tried Reynolds' radio and it was turned off. Deidre's threatening to shoot Reynolds on sight."

Despite everything, I smiled. "That sounds like Deidre."

"Stay on the line with me," Dash said, his voice gentler now. "I'm almost there."

The harbormaster tapped my shoulder, pointing urgently toward the window. "Someone's coming," he whispered.

I peered carefully through the blinds and my blood froze. Reynolds was approaching the office, his service weapon drawn, a dark stain visible on the side of his head even in the dim light.

"He's here," I whispered into the phone. "Reynolds is outside the office. I can see him through the window."

"Harris and Jackson are pulling in now," Dash said, urgency sharpening his tone. "Stay down."

"The door's locked," the harbormaster said, tugging me away from the window. "Get behind the desk."

Reynolds reached the door, trying the handle. When it didn't open, he pounded on it with his fist. "I know you're in there, Mabel!" he shouted. "Open the door!"

I clutched the phone, hearing Dash's voice but unable to make out the words over the pounding of my heart. Through the window, I could see Reynolds raise his weapon, aiming at the lock. I ducked lower, pulling the old man down with me.

The sound of squealing tires and sirens shattered the night. From my position behind the desk, I couldn't see what was happening, but I heard car doors slamming and then Harris's voice cutting through the chaos.

"Drop the weapon, Reynolds!" he shouted. "Hands where we can see them!"

There was a long, terrible moment of silence. Then the harbormaster, who was peering carefully over the desk, whispered, "He's putting the gun down."

I crawled to where I could see through the window. Reynolds stood with his hands raised, his face a mask of rage and defeat. Harris approached cautiously, kicking the gun away before spinning Reynolds around to cuff him.

The harbormaster helped me to my feet just as another set of headlights swept the parking area. Through the window, I saw Dash's SUV skid to a stop. He was out of the vehicle before it had fully stopped, scanning the scene until his eyes locked on the office. When he saw me through the window, something in his expression shifted—relief so profound it was almost painful to witness.

He jogged to the office, and the harbormaster unlocked the door, stepping aside as Dash burst in. Before I could say a word, he'd pulled me into a crushing embrace, one hand cradling the back of my head.

"Are you hurt?" he asked, holding me at arm's length to examine me.

"Just some scrapes and cuts on my wrists," I said, suddenly aware of how I must look—disheveled, bloodied, and probably sporting some kind of swamp creature on my face from hiding under the pier. "I knocked Reynolds out and escaped."

Dash's lips twitched despite the gravity of the situation. "Remind me never to make you angry."

"I'm pretty angry right now," I said, but there was no heat in it. I was too exhausted for genuine anger, the adrenaline that had kept me going now rapidly deserting me and leaving trembling weakness in its wake.

Reynolds was being led to a patrol car, his head bowed. As they passed by the office, he looked up, meeting my eyes through the window.

"It wasn't about the Harbor Development," he said loud enough for me to hear through the glass, his voice hollow. "That was just a cover story. You're looking in all the wrong places."

Harris tugged him forward, but Reynolds resisted. "He's more powerful than you think," he added urgently. "He's got friends every-where. You won't see him coming."

"Get him out of here," Dash ordered, and Harris complied, pushing Reynolds into the back of the cruiser.

"He was protecting someone," I said, watching the patrol car pull away. "Someone who killed Elizabeth and Vanessa. Someone who was supposed to meet us at the boathouse tonight."

"We'll figure it out," Dash promised, his arm sliding around my waist as he guided me toward his SUV. "But right now, let's get you home and cleaned up. Those cuts need attention."

I looked down at my wrists, where the rusty nail had left angry red gashes. "Tetanus shot too, probably," I sighed. "Not exactly how I planned to spend my evening."

"I don't know," Dash said, opening the passenger door for me. "Being kidnapped, assaulting a police officer, and hiding under a pier in the middle of the night? Sounds like a typical Wednesday for Mabel McCoy, intrepid investigator."

I narrowed my eyes at him as I slid into the seat. "Your bedside manner needs work, Sheriff."

His smile faded as he reached out, brushing a strand of hair from my face with surprising gentleness. "You scared ten years off my life tonight," he said, his voice low. "When the Silver Sleuths called saying you were missing…"

"I'm okay," I assured him, catching his hand in mine. "A little worse for wear, but okay."

He nodded, giving my hand a squeeze before closing the door and circling around to the driver's side.

As we drove back toward my house, I leaned my head against the cool window, watching the familiar streets of Grimm Island slide past. Nothing looked different, and yet everything had changed. Someone on this picturesque island had killed twice to protect a decades-old secret—and they were still out there, waiting.

"Reynolds said his mysterious boss knew about the ledger we found in the lighthouse," I said, breaking the comfortable silence. "Said nothing stays secret for long on Grimm Island."

Dash frowned, his fingers tightening on the steering wheel. "That means someone is feeding information back to our killer. Someone who knows what we've been investigating."

"It has to be someone close to the investigation," I agreed, a chill running through me. "But who?"

"That's our next step," Dash said as we pulled into my driveway. "But it can wait until morning. Right now, you need rest."

The porch light blazed, and through the front window I could see movement—the Silver Sleuths waiting anxiously for our return.

The front door flew open before we'd even reached the porch, and Dottie emerged, brandishing what appeared to be her pearl-handled revolver. Behind her, Walt, Hank, and Deidre crowded the doorway, their faces a comical mixture of concern and relief.

"Land sakes, girl, you look like you've been through a hurricane," Dottie exclaimed, tucking the gun into the pocket of her bathrobe. "Did you get that no-good Reynolds? Because if not, I've got plenty of ammunition."

"Reynolds is in custody," Dash assured her, guiding me inside. "A man who has nothing to lose will take desperate measures. Mabel needs to get cleaned up and rest."

"I'll put on some tea," Deidre declared, already heading for the kitchen.

"Tea won't cut it," Dottie said, following her. "Get out that bourbon Mabel keeps in the cabinet over the refrigerator. This calls for something stronger."

"First it calls for antiseptic and bandages," Hank corrected, eyeing my injured wrists. "Where's your first aid kit?"

"Upstairs bathroom," I said.

"I'll get it," Dottie said, heading upstairs.

I let them fuss over me, too drained to protest as they cleaned and bandaged my cuts, brought me tea (and bourbon), and helped me into fresh clothes. Their concern wrapped around me like a warm blanket, and I realized with a pang how much I'd come to care for this odd collection of friends.

"All right, enough," Dash finally said, his tone gentle but firm.

"Mabel needs sleep, and so do all of you. We'll regroup in the morning."

After a chorus of protests and several more fussings over my injuries, they finally retreated to their assigned rooms.

"You should get some rest too," I told Dash as we stood in the foyer, the house finally quiet.

"I'll be on the couch," he said, shrugging off his jacket and draping it over the banister. "Close enough if you need anything, but not so close as to scandalize the Silver Sleuths."

I smiled, despite the exhaustion weighing on me like a physical thing. "You know Mrs. Pembroke will still talk?"

"Let her," he said, stepping closer. His hand came up to cup my cheek, his thumb brushing lightly over my skin. "You scared me tonight, Mabel McCoy. And I don't scare easily."

The intensity in his gaze stole my breath. "I'm tougher than I look."

"So I've noticed," he murmured, leaning in slowly, giving me time to pull away if I wanted to.

I didn't.

His lips met mine, gentle at first, then with increasing urgency as I responded. This wasn't the tentative, questioning kiss from before. This was something else entirely—an affirmation of life, of possibility, of a connection neither of us had been looking for but couldn't seem to resist.

When we finally broke apart, both a little breathless, I found myself at an unusual loss for words.

"Get some sleep, Mabel," Dash said softly, his fingers lingering on my cheek for a moment before dropping away.

"Yeah, right," I said, rolling my eyes. "I'm going to sleep great now that you shot my blood pressure through the roof."

He grinned and turned toward the living room and his makeshift bed for the night.

"Good night, Sheriff," I called out loudly.

"Good night, Mrs. McCoy," he answered, and I could hear the laughter in his voice.

As I climbed the stairs, I realized two things with perfect clarity—we were getting closer to uncovering the truth about Elizabeth's murder, and I was falling for Dash Beckett far more quickly than was prudent for a proper Southern widow. When common sense kicked back in, I'd remind myself that I didn't know a thing about him.

Chowder was waiting on my bed, his wrinkled face somehow managing to convey both relief and judgment as I slipped beneath the covers.

"Don't you start," I muttered, scratching behind his ears. "It's been a long night."

He snorted, turning in three circles before settling against my side, his solid warmth a comfort I hadn't realized I needed.

As I drifted toward sleep, Reynolds' words echoed in my mind—*It wasn't about the Harbor Development. That was just a cover story. You're looking in all the wrong places.*

If not the development scandal, then what? What secret was worth killing for—not once, but twice?

The answer was out there somewhere. And tomorrow, we'd find it.

# CHAPTER
## SEVENTEEN

I woke with a jolt, my heart hammering against my ribs like a trapped bird. The bandages on my wrists were stark white in the morning sunlight, a painful reminder that last night hadn't been a nightmare. My muscles screamed in protest as I pushed myself upright, every inch of my body cataloging new injuries. The skin on my feet felt raw and tender, peppered with splinters from my barefoot sprint across the marina docks.

But instead of the fear I expected to feel, something else surged through my veins—a fierce, crackling energy that had my lips curving into a smile despite the pain. I'd escaped a dirty cop, outsmarted a killer's plan, and lived to tell about it. Not bad for a tea shop owner whose most dangerous daily activity was usually deciding between Earl Grey and Darjeeling.

*"I am woman, hear me roar,"* I belted out as I slid from the bed, wincing as my battered feet met the cool hardwood. *"In numbers too big to ignore…"*

Chowder lifted his wrinkled face from his pillow, his expression a perfect blend of judgment and concern. He snorted once, as if to comment on my newfound feminism, then rolled over to continue his beauty sleep.

"Don't be such a grump," I told him, limping to my closet. "Some of us had a very exciting night."

I stood in my closet in my underwear and bypassed my usual safe choices, pulling out a black-and-white polka-dot halter dress that was very glam Hollywood. The halter neckline plunged lower than my usual styles, and the fitted bodice hugged curves I typically kept under wraps. The bandages on my wrists stood out in stark contrast against the playful pattern—visual proof that I wasn't the same woman who'd gone to bed two nights ago.

"What do you think?" I asked Chowder, who had deigned to open one eye. "Too much?"

His response was a deep sigh that seemed to originate from his very soul.

"I'll take that as approval," I decided, slipping into the dress with only minor contortions to accommodate my injuries.

The house was unusually quiet as I made my way downstairs, each step a reminder of my tender feet. The aroma of bacon and coffee wafted up from the kitchen, making my stomach growl in response. It was after eleven according to the grandfather clock in the hall—we'd all slept late after the previous night's excitement.

"She lives!" Deidre declared as I entered the kitchen. She stood at the stove in another pair of plaid culottes and a white eyelet blouse. She was wielding a spatula with the confidence of a samurai. "And look at that dress. Someone is feeling feisty."

"I had a dress like that once in my day," Dottie said, sitting next to Walt at the table, her hands cupped around a teacup. For some reason she was dressed in baggy denim overalls and a white shirt rolled up to her elbows. "I used to love to go dancing."

"Which makes it even more perplexing as to why you're dressed like Farmer Dale," Bea said, eyeing Dottie's overalls.

"The lady at the shop told me they were all the rage," Dottie said. "It's the twenty-first century, Bea. There's no need to dress like you're a cast member from *Three's Company*. We're never too old to get with the times."

Bea was wearing one of her favorite wigs today—a chin-length bob with spiky bangs—and she'd added a streak of turquoise eyeshadow to the tops of her papery thin lids. Her caftan was decidedly Mrs. Roper from *Three's Company* in shades of lime green and her signature turquoise, and I suspected she knew it, otherwise she wouldn't have looked so put out by Dottie's comment.

Walt sat at the kitchen table, today's crossword set before him, though his attention remained fixed on the window. He'd positioned his chair for optimal surveillance of the street.

"I miss my house," he declared. "I'm too old to sleep in someone else's bed."

"That's not what I heard," Bea piped in, her Cheshire Cat smile glowing. "A little birdy told me why you missed the historical society fundraiser. Fraternizing with the enemy aren't you, Walt?"

Walt straightened in his chair and slapped his newspaper onto the table. "I would never betray my country," he said.

"Hmm," Bea said. "And how was the opera? That is where you took her, isn't it? And then a little nightcap at her place?"

I looked at Dottie because she normally kept Bea in check, but she was locked into the story, waiting to hear Walt's answer. The look Walt was giving Bea made me think he might be okay with a midnight mission to stuff her face in a pillow.

"Patrick took me to an opera once," I said, taking a step between them to break their line of sight. "*The Magic Flute.*"

"Hmmph," Walt said. "German."

"Oh, give it a rest, Walt," Dottie finally piped in. "No one wants to listen to an American opera. And I don't know who you think you're fooling trying to keep some clandestine arrangement with a woman. You knew Bea would find out. You can't act all suspicious and not expect her to nose around. It's what she does."

Walt hmmphed again and went back to his crossword.

Deidre rolled her eyes at men and mouthed, "Men," and then she opened the oven and took out a casserole that smelled like heaven. Once she'd put it on the table in front she said, "Walt, why don't you tell Mabel what you told me a bit ago. About Clint Harrison."

That got my attention. "What about him?" I asked.

"He drove by the house," he reported, putting aside his crossword so Deidre could put his plate in front of him. "Slowed down so I was able to get a good look at him."

"Well, that's not suspicious at all," I said. Walt's mouth quirked in his version of a smile.

"Hank," Dottie yelled. "Get in here. The food is ready and I'm starving."

Hank entered the kitchen from the living room, his seersucker suit pristine, his cheeks rosy and his white eyebrows in need of a trim. "You've made the front page," he announced, handing me the *Grimm Island Gazette*. "'Local Woman Escapes Corrupt Deputy.' I have a mind to go down to the *Gazette* and talk face-to-face with Loretta Hampton. She made it sound like you and Mark Reynolds were having a leisurely stroll at the docks rather than him kidnapping you and you whomping him in the face with a fishing sinker."

"Isn't Loretta Hampton his grandniece?" Deidre asked.

"Doesn't matter," Hank said. "Right is right and wrong is wrong. And her uncle is a dishonest pig who deserves to rot in prison. I'm tired of having corrupt cops on this island. It makes me want to be on the bench again. I'd send them away for life."

"Have some breakfast casserole, Hank," Dottie said, pulling out a chair for him. "Virginia Gerber brought it by this morning. She's an excellent cook."

"People are still bringing food by?" I asked, noticing there were an abundance of fresh baked breads and desserts on my countertop.

"For as long as something is newsworthy at this house there will be a casserole," Deidre said. "It's the Southern way."

"And the only way to find out what's really happening," Bea said. "Casserole delivery is the oldest trick in the book. Kind of like women's prayer meetings. I used to belong to one of those at the Methodist church. All those ladies would get together and gossip about everyone on the island and then ask us to pray for that person at the end of the meeting so it sounded legitimate instead of like they were spreading people's business."

Dottie snorted out a laugh but didn't disagree.

"Where's Dash?" I asked.

"Went to the station," Deidre said. "Said he needed to be there when Reynolds was processed. Left at dawn but said he'd be back." She peered at me over her glasses. "How are those wrists? You look like you've been in a wrestling match with a gator."

I glanced down at my bandaged arms. "They sting a little, but I'm fine."

"Well, sit down before you fall down," she said. "Your feet must be killing you."

I didn't argue, sliding into a chair as Dottie placed a steaming mug of coffee before me. The rich aroma hit my nose, instantly making my eyes water with pleasure. And then she put a plate in front of me heaped high with breakfast casserole, banana bread, bacon, and what looked like banana pudding.

"Banana pudding?" I asked.

"It's fruit," she said. "And Walt said he's getting a toothache so I figured he'd want something soft."

The kitchen door swung open, and Dash entered, the weariness of a sleepless night evident in his posture. His uniform was as crisp as ever, but shadows darkened the skin beneath his eyes, and a day's worth of stubble shadowed his jaw, giving him that rugged, intense look that somehow made him even more handsome. When his gaze found mine across the kitchen, something in his expression softened, the fatigue momentarily vanishing from his features.

"Good morning," he said, his eyes taking in my dress with a flash of surprised appreciation that sent heat rushing to my cheeks. "You look…"

"Like a woman who escaped a kidnapping and beat a deputy senseless with a fishing weight?" I supplied.

His lips quirked. "I was going to say recovered, but your version has more dramatic flair."

"Have some brunch," Dottie insisted, already loading a plate. "You look dead on your feet."

I had an odd moment where I felt like I was having an out-of-body experience. It was such a surreal scene in my kitchen—the Silver

Sleuths gathered around the table, Dash coming home from a hard day's work, all that was missing was him kissing me on the head in greeting and a couple of kids to run in and hug him around the neck.

"Mabel?" Dottie said. "Mabel did you hear me?"

I shook my head, trying to get the vision out of my head.

"Maybe she's addled," Hank said. "Could've hit her head last night. She should go back to bed."

"I'm fine," I said. "Was just thinking."

"About what?" Bea asked, curiously.

"I can't remember now," I lied. "What were you saying, Dottie?"

"I was just asking if you wanted more casserole."

I looked down at my full plate and said, "I think I'm okay."

"So tell us the scoop," Walt said. "Is Reynolds talking yet?"

"Barely," Dash replied, accepting the coffee Deidre thrust into his hands with a grateful nod. "He lawyered up pretty quick. He's got an alibi for the night Vanessa was murdered so he knows he's clear on that. He's trying to work a deal, hinting he can give us Elizabeth and Vanessa's murderer."

"I'm surprised he was working alone all these years," I said. "What about Larson? They always seemed thick as thieves."

Dash shook his head. "That's the interesting part. Larson was actually the one who helped us catch Reynolds. He noticed the discrepancy in the radio logs—that Reynolds had turned his off when he left with you."

"Larson?" Walt's eyebrows shot up nearly to his hairline. "I thought he was gunning for your job from day one, Sheriff."

"Turns out he's been quietly investigating corruption in the department for years," Dash said. "Found inconsistencies in Reynolds' reports dating back years. He just didn't trust me enough to share what he knew."

"Why the change of heart?" Dottie asked, clearly skeptical.

Dash's lips twitched slightly. "When Reynolds put Mabel in danger, Larson drew the line. Seems he hates dirty cops more than he distrusts outsiders. He was the first one at the station when they brought Reynolds in—looked ready to take him apart."

"So he's one of the good guys?" Dottie asked skeptically.

"Let's say he's complicated," Dash replied. "But he's thorough, and right now, I need thorough. With Reynolds in custody, we're down another deputy. I need everyone I can trust working this case."

"Speaking of Reynolds," Hank interjected, leaning forward with his elbows on the table. "Don't let him cut any deals. We'll find out who did it without his help." His blue eyes narrowed menacingly. "It makes me wish I was still on the bench. I hate dirty cops. He deserves to go away for a long time."

"I agree with you," Dash said. "One thing he did say that was interesting was that we'd been looking at it all wrong."

"That fits with what he told me last night," I said, pushing my plate away. "He said it wasn't about the Harbor Development—not really."

"We know something was going on with the Harbor Development," Walt said. "There's all kinds of evidence that those guys were doing dirty deals."

"But that doesn't necessarily mean it had anything to do with the murder," I said.

"Then what else could it be about?" Hank said.

"The watch," Dash said. "I think that's our key."

"Speaking of which," Deidre interjected, her eyes brightening with the fervor of new information, "Dottie and I have been making calls all morning."

"We might have a lead," Dottie added.

All eyes turned to them, and Deidre sat up straighter, clearly relishing her moment in the spotlight.

"We called every high-end jeweler in Charleston," she continued, "And on our seventh try, we struck gold. Marconi's Fine Jewelry on King Street."

"The salesman nearly swallowed his tongue when we described the watch," Dottie added with relish. "Started babbling about client confidentiality faster than Bea can down a sidecar."

"Speaking of," she said, scooting back from the table and going over to the bar. "It's almost noon. Anyone else?"

"How are you not pickled, Bea?" Dottie asked. "I've seen body parts in formaldehyde jars that aren't as well preserved as you."

"Should tell you something," Bea said, slicing an orange.

"Anyway," Deidre continued. "The jeweler wouldn't give us a name, but he confirmed he did an engraving for a watch that matches our description. That's all he would tell us."

"When did he come in?" Dash asked.

"Last week," Deidre confirmed with a triumphant smile. "Paid extra for a quick turnaround."

"Whoever ordered it knew exactly what the original looked like," Dash said.

"Too bad Mr. High and Mighty at the jewelry store wouldn't give us a name," Dottie said.

"Time to get a warrant," Dash said, pulling out his phone.

"Does that mean we're taking a road trip to Charleston?" I asked.

Dash's eyes met mine, a silent question in them. "You sure you're up for it after last night?"

"As long as we're not walking there I'm fine," I said, grinning.

▭

Within the hour, Dash and I were on our way to Charleston, cruising along the coastal highway in his SUV. The bandages on my wrists itched, and my feet still smarted from the splinters, but the discomfort felt distant, overshadowed by the anticipation of getting answers.

"Have you ever been married?" I asked as we crossed the causeway, surprising myself with my directness.

Dash glanced at me, a hint of amusement in his eyes. "Personal questions equal a date," he said. "The level of question determines the level of date."

I paused for a second and pressed my lips together. "Dinner. But not on Grimm Island. I've had enough of people staring at me for a while."

"Deal," Dash said, looking much too smug for my liking. "Then to answer your question, no, I've never been married. Came close once, during my time with the DEA. Job got in the way—undercover work isn't exactly conducive to healthy relationships."

"Do you regret it?" I pressed, feeling bold in my polka dots and bandages.

"Not anymore," he replied.

Marconi's Fine Jewelry occupied a prime corner of King Street, its elegant façade and discreet signage suggesting old money and refined taste. As soon as we stepped through the door, my senses were assaulted by the overwhelming scent of vanilla and sandalwood—an expensive cologne trying too hard to create an ambiance of luxury. The lighting was calibrated to make every surface gleam, from the polished mahogany display cases to the diamonds nestled on velvet cushions.

A man materialized from the back, moving with the theatrical flourish of someone who'd once dreamed of Broadway but settled for retail. He was tall and rail thin, with a shock of silver hair styled in a gravity-defying pompadour that added a good three inches to his height. His charcoal suit was impeccably tailored, and he wore more rings than Dottie—no small feat.

"Welcome to Marconi's," he greeted, his voice carrying just enough Italian accent to seem exotic without being difficult to understand. "A couple in love. Here for an engagement ring. How wonderful?"

His smile dimmed as Dash showed him his badge. "One of my deputies called earlier and spoke to someone about a watch."

"That was one of your deputies?" he asked. "The elderly woman?"

Dash paused before he answered, but said, "Yes."

"Interesting," he said. "I am Vincent Marconi. How can I be of service?"

"The watch," Dash said, pulling out a picture of the one that was left on my island counter.

Vincent's dark eyes flickered with recognition and he said, "Yes, as I told the fine deputy this was one of our higher quality watches. The customer paid cash, and paid extra for an expedited engraving. But I'm afraid I have a reputation for keeping my clients' privacy. That's all I was able to tell her."

"He asked for this watch specifically when he came in?" Dash asked.

Vincent opened his mouth to speak, and then paused. "Well, now that you mention it, no. He came in with another photograph. An older photograph. I assumed it was an heirloom he'd lost and was trying to replace."

"He was looking for that specific watch?" I asked.

"He was looking for someone who could do a custom commission and replicate it. But I told him a piece like that would take at least two months, and it would cost him. He didn't seem to care about cost though. But he did seem upset that I couldn't get the piece commissioned sooner. That's when I suggested this piece. It's very similar, though the scrollwork is a bit different, as well as the diamond face. It's a fine piece."

"He was in a hurry," I said to Dash.

"Very much so," Vincent said, his hands as animated as his expressions. "As soon as he made the decision to purchase, he told me he had to have it engraved in twenty-four hours. Paid for it too."

"I need to know a name," Dash told him.

Vincent put his hand to his heart. "I wish I could help you, but my reputation is how I've stayed in business for thirty years."

"I think a homicide trumps your reputation," Dash said.

Vincent's olive complexion paled to the color of dirty dishwater. "Homicide?" His voice rose an octave. "I—I don't understand."

"I think you do," Dash said, reaching into his jacket and producing an official-looking document. "This is a warrant for your business records related to the creation of this specific watch, including any names or personal information you collected."

"Well then," he said, taking the handkerchief from his jacket pocket and dabbing his forehead. "Follow me."

He led us through a door behind the main counter, into an office that looked like it had been decorated by someone with unlimited funds and questionable taste. Everything gleamed with gold leaf, from the ornate picture frames to the baroque desk that dominated the space. The walls were lined with antique clocks, all showing slightly different times, their ticking creating a cacophony of tiny heartbeats.

"This is highly irregular," Vincent said. "I've never been involved in a murder investigation before. The man didn't look like a murderer."

I wanted to ask him what murderers were supposed to look like, but didn't figure now was the time.

"I need a name," Dash said.

"Let me check my records," he said, moving to a file cabinet behind his desk.

I would've bet dollars to donuts that he had the name memorized, but he was enjoying his moment in the spotlight.

"Here we go," Vincent said, pulling a single sheet of paper from the file. "He didn't leave an address or phone number. Which was odd because I told him I needed it so I could call him when the engraving was finished. But he told me he'd be here at three o'clock and that the watch had better be ready."

Vincent handed the paper to Dash and I looked down at the name printed neatly at the top.

"Clint Harrington," I said.

Dash's expression remained carefully neutral. "Can you describe him?"

"Of course," Vincent said. "I'm excellent with names and faces.

━━

"That wasn't Harrington he described," I said once we were back in the SUV, the air-conditioning cooling my flushed skin. "Not even close."

"No," Dash agreed, his expression grim. "It wasn't."

Dash made a sharp U-turn, heading back toward the causeway.

"Where are we going?" I asked, watching his profile as he navigated through Charleston's narrow streets.

"To have a chat with Clint Harrington," he said, his jaw tight. "Pull up the address on the MDT."

"What the heck is an MDT?" I asked, looking all over the inside of the Tahoe.

He pushed what looked like a laptop attached to a swivel arm in my direction. "Mobile Data Terminal," he said. "Just type it in and the directions will come up on the screen."

"So it's a big GPS?" I asked, arching a brow.

"Among other things," he said. "Type in Clint Harrington's name and see what comes up."

Once I'd put the map on the screen I did as he suggested. "There are seven Clint Harringtons in South Carolina." Then I looked at the screen closer. I could narrow it down further by city and age. "He's got a couple of parking tickets."

"I'll make sure to mention it when I ask him why someone would be using his name."

"You think he's involved?"

"I think it's quite a coincidence," Dash replied. "And I don't believe in coincidences."

We drove in thoughtful silence, the air-conditioning doing little to cool the heat of suspicion that had settled between us. The Harrington Construction headquarters came into view, its modest exterior belying the millions that flowed through its accounts.

"He probably won't even be here," I said as Dash pulled into a parking space. "It's after four o'clock."

"There's a brand-new King Ranch pickup truck in the president's spot," Dash observed, nodding toward the reserved parking space near the entrance. "Must be our lucky day."

The receptionist looked surprised to see me again but gave us a hesitant smile. Harrington's office door was open behind her and he was on the phone, feet propped on his desk in a casual pose that stiffened instantly when he saw us. He muttered a quick goodbye and hung up.

"Twice in one week," he said to me, dropping his feet to the floor. "And you've brought the sheriff this time." He extended his hand to Dash. "Clint Harrington."

"Sheriff Beckett," Dash replied, shaking his hand firmly.

"We need to clear up a few things," I said, declining the offered seat. "A high-end watch was purchased recently at Marconi's Fine Jewelry in Charleston. Under your name. The watch was a replica of one that belonged to Elizabeth Calvert. Gold with diamonds around the face. Inscription on the back that said *Seek Truth. Stay True.*"

The color drained from Harrington's face. "That's impossible."

"That's what we thought," I said. "Especially since the man who bought it looks nothing like you."

Harrington rubbed a hand across his stubbled jaw. "Someone used my name?"

"That's what we're trying to figure out," Dash said.

"You know the watch I'm talking about," I added, "It's the one I specifically asked you about when Walt and I were here."

Harrington's expression shifted, something like pain flashing in his eyes before he masked it. "I gave her that watch," he said quietly. "We were stupid kids. And I was a stupid kid with a trust fund. When we decided to reconcile I found the watch and thought it suited her. And then I decided to have the inscription added. Elizabeth was always about finding truth. But I wanted her to remember who was with her for the long haul. Jason Brooks romanced her and played to her ego, and she didn't give a second thought to dropping me for him.

"She told me it was because he was more mature and sophisticated. She needed someone who could challenge her ideas, and apparently that wasn't me. But I guess Brooks wasn't all he was cracked up to be. They fizzled out pretty quick and she came back. I wanted her to remember when she looked at that watch that she'd been a fool not to stay true to me. And to remember that the next time some slick-talking Don Juan threw her a little attention."

I felt the heat rise up from my neck. Apparently Jason Brooks hadn't changed too much over the last decades. He was still a slick-talking Don Juan.

"Why'd you lie about the watch?" Dash asked.

"Because I didn't want to look even more suspicious," he admitted. "I've already got motive written all over me. Ex-boyfriend, argument the night she died, family business at stake." He shook his head. "I don't know what happened to the watch. She only had it a couple of weeks before she died."

"When did Jason Brooks find out the two of you were reconciling?" Dash asked.

Clint looked older—worn and weary. "I'm not sure he ever did. That's the thing with Elizabeth. As long as Brooks was of use to her for her story, there's no doubt in my mind she would have strung him along. I know it makes Elizabeth sound like a terrible person, but she wasn't. When I tell you she'd do anything for the truth, I mean that. She would've been a heck of an investigative journalist if she'd lived. And with some age and seasoning on me, I realize now that we never would've made it. She'd have gone somewhere halfway across the world and I'd have never seen her again. But first loves are always a bit foolish, right?"

In that moment I felt sorry for Clint Harrington—for his grief in losing someone he loved, but also in the way he was rewriting history to soften that grief. Patrick had been my first love, and I'd been about the same age as Elizabeth when we'd met, and not too much older when he'd died. But I wasn't buying Elizabeth's quest for truth as being so noble as to betray and lie to and cheat on someone who loved her. And the sad thing was, I wasn't sure Clint bought it either.

"Where were you last Thursday afternoon around three o'clock?" Dash asked.

Harrington blinked at the sudden shift. "Thursday?" He opened the screen on his computer and said, "I was in Savannah. Had a meeting with potential investors for a new development. Stayed overnight."

"Anyone who can verify that?"

"About fifty people," Harrington replied. "It was a cocktail reception at the Hyatt after the meeting. I've got the hotel receipt somewhere if you need it."

Dash studied him for a long moment before nodding. "I'd appreciate it. We'll need to verify just to eliminate different avenues of the investigation."

"Look," Harrington said, leaning forward. "I'm not involved in this. I did love Elizabeth. Still think about her sometimes, even after all these years. We'd known each other for years in school." His voice grew softer. "Her death was not just something I was able to get over. But it's been a long time. I don't know what else I can tell you."

"Who would use your name?" Dash asked. "Who would know about that watch and its significance?"

Harrington thought for a moment and shrugged. "Honestly, it could be anyone trying to bring me trouble. I've made plenty of enemies over the years, especially after my father passed and I was left to clean up all his messes."

"Is Jason Brooks an enemy?" I asked.

Something hardened in Harrington's eyes. "Brooks and I have a complicated history, but we're both prominent men in this city. We run into each other from time to time. And we're friendly enough. That's it. But a guy like Brooks isn't one to get his hands dirty. It's why he left the DA's office. There was too much work involved with people he didn't want to be associated with. He always had a taste for the finer things."

"Thanks for the time," Dash said, handing Clint a card. "If you could send over that information so we can confirm your trip to Savannah I'd appreciate it."

As we headed back to the car, I glanced at Dash. "Do you believe him?"

"About the watch, yes," Dash said. "About not knowing who might use his name? Not for a second. He definitely had some ideas. That's a man who should never play poker."

"What now?" I asked as we climbed back into the SUV.

"Now we go back to your place and tell the Silver Sleuths what we found out," he said, starting the engine. "And we figure out how to set our trap."

We drove back to Grimm Island in thoughtful silence. The island looked different somehow as we crossed the causeway—still picturesque, still charming, but now I could see the shadows lurking behind the quaint façades, the secrets buried beneath the Spanish moss.

The Silver Sleuths were waiting eagerly when we arrived, Chowder waddling over to greet us with unusual enthusiasm. His cold, wet nose pressed against my bare leg, making me yelp in surprise.

"Traitor," I told him, scratching behind his ears. "Now you're happy to see me."

"What did you find out?" Dottie demanded, practically vibrating with impatience. "Did the jewelry man crack?"

"Like an egg," I confirmed, stepping fully into the living room. "But before we get into it—"

"Wait," Walt interrupted, raising his hand. His eyes narrowed as he peered through the front window. "You said a dark sedan had been following you. One has been parked down the street for almost an hour."

There was no fear at this revelation. Instead a burning rage came from out of nowhere. "Oh, really?" I asked. "Let's go see who it is."

I walked past gaping Silver Sleuths and Dash and slammed open my front door. The old me would've winced. I wasn't a door slammer. And then I marched down the front walk and down the middle of the street.

The black sedan was parked half a block away, partially obscured by a live oak draped in Spanish moss that swayed gently in the afternoon breeze. As I approached, I could see a figure hunched behind the wheel, watching my house through the windshield.

The driver looked startled when I rapped sharply on the window, his weathered face going slack with shock. For a moment, I thought he might speed away, but then he slowly rolled down the window, the electric motor whining in protest.

"Why are you following me?" I demanded, hands on my hips.

The man behind the wheel was older than I expected, probably in his late sixties, with the leathery skin and sun-spotted hands of someone who'd spent decades outdoors. His white hair was sparse and wispy, like dandelion fluff, and deep grooves lined his face, telling a story of hard years and harder decisions. He blinked up at me in surprise, then cleared his throat nervously.

"You're Mabel McCoy?" he asked, his voice gravelly with age or cigarettes or both.

"Yes," I confirmed. "And you are?"

"Frank Donovan," he said, offering a calloused hand through the window. "I used to work security at the marina. Back in '96."

The marina. Where Elizabeth had been found. My interest immediately sharpened, and the hairs on the back of my neck stood at attention.

"That doesn't explain why you've been following me," I said.

Frank sighed, looking suddenly exhausted. The scent of peppermints and Old Spice wafted from the car.

"I saw on the news about that deputy getting arrested. Reynolds." Frank's gaze flickered past me to where Dash now stood a few feet away, watching carefully. "Heard rumors around town that the Elizabeth Calvert case was being reopened." He paused, his weathered hands gripping the steering wheel so tightly his knuckles whitened. "I was there that night. The night she died. I saw something."

My pulse quickened, sending a rush of blood to my head that made me momentarily dizzy. "Why didn't you come forward before?"

"I tried," Frank said, his expression hardening like cement setting. "Went to Sheriff Milton the very next day. He told me to keep my mouth shut if I wanted to keep my job." His hands trembled slightly on the steering wheel. "I had young kids back then. Couldn't afford to lose that paycheck."

I exchanged a look with Dash, who nodded almost imperceptibly.

"Would you like to come inside, Mr. Donovan?" I asked. "You look like you could use some tea."

Frank hesitated, then nodded. "Been trying to work up the nerve to come talk to you for days," he admitted. "Figured following you was the easiest way to get a chance to do it without being seen."

Ten minutes later, Frank was settled in my living room, a steaming cup of Earl Grey in his weathered hands. He didn't seem too shocked to be surrounded by the Silver Sleuths. I had to give him props for that.

"Start from the beginning," Dash encouraged, his voice gentle but firm. "What did you see the night Elizabeth died?"

Frank took a sip of tea, his hands steadier now. The scent of bergamot filled the room, calming my nerves like it always did. "I was working the night shift at the marina. Security guard, walking the perimeter every hour or so. It was quiet that night—Tuesday, not many boats coming or going."

He set the cup down carefully on its saucer, the porcelain clinking softly. "Around nine, I saw a young woman by the docks. Pretty girl, blond hair. She seemed agitated, kept checking her watch. Then a man showed up—not who she was expecting, I could tell that right away from her body language."

"How so?" Hank asked.

"They immediately started arguing," Frank explained. "You could tell they knew each other. I couldn't hear everything, but their voices carried across the water."

"What were they arguing about?" I asked, leaning forward despite myself.

Frank frowned, concentration furrowing his brow even deeper. "She kept saying something about telling the truth and going public. He was trying to convince her not to, said she didn't understand what she was getting into." Frank's voice darkened. "When she turned to leave, he grabbed her by the wrists." He demonstrated, his hands closing around invisible arms with enough force that I could almost feel the bruising pressure.

A chill ran through me, raising goose bumps on my bare arms as I remembered the autopsy report that mentioned bruising on Elizabeth's wrists. Beside me, Dottie's sharp intake of breath told me she'd made the same connection.

"I was about to intervene," Frank continued, "But then my supervisor radioed. There was a boat emergency on the other side of the marina—a guy had been drinking and went overboard. Hit his head and knocked himself out. By the time I got back, maybe an hour later, they were both gone." His voice dropped. "Never saw her alive again."

"Can you describe the man?" Dash asked.

Frank nodded slowly, his eyes distant as if seeing the scene replay before him.

"Would you recognize him if you saw him again?" Dash asked.

"Maybe," Frank said. "It's been thirty years, and it was dark. But I'll never forget the way he grabbed her wrists, or how she looked at him. She was angry. Looked like she might throw a punch."

"Would you be willing to come in tomorrow and give a formal statement and look at some photographs?" Dash asked.

Frank nodded firmly. "That's why I'm here. Should've done it thirty years ago, no matter what Milton said." He looked at me directly, his faded blue eyes suddenly intense. "When I heard what happened to you last night—that Reynolds tried to kidnap you—I knew I couldn't stay silent anymore. History repeating itself, you know?"

Once Frank left, Dash spread out the timeline we'd constructed, his fingers tracing the connections we'd drawn. "Let's look at what we know for certain. Elizabeth was researching corruption related to the Harbor Development. She stumbled across financial impropriety and documented dates and amounts in her ledger, along with the names of Roy Milton, Paul Cromwell, and Clinton Harrington Sr. Plus about half a dozen or so others. The information she had was enough to send a lot of people to prison for a long time. So there's motive there.

"We already know from what Clint Harrington told us that he'd made plans to meet Elizabeth at the docks at ten o'clock the night she was murdered. His alibi is shaky since he can't be accounted for from the time he left the Charleston Symphony fundraiser with the parents to when he returned."

"We know from Frank that she was at the docks around nine and that she was arguing with a man there," Hank said.

"Which means we can't rule out that it was Clint Harrington," Dash said, "because he doesn't have an alibi for that time, even though he said he'd left Charleston around nine."

"Except," I said, looking at Dash. "The description the jeweler gave of the man who bought the watch does not match Clint Harrington or Reynolds."

"That's all the past," Deidre said. "What about the present? Vanessa Garfield is dead, strangled just like Elizabeth."

"And we know from her bank account that she made a large deposit in cash the day before her murder," Walt said. "Someone paid her for something. The reason people get paid in cash or in an amount like that is if they have information to sell, or if they're blackmailing someone."

"And the reason she's dead could be because of either of those things," Dash said.

"What about her phone records?" I asked. "Did we ever get those?"

"Harris was supposed to get them and bring them by," Dash said, pulling out his phone and dialing. His conversation was short before he hung up.

"He's on the way over with them," Dash said. "He said the woman at the phone company kept asking him questions about the case so she took forever printing out Vanessa's phone records."

"Darla Hedgeseth," Bea said, shaking her head. "She's worked at the phone company a long time. Knows everything about everyone."

"Another one of your informants?" I asked Bea, grinning. She just grinned back, but didn't confirm.

"So what's our next move?" Dottie asked.

"We set a trap," Dash said.

"How?" Deidre asked. "Don't get me wrong. I like all this excitement. But I'm not forty years old anymore. I can't keep up this kind of pace."

"We should go on that seniors cruise when this is over," Bea said. "Those senior cruises are like a game of chance. Once you get out to sea those old people start dropping like flies. They keep all the bodies in a cooler down below."

"I'll go," Dottie said. "But I want to hear about this trap we're supposed to set. And then I'm going to take a nap. I'm full of carbs and indigestion. Go ahead, Sheriff."

Dash looked like he wanted to yank Bea's sidecar out of her hand and knock it back. But he showed admirable restraint.

"We let it be known that Frank has come forward," Dash explained. "That he saw everything that night and is prepared to identify Elizabeth's killer in a lineup."

"Won't that put Frank in danger?" I asked, concerned.

"We can protect him," Dash assured me. "But we need to force the killer's hand—make him panic, make him act."

"And when he does," Walt said, nodding with approval, "we'll be ready."

There was a knock on the door and I could see Deputy Harris through the glass before he let himself in. He held a manila envelope in his hand.

"Must be something good in here," Dash said, studying Harris's face.

"It certainly paints a picture," Harris said.

"What about text messages?"

Harris looked every bit of his twenty-two years as excitement flushed his cheeks. "You've got those too."

Dash pulled out the papers and laid them out of the table. "Huh," he said. "I guess Reynolds was right. We were looking in all the wrong places."

# CHAPTER
# EIGHTEEN

"Holy Moses," Dottie breathed, leaning so far over the table I thought she might fall face-first into the phone records. "Would you look at that?"

My finger traced the pattern of calls laid out in neat columns and timestamps. Twenty-three calls between Vanessa Garfield and Jason Brooks in the two weeks before her death. The last one—a seventeen-minute conversation—just hours before she'd been strangled.

"There it is," I said, a chill creeping up my spine despite the warmth of the kitchen. "I guess Reynolds was right."

His words from the boathouse echoed in my mind—*It wasn't about the Harbor Development. That was just a cover story. You're looking in all the wrong places.*

Walt adjusted his reading glasses, jabbing his finger at the call log. "Look at the pattern. Short calls every couple of days, then suddenly a flurry of activity the day before she died."

"Maybe she was threatening him," Hank suggested. "Blackmail usually starts with a calm negotiation before it turns ugly. And then there's the ten thousand dollars."

I scanned the text message log Harris had included, noting the increasingly frantic tone of the exchanges.

*Need to talk. Important.*

*This isn't something we should discuss over text.*

*I'm not playing games. Meet me or I go public.*

The final text from Vanessa, sent just hours before her death—*I know what you did to Elizabeth. $10,000 by midnight or I go to Beckett.*

"Jason Brooks," I said, the name feeling like a betrayal on my lips. The charming attorney who'd flirted with me, who'd asked me to dinner—who'd killed not once, but twice. "What a jerk! I can't believe he wanted to go out with me."

"Murderers are looking for love too, Mabel," Bea said, patting me on the back. "There's a whole reality show about it."

"It fits," Dash said, his hand moving to the small of my back, steadying me though I hadn't realized I was swaying. "Frank put Brooks at the marina with Elizabeth the night she died, arguing about going public with some discovery. The jeweler's description of the man who ordered the watch matches Brooks, not Harrington."

"It's all just circumstantial," Hank said.

"He wanted to frame Harrington," Deidre said, tapping her pencil against her notepad. "Old rivalries die hard."

I sank into a kitchen chair, my mind racing to reconcile the smooth-talking attorney with a cold-blooded killer. "But if it wasn't about the Harbor Development, what secret was worth killing for? What did Elizabeth really find?"

The kitchen fell silent as we all pondered the question. Dash leaned against the counter, arms crossed over his chest, his expression unreadable except for the muscle working in his jaw—a tell I was beginning to recognize as suppressed anger.

"I think I might have an idea," I said, looking up at Dash.

"What's that?" he asked, raising a brow.

I took a deep breath. "What if I accepted his dinner invitation? Wore a wire? He already thinks I'm interested in him—if I can get him talking about Elizabeth…"

"Absolutely not," Dash said immediately, straightening to his full height. "We've got enough to bring him in for questioning. We're not putting you in danger again."

"It's just..." I hesitated, searching for the right words. "What if bringing him in isn't enough? He's a lawyer—he knows exactly how to shut down an interrogation. But he doesn't see me as a threat. He thinks I'm just a sweet tea shop owner." I looked around at the Silver Sleuths. "He'd never suspect I was trying to get a confession."

Walt shook his head, military straight in his chair. "Too risky. Too many unknown variables."

"I'm with Walt on this," Deidre added. "After what you went through with Reynolds, I don't think—"

"Maybe that's why it would work," I suggested softly, not wanting to push too hard but unable to let the idea go. "Brooks has no idea we suspect him. He thinks I'm just a naïve widow who's easily charmed."

Dash studied me, his dark eyes searching mine. "You've been through enough already, Mabel. This isn't your responsibility."

"I know," I said, holding his gaze. "But I want to help. For Elizabeth. For her father." I swallowed hard. "If you think it's too dangerous, I understand. You're the expert here. But if there's a way to make it safe..."

Something in his expression shifted—a flicker of consideration replacing outright refusal. "You're serious about this?"

"I am," I nodded. "But only if you think we can do it without unnecessary risk."

Dash ran a hand through his hair, his internal debate visible on his face. "If—and that's a big if—we did something like this, there would have to be strict protocols. Public location. Full surveillance. Armed officers within seconds of your position."

"Of course," I agreed quickly. "Whatever you think is best."

"The Crab Shack," I suggested after a moment's thought. "Weeknight evening crowds are thin. You'll have good line of sight."

"Plenty of exits," Walt added, warming to the idea despite his initial resistance.

"And we could position deputies in plain clothes on the dock," Dash continued, working through the logistics. "A couple of others in the parking lot and then a female and male in plain clothes inside the restaurant."

"Sounds perfect," I said, a flutter of nervous excitement replacing the dread in my stomach.

"I still don't like it," Dottie interjected, crossing her arms.

"Neither do I," Dash admitted. "But Mabel's right about one thing—Brooks might shut down completely in an interrogation room. This might be our best shot at finding out what really happened to Elizabeth."

Dash nodded, his decision made. "We do this by the book. Full tactical plan. Panic button. And at the first sign of trouble—the very first hint—we move in. No heroics."

"Understood," I promised.

He extended his hand, and I took it, his warm fingers curling around mine with gentle strength. The calluses on his palm scraped deliciously against my skin, sending little sparks racing up my arm.

"I hope you know what you're doing, Mabel McCoy," he said softly. "I've got plans for you that don't include you ending up dead."

"Well," I said, fighting the urge to fan myself. "That ought to give me incentive."

Bea's delighted cackle broke the tension. "If we're setting a trap for a murderer, I'm going to need another drink. Who wants a sidecar?"

Brooks sounded genuinely pleased when I called to accept his dinner invitation, though he tried to steer me toward The Blue Crab instead.

"It's a bit more...refined," he suggested. "Better wine list."

"Oh, I've been to The Blue Crab," I said innocently. "But The Crab Shack is more my speed." I tapped my nail absently against the back of my phone. "Besides, they have the best crab claws on the island."

He chuckled, his voice warm through the phone. "The Crab Shack it is, then. This will be a first for me. Eight o'clock?"

"Perfect," I replied, hoping he couldn't hear the thunder of my heart. "Be casual and comfortable. It's not fancy, but the food is incredible."

"I'm looking forward to it," he said indulgently. I was starting to intensely dislike Jason Brooks, and it wasn't altogether because he was suspected of being a murderer.

After I hung up, I turned to find Dash watching me with an unreadable expression.

"What?" I asked, suddenly self-conscious.

"Nothing," he said, the corner of his mouth lifting slightly. "You're a natural at this. Had me almost convinced you were looking forward to dinner with a murderer."

"I'm a real Grace Kelly," I said dryly.

Two hours later, I stood in my bedroom, staring at the floral sundress I'd laid out on the bed—a vintage piece with a pattern of green leaves and yellow daisies that reminded me of summer picnics and simpler times.

"I'll probably never be able to wear this again after tonight," I said as Dash helped me get wired—a surprisingly intimate process that involved threading a tiny microphone up through the fabric and securing it just below my collarbone.

His fingers brushed against my skin, and despite the gravity of the situation, I felt heat rush to my cheeks.

"Good," he said, his voice low as he taped the transmitter to the small of my back. "It's not one of my favorites."

I jerked my head up to meet his eyes, surprised by the teasing. "Since when do you have opinions on my wardrobe, Sheriff?"

That half smile I was coming to adore spread across his face. "Since I started paying attention. Maybe you could wear that polka-dotted number again. I liked that a lot."

My pulse skittered traitorously, and I blamed the warmth in my cheeks on nerves rather than the way his fingers skimmed the bare skin at the small of my back.

"You sure about this?" he asked, his voice serious again as he stepped back to inspect his handiwork. "Weather service just issued a storm watch for tonight. Might work in our favor though—keep more people inside where our plainclothes officers can maintain visual contact."

"No," I admitted, decided I wasn't sure about anything. "But I'm doing it anyway. Rain or shine."

The Crab Shack was a weathered building perched on stilts over the water, its wooden deck extending out over the harbor like a gangplank into the darkness beyond. Paper lanterns strung along the railings cast an amber glow over weather-beaten tables, transforming the humble restaurant into something almost magical against the darkening sky. The scent of fried seafood and Old Bay Seasoning hung in the humid evening air, mingling with the briny tang of salt marsh and the promise of rain.

I arrived fifteen minutes early, giving myself time to get the lay of the land and identify Dash's people. The hostess—a college-aged girl with a messy ponytail and a sunburn across her nose—led me to a table with a clear view of both the entrance and the deck beyond. Perfect.

As I settled in, I surveyed the room casually, mentally mapping exits and identifying Dash's undercover officers. Near the bar, a young couple was being seated—the woman wore a sundress, but her alert posture and the way her eyes continuously scanned the room marked her as law enforcement. Her "date" kept his back to the wall, his jacket slightly bulky on the right side where his holster would be. They looked relaxed to anyone who didn't know better, but I recognized Officer Lee's dark ponytail and the set of Detective Reyes' shoulders despite his casual attire.

Through the window, I could see Harris down on the dock, looking absurdly young in cargo shorts and a faded baseball cap pulled low over his eyes. He was pretending to work on a fishing line, positioned where he'd have a clear view of both the restaurant deck and the water below. I almost didn't recognize him without his usual starched uniform and serious expression—he looked like any other island teenager killing time before curfew.

My gaze swept across the other diners—a family with two bored teenagers, an elderly couple sharing a plate of hush puppies, a rowdy table of sunburned tourists who'd clearly started happy hour early.

Dash had positioned his people well, blending them seamlessly into the normal Thursday night crowd.

I'd chosen this place not just for its out-of-the-way location, but for the half dozen exits and the clear sight lines that would give Dash and his team perfect visibility from every angle. Nothing said romance like tactical advantages.

I'd paired my floral sundress with peep-toe sandals that could be kicked off in an instant if I needed to run. My hair hung loose around my shoulders, and for once, I hadn't bothered with my usual red lipstick. Tonight wasn't about playing dress-up or impressing anyone. It was about justice. It was about Elizabeth.

Brooks arrived right on time, smooth as a shark gliding through calm waters. He looked casually elegant in khakis and a blue button-down with the sleeves rolled up, revealing tanned forearms. His own thick mane caught the golden light from the lanterns and made the silver at his temples gleam, and his smile when he spotted me was warm and seemingly genuine. But I didn't miss the way his eyes darted around the weathered building, taking in the paper towel rolls on each table and the uneven planks beneath our feet with barely concealed disdain.

He might have dressed down for the occasion, but it was obvious he wasn't used to slumming it with the regular folks. Money and privilege clung to him like expensive cologne—impossible to wash off no matter how casual the clothes. According to Deidre, he'd come from nothing and was determined never to go back there.

"Mabel," he greeted, leaning in to kiss my cheek, his cologne expensive and subtle, like everything else about him. "You look lovely."

"Thanks for meeting me on such short notice," I said, returning his smile with one I hoped looked authentic while my skin crawled from his touch. "It's been a crazy few days."

"So I've heard," he replied, settling into the chair across from me with the easy grace of a man accustomed to having the best seat in the house. "The whole island is buzzing about your adventure with Reynolds. You're very brave." His tone was light, but something in his eyes flickered—calculation, perhaps, or resentment. "My sister called me in near hysterics—she lives near Grimm Park, you know. Said she saw the whole thing on the news."

He leaned forward, his expression a perfect mask of concern that didn't quite reach his eyes. "You're lucky to be alive, Mabel. I've been worried about you ever since you and Hank came to my office. Civilians getting mixed up in police business…" He paused, his voice dropping to a confidential murmur. "It rarely ends well."

The concern in his voice sounded genuine, but something in his eyes sent a warning shiver down my spine. Predators often play with their food before devouring it.

"I have good backup," I said, thinking of my crew of armed senior citizens.

A waitress appeared with menus, and Brooks signaled her with a barely perceptible nod—the kind of subtle gesture that expected immediate attention and usually received it.

"We'll both have the grilled grouper," he said decisively, not bothering to check if that's what I wanted. "And a bottle of the Sancerre." He glanced at me with a smile that didn't quite reach his eyes. "Trust me, Mabel. You'll love it."

I bit the inside of my cheek to keep from saying something sharp enough to draw blood. Patrick had always insisted we try new things together, but he'd never dreamed of ordering for me. Even Dash, with all his take-charge attitude, had respected my choices enough to ask first. The small presumption spoke volumes about the man across from me.

"Actually," I said, smiling sweetly at the waitress, who looked caught between two opposing forces, "I'll have the crab claws and a glass of Moscato. That's why I suggested this place, after all."

Brooks' expression flickered—a momentary tightening around the eyes that vanished so quickly I might have imagined it. But the temperature between us dropped ten degrees, the change as palpable as the gathering storm outside.

"Of course," he said smoothly, a master at recovery. "How thoughtless of me."

I took a sip of water, studying him over the rim of my glass. "You're a man of many layers," I said. "Prestigious law career, deep island connections...yet I hardly see you around. Charleston must keep you busy." I kept my tone light, conversational, as if I were merely making small talk rather than fishing for information.

His eyes met mine, assessing. "I've found it's better to let my work speak for itself rather than my presence. Besides, the island holds... complicated memories."

Something flickered in his expression—a shadow that passed so quickly I might have imagined it. His smile remained firmly in place, but it didn't quite match the sudden guardedness in his eyes.

"Complicated how?" I asked, treading carefully.

He toyed with the stem of his wine glass, his gaze drifting past me toward the harbor. For a moment, he seemed to be looking at something far beyond the water—something only he could see.

"You grow up here, you leave, you come back different," he said finally. "Not everyone appreciates the change." His focus returned to me, sharp and present. "Small towns have long memories, and not all of mine are pleasant. Keeping a low profile has served me well over the years."

"I imagine things were especially complicated when you worked for the DA's office," I said, watching his reaction carefully.

"Different time, different place," Brooks replied. "Small-town law enforcement was challenging to say the least."

"Because of Sheriff Milton?" I ventured.

"Milton was just a symptom of a larger problem," Brooks replied. "The whole system here was built on relationships rather than rules. Like I said...challenging."

"I've heard some troubling things about the old cases," I said, carefully watching his expression. "The Charleston Medical Examiner was just telling Dottie—you know Dottie Simmons?—that she's been reviewing some of the autopsy reports from cases during Milton's tenure. Apparently there were some inconsistencies that were overlooked. Looks like Milton had someone to do dirty work for him at the ME's office."

Brooks didn't flinch, but something in his posture changed—a subtle tensing. "Like what?"

"In Elizabeth's case, for one," I said, taking another sip of wine to steady myself. "They've confirmed she was strangled before she went into the water. That throws Milton's ruling of accidental drowning right out the window." I watched his face carefully. "Turns out we've had an unsolved homicide on this island for almost thirty years."

His expression remained carefully controlled, but I caught the slightest twitch at the corner of his eye. "So Sheriff Beckett is really digging into the evidence himself, not just delegating? Impressive dedication for a new arrival."

"He's nothing if not thorough," I replied, watching the calculation behind his casual demeanor. "Seems determined to clean up every loose end Milton left behind, no matter how old."

"Good for him," Brooks said, though his tone didn't match his words. "Closure is important." He signaled the waitress for another glass of wine with a casual flick of his wrist. "Though I imagine not everyone appreciates having old wounds reopened."

I nodded, waiting a beat before continuing. "They've found some interesting things. Like the watch, for instance."

"The watch?" he repeated, his voice carefully neutral.

"Elizabeth's gold watch. The one Clint Harrington gave her with the inscription about seeking truth." I watched his face closely. "Odd thing is, someone went to a lot of trouble to have an exact replica made recently. Left it on my kitchen counter as a warning."

Brooks frowned, the picture of concern. "That's disturbing. Have you told the sheriff?"

"Of course," I said. "We found the jewelry store where it was sold. The salesman gave us the receipt and you'll never guess whose name was on it."

"I'm on pins and needles," Brooks said.

"Clint Harrington."

He arched a brow, looking contemplative. "You don't say."

I paused for dramatic effect, swirling the wine in my glass. "But here's the interesting part—the salesman's description of the buyer didn't match Harrington at all. It was only someone pretending to be him."

Brooks maintained his composure, but I caught the slight tightening around his eyes. "And who did it match?"

I looked directly into his eyes. "Why you, of course."

The air between us crackled with sudden danger, like the static charge before lightning strikes. Brooks' expression didn't change, but his eyes turned cold, calculating, as if seeing me clearly for the first time. The mask of civility slipped, just enough for me to glimpse the predator beneath.

"You shouldn't play detective, Mabel," he said softly, his voice barely carrying over the restaurant's ambient noise. "It's dangerous."

My mouth went dry, but I forced myself to hold his gaze. "So I've been told," I replied, my heart pounding so hard I was certain he could hear it. "But I've never been very good at following advice. Just ask the Silver Sleuths."

"Those old fools," he said, his mask slipping further with each word. "They should have minded their own business. And so should you."

The dinner around us continued—servers carrying plates, diners laughing, wine glasses clinking—but it all seemed to recede, like we were sitting in our own deadly bubble of truth.

I leaned forward so only he could hear my words. "Why did you kill her, Jason?" I forced myself to maintain eye contact despite the fear creeping up my spine like ice water. "Elizabeth, I mean. Was it because she was going back to Harrington? Or because she was going to expose what she'd found?"

He laughed, the sound so normal it sent chills down my back. "You know, Mabel, you'd make a lousy cop." His voice was almost gentle, like he was offering helpful career advice rather than threatening me. "Coming out with an accusation like that? No finesse, no build-up." He shook his head, tutting softly. "You'd be laughed out of any interrogation room in the country."

His condescension made my blood boil, burning away some of the fear. I kept my expression neutral as he continued, hoping the wire beneath my dress was picking up every damning word.

"Besides," he added, leaning back with the casual confidence of a man who'd never faced consequences. "You don't know what you're talking about."

He pushed back from the table, but I put my hand on his wrist to stop him, surprising us both with my boldness. His skin was cool beneath my fingers, and I could feel his pulse—steady, unhurried. A killer's pulse.

"I think I do," I countered, my voice steadier than I felt. "We found Frank Donovan—the security guard who saw you arguing with Elizabeth at the marina that night. He heard you trying to convince her not to go public with what she'd found. When she refused, you grabbed her wrists." I lifted my chin. "Those bruises showed up on her autopsy. We have her diary, Jason. We know everything."

Brooks' gaze darted around the restaurant, assessing exits, witnesses.

He leaned back in his chair, an eerie calm settling over him. "You know what? I think I'll indulge this little fantasy of yours for a moment." His smile turned cold, predatory. "Enjoy your wine, Mabel. It's probably the last glass you'll ever have."

I felt a chill run through me, but kept my expression neutral. "Is that a threat?"

"It's reality," he said softly. "Someone in my position understands how the world really works. Problems arise. Problems get eliminated." He took a slow sip of his wine. "You're just a small problem, Mabel. One that can be dealt with quietly. And afterward, I'll make a hefty donation to the sheriff's campaign fund to encourage him to keep fighting for justice." His voice dripped with sarcasm. "That's how things work in the real world."

"You seem very confident," I said, surprised at how steady my voice sounded.

He smiled, swirling the wine in his glass. "You know what Elizabeth was actually investigating that summer? Not just some small-town corruption or petty bribery." He leaned forward, lowering his voice. "She stumbled onto something much bigger. Those girls who went missing after graduation in '94. The Simmons girl, the Baker twins."

My breath caught. I knew the story. Everyone on Grimm Island knew it—three eighteen-year-old girls who'd disappeared right after high school graduation. They'd supposedly gone on a celebratory road trip and decided not to come back to the island. With them being legal adults, the investigation had been minimal.

"Everyone thought they'd run away," I said carefully. "Their parents were the only ones who kept searching."

"Because that's exactly what we wanted people to think," Brooks replied, a cold pride in his voice. "Those girls were never meant to be found. They were in the wrong place at the wrong time—sneaking onto the wetlands property to get high. Unfortunately for them, they overheard a conversation between Cromwell and Harrington that they shouldn't have."

He took another sip of wine, as casual as if discussing the weather. "Milton had them buried in the wetlands that were later developed into the harbor project. The perfect hiding place—or so we thought. But Elizabeth somehow connected their disappearance to the development timeline. Found a construction worker who swore he dug up part of a body."

"And when she confronted you about it?" I asked.

"I tried to reason with her," he said, and for a moment, I caught a glimpse of the man he must have been back then—ambitious, calculating, desperate to protect his future. "I told her to drop it, to go to Duke and forget what she'd found. I even offered to go with her, to start fresh somewhere else."

"But she wouldn't let it go," I guessed.

He shook his head, a sad smile playing at his lips. "Elizabeth was relentless when she caught the scent of a story. She'd even hidden evidence in that stupid lighthouse as insurance. Told me that if anything happened to her, the truth would still come out. I thought she was bluffing."

"And Vanessa?" I asked. "How does she fit into all this?"

"Vanessa always had a talent for finding things she wasn't supposed to," Brooks said, contempt dripping from every word. "While she was married to Milton, she had access to everything in his home office. Apparently, our esteemed former sheriff kept souvenirs from his more profitable arrangements."

"Like records of the cover-up," I guessed.

Brooks nodded. "After Milton was arrested, she contacted me. Said she had documents that mentioned my name, suggested we could come to an arrangement." His lips curled into a sneer. "She was always looking for an angle, always trying to turn a profit. When she realized what she had, she thought she'd hit the jackpot."

"So you killed her too," I concluded. "Just like Elizabeth."

Brooks reached for his wine glass with a steady hand, taking a careful sip. "You're making very serious accusations, Mabel. Based on what? Speculation? The ramblings of an old security guard?" His tone was calm, reasonable—the voice of a man used to persuading juries. "I thought we were having a pleasant dinner."

"That's why sent me the watch," I said, understanding dawning. "To frighten me off the case by reminding me what happened to Elizabeth."

"With the added bonus of throwing suspicions Clint's way," he said. "Never could stand that guy. You're a smart woman, Mabel. I thought you'd take the hint. But I guess you're stubborn—just like she was."

His hand slipped beneath the table, and the unmistakable sound of a gun being cocked froze the blood in my veins. I felt my entire body go rigid.

"Don't make a scene," he said, his voice barely above a whisper. "That would be unfortunate for everyone here."

I swallowed hard, fighting to keep my expression neutral despite the terror clawing at my throat. "You won't get away with this."

"I already have," he replied, placing a hundred-dollar bill on the table with his free hand. "Twice before. Now, here's what's going to happen. You're going to get up slowly, smile like you've had a lovely evening, and walk toward the exit. I'll be right behind you."

My mind raced, desperately searching for options. The wire beneath my dress suddenly felt flimsy, inadequate protection against the cold steel I knew was pointed at me under the table.

"Now, Mabel," Brooks said, his voice hardening to steel.

With trembling legs that threatened to buckle beneath me, I rose from my chair, scanning the restaurant desperately. At the corner table, I spotted Lee and Reyes. Lee met my gaze briefly, giving me a nearly imperceptible nod. They'd heard everything through the wire.

Brooks stood smoothly, stepping in close behind me, one hand resting at the small of my back where I could feel the hard press of the gun barrel through the thin fabric of my dress. The cold metal against my spine sent tendrils of ice through my veins, my mouth going desert dry with terror.

"Perfect," he murmured, his breath warm against my ear, the scent of the wine on his breath making my stomach turn. "Just like we're a couple having a lovely evening. Smile, Mabel. Like your life depends on it."

The irony wasn't lost on me.

I forced my lips into what must have been a ghastly approximation of a smile, my facial muscles stiff with fear. My eyes darted around the restaurant—couples laughing over wine, a family celebrating a birthday, waitstaff bustling between tables—all oblivious to the life-or-death drama unfolding in their midst. So many people, yet I'd never felt so alone.

As we neared the door, the undercover officers rose casually from their table, the woman whispering something to her partner as she pretended to gather her purse. They moved toward the bar with nonchalance, positioning themselves to intercept us.

Reyes' hand moved toward his concealed weapon beneath his windbreaker. "Jason Brooks," he said. "We need you to stop right there. You don't want to make a scene."

Brooks froze for a split second, a statue of surprise, before yanking me against him with unexpected strength. The gun, no longer hidden, now pressed openly against my temple, the cold metal burning against my skin.

"Back off!" he snarled, his cultured voice replaced by something feral and desperate. "Or she dies right here."

The restaurant fell silent, a record scratch of shock freezing the scene. A child whimpered somewhere. A glass shattered. The female officer had her weapon drawn now, her stance wide and stable, but she couldn't risk a shot with me in the way.

"You're surrounded, Brooks," she said calmly, her voice steady despite the tension crackling through the air. "There's no way out of this."

"Oh, there is," he replied, backing toward the door that led to the deck, dragging me with him, my heels scraping against the wooden floor. "She's my ticket out. Anyone follows us, I pull the trigger."

My heart hammered against my ribs like a trapped bird, each breath shallow and panicked. This was no longer a game of cat and mouse. This was survival.

The first drops of rain began to fall as Brooks forced me onto the deck, cold pinpricks against my bare arms. The darkening sky mirrored the desperation of the moment, the distant rumble of thunder like a celestial warning. Wind whipped across the water, carrying the scent of salt and storm, as he moved backward toward the stairs leading to the dock, keeping me in front of him as a human shield.

"Keep moving," he hissed, the gun pressing painfully against my temple, each step taking us farther from help, closer to whatever end he had planned for me.

Through the gathering rain and gloom, I spotted movement at the far end of the dock—a shadow slipping between the pilings. Dash. Our eyes met across the distance, his filled with fierce determination that steadied something in me. In that heartbeat of connection, I knew what I had to do.

I sucked in a deep breath, tensed every muscle in my body, and then did the opposite of what instinct demanded. Instead of fighting, I surrendered—went completely limp, dropping my full weight downward like a puppet with cut strings.

The sudden deadweight caught Brooks off guard. He staggered, his grip loosening as he tried to maintain his balance on the rain-slicked deck. The gun shifted away from my head for just a fraction of a second—the smallest window of opportunity, but the only one I'd get.

The crack of a gunshot split the air like thunder, echoing across the harbor. Brooks staggered backward, his face a mask of shock as he clutched his shoulder, crimson blooming between his fingers. The gun clattered to the deck as he fell, skidding across the wet boards away from his reach. I scrambled away on hands and knees, my palms scraping against rough wood, my dress a beacon in the gathering darkness. The rain was falling harder now, plastering my hair to my face and neck, washing away the scent of Brooks' cologne that still clung to my skin.

Officers swarmed from every direction—from the restaurant, from the parking lot, from positions I hadn't even realized were manned. In seconds, Brooks was surrounded, the predator becoming prey.

Dash reached me first, holstering his weapon as he knelt beside me on the rain-slicked deck. His eyes scanned me frantically, looking for injuries, his hands hovering over me as if afraid to touch.

"You okay?" he asked, his voice rough with emotion.

"Probably not," I managed to say between chattering teeth, my whole body trembling not just from the cold rain but from the aftershocks of adrenaline and fear. "It probably won't be too long until I have a total meltdown. Just FYI."

"Completely understandable," he said.

The rain was falling in earnest now, silver sheets illuminated by flashes of distant lightning. Behind us, officers secured Brooks, who was cursing through clenched teeth as they handcuffed him despite his wounded shoulder. His expensive shirt was ruined, blood and rain mingling to create a macabre watercolor.

"It's over," Dash said, finally touching me, his arm steady around my waist as he helped me to my feet. His warmth seeped through my rain-soaked dress, an anchor in the storm. "You're safe."

The undercover officers approached, the woman offering me her jacket. "That was quick thinking," she said. "Giving us the signal, then dropping like that."

I nodded, though in truth it had been pure instinct rather than careful planning. The weight of what had just happened—how close I'd come to death—began to settle over me like a physical thing.

"We got his confession on the wire," Dash said, his voice tight with barely contained emotion. "Everything about Elizabeth, Vanessa, the missing girls—all of it."

I watched as they led Brooks toward a waiting patrol car, his once-immaculate appearance now disheveled, blood staining his expensive shirt. He caught my eye as they guided him past, his face a mask of hatred.

"This isn't over," he said, his voice weak but still menacing.

"Yes, it is," Dash replied, stepping between us. "Jason Brooks, you're under arrest for the attempted murder of Mabel McCoy and for the murders of Elizabeth Calvert and Vanessa Garfield."

Things were kind of a blur after that. Outside, the rain had intensified, drumming on the roof of the car in a steady rhythm. I remember Dash putting me in his Tahoe and getting in next to me, his warmth a stark contrast to the chill that had settled into my bones.

"You're in shock," he said gently. "Just breathe."

I nodded again, focusing on the steady in and out of my breath, on the solid presence of him beside me.

"Take me home," I said, laying my head back on the seat. "I'm stick a fork in me done."

***

When we got back to the house we were greeted with the Silver Sleuths, hovering on the porch as they watched Dash help me out of the car.

"Honey, you're the color of old oatmeal," Deidre said, pressing a warm hand to my cheek. "Shock will do that. You need a blanket and something warm to drink."

"And a shot of bourbon," Bea added, appearing at my elbow with suspicious timing and a glass of amber liquid. "Medicinal purposes only."

"Stand back, stand back," Walt said. "Let the poor girl get in the house and settle before you start hounding her."

"He was worried sick," Dottie whispered to me. "We all were. We were listening to the whole thing on Walt's police scanner. You were so brave."

"I didn't feel very brave," I said. "I felt like a big fat chicken when he held that gun to my head."

"I have half a mind to get my revolver and go finish him off," Bea said, looking at Dash. "Too bad you didn't kill him."

"There's a lot more paperwork when someone dies," Dash said, leading me to the couch. He sat me down and then sat down next to me, so close he had to put his arm around me. It was a good thing too, because I hadn't stopped shivering since we'd left the restaurant.

"Will he confess?" I asked Dash.

"He already has," Dash replied. "Everything he said at the restaurant is on tape. Between that and the DNA evidence from both crime scenes, he's done."

I absorbed this, feeling a complex mix of emotions—triumph and exhaustion, relief and a lingering sadness for lives cut short by one man's ambition. "Elizabeth deserved better," I said quietly, the words catching in my throat.

"She did," Dash agreed, his fingers finding mine and squeezing gently. "But thanks to you and the Silver Sleuths, she's finally getting justice. You finished what she started."

We sat in companionable silence for a few minutes while the Silver Sleuths bustled around the house, plying me with blankets, tea and alcohol. Chowder had launched himself into my lap and was doing his best to console me by promptly going to sleep and snoring.

"Where'd you learn to shoot like that?" I asked Dash softly. "I can't tell you how grateful I am for your accuracy."

He smiled and tucked a piece of hair behind my ear. "You know the deal," he said. "That's a personal question."

"Another dinner?" I asked, my mouth quirking in a smile.

"With a twist," he said. "Dinner at my house. Chowder can be our chaperone."

I couldn't help myself. My gaze dropped to his lips and the urge to lean in and taste him was more than my already overburdened senses could bear. So I straightened my spine and cleared my parched throat.

"Dinner," I said, nodding, and then I leaned into him and let him hold me.

It had been so long since a man had held me. And I ached as those needs—those feelings—rushed through me after lying dormant for so long.

"Penny for your thoughts?" Dash asked, his voice gentle in the quiet. He massaged the tension in my shoulder until I relaxed against him again.

I sighed and said, "I was just thinking about how sometimes you have to disturb the surface to see what's been hiding in the depths all along."

"Profound," he said. "What does that mean?"

"I have no clue," I said. "Just the inner musings of a thirty-four-year-old widow and tea shop owner. Don't pay her any attention."

"That's going to be a problem," he said. His thumb was making small circles on the back of my neck and it was driving me to distraction. "I plan to pay her attention every chance I get. You see, ever since I met her I can't stop thinking about the thirty-four-year-old widow and tea shop owner. Thoughts of her keep me up at night."

My lips twitched with good humor. "I'll send you home with some chamomile tea to help you sleep."

"I think you're going to be a real handful, Mabel McCoy," he said, rubbing Chowder between the ears.

"And?" I asked.

"And I wouldn't want it any other way."

I laid my head on his shoulder and closed my eyes, breathing in his familiar scent and letting the last week fall away. Elizabeth's case was closed, but my story—our story—was just beginning to unfold.

And for the first time in ten years, I couldn't wait to turn the page.

# PRE-ORDER DIRTY VALENTINE

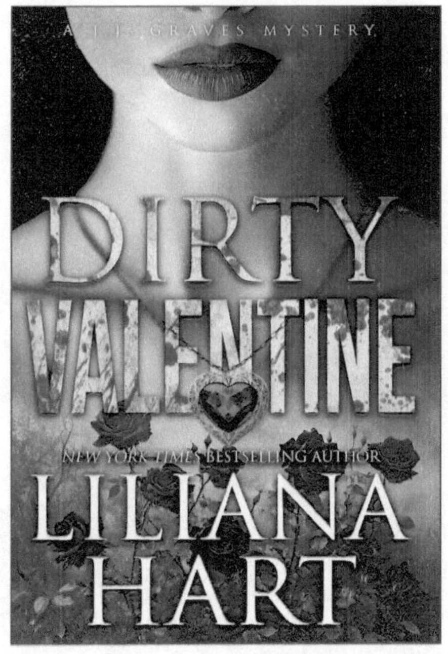

Dirty Valentine

September 30, 2025

When a brutal murder in the historic town of Bloody Mary seems out of place, coroner JJ Graves and Sheriff Jack Lawson are thrust into a high-stakes investigation.

As they delve deeper, they uncover connections to a chilling two-hundred and fifty-year-old murder. With dark secrets and hidden truths surfacing, JJ and Jack race against time to piece together clues spanning generations. The town of Bloody Mary, renowned for its historical roots, becomes a treacherous ground where past and present collide.

With each revelation, the danger intensifies, and the line between ally and enemy blurs. Will JJ and Jack unravel the truth before it's too late, or will Bloody Mary be forever haunted by its bloody past?

Join JJ Graves in this heart-pounding crime thriller, where betrayal, dark secrets, and suspense collide in a web of danger and deception.

# THE LIES WE TELL

By her calculations, Grace Meredith had exactly five and a half seconds to take out six targets before an alarm sounded. She had a round in the chamber and five in the magazine of her M40A5. Piece of cake.

She ignored the mosquitoes the size of hummingbirds searching for exposed flesh, and she disregarded the sweat that dripped steadily down her spine as she looked through the scope of her rifle. The temperature was in the mid-nineties, but the canopy of trees that blanketed the area held the heat in like an oven and slowly baked anyone who didn't have shelter with a running AC. Her body and mind were disciplined, so the discomforts barely registered.

Colombia wasn't known for its gentle climate. Or gentle anything for that matter. Gemino Vasquez was Colombia's baddest arms dealer, and lately his biggest client had been North Korea. But Vasquez had something Grace wanted very badly. Something that would bring in a big, fat paycheck from the South Korean government.

She shifted slightly, and the bark of the large tree branch she'd lain on for the last four hours ground against her stomach. But her focus was absolute. Not even the hundred-and-fifty-foot drop to the ground could distract her.

The orange sun blazed just over the tops of the trees, but it would disappear completely in another twenty minutes. By the time it was gone, she'd have the flash drive in hand and already be across the border to Venezuela.

Grace did one final check of all her equipment and took a deep, steadying breath, slowing her heartbeat so her pulse would be in time with-b each shot. She'd hit the sentry at the top of the Vasquez compound first and then take the rest in order from left to right. She pushed her feet against the tree for balance. The clock ticked in the background of her mind as she put the slightest amount of pressure on the trigger.

"One," she whispered. She didn't wait to watch him fall but moved to the next target. Five seconds until the report from her rifle reached their ears. Five seconds for five more kills.

*Two…*

*Three…*

*Four…*

*Five…*

*Six…*

Grace didn't stop to check the accuracy of her shots. She never missed a target. She hung her rifle on a tree branch, already missing the feel of it in her hands. Time was of the essence now, and she couldn't afford to be burdened with too much equipment—she'd have to leave it behind. The new guards would be driving up soon for the shift change, and she had to be long gone by then.

She unzipped her supply pack, pulling out a lightweight pipe no longer than her forearm. It looked completely worthless at first glance. In reality, it was a military prototype she'd borrowed from her former life. She hit the button on each end of the pipe and it expanded in length until it was almost as tall as she was, and then she hit the button in the center and waited as wings made out of a synthetic material unfurled to complete the hang glider.

"No time like the present," she said, swallowing as she perched on the edge of the tree and looked out across the jungle. She had a straight shot into the compound, but any shift in wind would have her hurtling into trees. Falling to her death wouldn't bring her the money she needed, so she had no choice but to take a leap of faith. Literally.

*Fifteen minutes until all hell breaks loose.*

Grace grasped the bar and jumped. The bottom dropped out of her stomach as she free-fell for just a brief moment, and then the air caught beneath the wings and she soared through the treetops like a phantom. It took all her strength and concentration to keep the glider on a straight path to the compound roof, and when her feet touched the ground her muscles were fatigued and her skin coated with perspiration.

She hit another button on the long metal tube and the glider folded itself back up until it was small enough to fit back in her pack.

The body of the first sentry she'd shot lay face down in the greenish-blue water of the swimming pool. A hazy cloud of blood ballooned from under him, and his arms and legs floated like waving ribbons.

Her eyes and ears were alert, but all that greeted her was growing darkness and silence. Even the animals and birds in the jungle knew something bad was about to go down.

Grace unhooked the harness and pulled her SIG from a thigh holster. She stood silently next to the gray door that led from the roof down a set of stairs to the main floors of the house. Two heartbeats passed before she opened the door and slipped inside. It was quiet, but that wasn't unusual at this time of the day according to her intel— six sentries on duty surrounding the compound, only two guarding Vasquez's private suite of rooms.

Vasquez's stupidity only made her job easier.

Grace walked silently down the thickly carpeted hallway as if she weren't about to steal the schematics for a new superweapon—a weapon that used state-of-the-art laser technology—and sell it to another country. But the closer she got to Vasquez, the more her spine tingled in awareness that something was wrong. That tingle had saved her life more than once, and she never ignored it. The hallway opened up into a landing just as she reached Vasquez's private rooms. Weak light filtered through the windows and cast rainbows as it pierced the glass chandelier that hung overhead.

She saw firsthand exactly why her spine was tingling.

Both sentries were slumped against each other—a dead man's embrace—one with a broken neck and the other with a hunting knife in his carotid. Efficient work considering the size of the sentries.

She pushed the bodies out of her way with her foot and eased the door open, her trigger finger at the ready on her SIG. All that mattered was the flash drive. If she didn't produce it, then she didn't get paid.

She crept into the room. The smells of new death were thick and cloying in the heat, and she could taste the fresh blood in the back of her throat with every breath she took. Dust motes danced in the air, and long shadows were cast in the fading sunlight.

Grace waited for her eyes to adjust and listened for sounds of footsteps, but all she heard was the gentle whir of the wicker fans that rotated slowly on the ceiling. She moved silently, staying close to the wall as she checked his suite.

Vasquez's bedroom was bigger than her whole apartment—the furniture oversized and ornate, the colors garishly red. He was set up for sex. The interesting kind of sex by the looks of things. Restraints and various whips and other tools lined one whole wall, and torn condom packages littered the floor. It looked like Vasquez had a busy day. Too bad his afternoon hadn't turned out so hot.

Gemino Vasquez's body lay spread-eagle on his bed. He was naked, and his eyes were open and unseeing. Two shots to the center of the forehead screamed of a professional hit. He hadn't been dead long. She couldn't stop the bitter disappointment when she saw the flash drive was gone from the chain on his right wrist.

"Hell," she whispered and moved to check the covers of his bed, just to make sure it hadn't come off in the struggle. But she knew in her heart it was long gone. Professionals didn't leave loose ends behind. And this was definitely professional. What ticked her off even more was that whoever did it managed to sneak in right under her nose. He had to have known she was watching through her scope and snuck in through the one blind spot she had at the back of the compound.

The stir of air behind her was the only warning she had before an arm locked around her throat.

"Looking for this?" a deep voice whispered in her ear. He held the flash drive in front of her face.

He pressed close against her back and squeezed his arm tighter around her throat so she had to breathe shallowly through her nose. Grace winced as he pressed his fingers against the pressure points of her wrist, and her pistol fell uselessly to the floor with a dull thunk.

Fear never had a chance to take hold. It was anger that drove Grace. Anger that had kept her alive the last couple of years. And she knew how to wield it. She threw her head back and aimed her heel at his knee simultaneously. He dodged her blows as if he'd been expecting them, but the distraction was enough for him to loosen his grip. She swept her leg and brought him to his knees, reaching down for the knife in her boot. The blade gleamed once in the fading sunlight just before it was knocked out of her hand and across the room.

He outweighed her by close to eighty pounds, and he had a good eight inches on her in height. They grappled and rolled, each one blocking the other's strikes with only seconds to spare. It was a well-choreographed dance.

A familiar dance.

The surprise of recognition took her off guard, and she looked up into laughing blue eyes framed by thick, dark lashes she'd always been jealous of. She had time to register that he'd let his hair grow—a shaggy mane of ink black that curled just over his ears and collar,and a face that was covered in a short, stubbled beard—just before her legs went out from under her. She hit the carpet with a thud. A hard body pressed her into the floor, and he held her wrists captive above her head.

"Hello, darling." His breath whispered against her skin. "You've been practicing. Who's your new sparring partner?"

"Gabe," she said. "What do you want?" She bucked beneath him, annoyed at the familiarity of his weight on her.

"I want you, of course." His lips glanced across her cheek to the corner of her mouth, and she sucked in a breath that brought her body even closer to his. After everything he'd done, he was still the only man who could make her feel less than whole when their bodies weren't fused together. She hated him for it. She hated herself for it.

"Go to hell." She struggled against him, but he shifted his weight to hold her down.

"I've been there, thanks." He cupped his hand against her cheek—gently—softly. "You still feel good against me. Stop wiggling and we'll talk. Don't you want to at least hear my offer? Especially since I did your dirty work for you."

She stilled her body and relaxed, hoping he'd get distracted long enough for her to make a move, and she spoke through gritted teeth. "I don't want anything you have to offer. Just give me the flash drive."

"I figure we have exactly four minutes to get out of this place before the new guards show up for the shift change and Armageddon begins. All I'm asking is that you come back with me and hear me out. If you decide to turn me down, then I'll give you the flash drive with no hard feelings, and you can claim your bounty."

Grace stared at him and tried to decide if he was bluffing. "You know I don't trust you."

"Yes, I believe you've told me that before," he said, his gaze hard. "But what I'm offering will pay more than double any of the jobs you've recently taken. Hear me out."

"Fine." She knew her options were limited. "What are we waiting for?"

"Our rendezvous point is on the other side of the border," he said, rolling off of her. She ignored the hand he reached out to help her up. "We've got twenty minutes to get there or we miss our ride."

Grace had no choice but to follow him out of one hell and into another.

***

The woman hadn't changed a bit in all the years he'd known her. She still kept her deep auburn hair braided tightly down her back while she was working. But he knew what it looked like spread across his pillow, and he knew what it felt like as it slithered like silk across his chest—glorious—a bright flame that was cool to the touch.

He looked at her critically, trying to decipher exactly why he was still attracted to her after the two years they'd spent apart. There wasn't just one thing about her that stood out, but the entire package. Her face was thinner now—her cheekbones more pronounced—but it was still the face of a sea goddess. Eyes the color of emeralds, slightly tilted at the corners, and full lips that haunted his dreams. She was every desire he'd ever had wrapped in one tiny package.

He let his gaze drift down her body. She was thinner all over. The lush curves he remembered were gone, replaced by a compact body of pure muscle and athleticism. She glanced back at him and raised a brow at where his gaze had landed.

Gabe smiled, but it didn't reach his eyes. He'd been wrong. She'd changed a lot. There was a hardness about her now that hadn't been there before. When she'd first started with the CIA, there had been hope and an ideal of the greater good. Now there was just emptiness —a cold, green stare that didn't believe in anything—and it scared the hell out of him. Because it was no one's fault but his own.

"We've just crossed the border into Venezuela by my calculations," she said, slowing to a jog. "How much farther is your rendezvous point?"

"About another mile. Keep the sound of water to your immediate left." He put his hand on her arm before she could take off again. "Wait."

She stopped dead in her tracks, and Gabe could tell she was trying to hear what he had. They were silent for a few more seconds before the sound came again.

She blew out an annoyed breath. "It's the new guards. You always did have ears like a bat."

"What do you have on you?" he asked.

"My SIG and a hunting knife. How many do you think there are?"

"No more than a dozen. They're noisy bastards. And not too fast." He pulled his own pistol from the small of his back and checked the magazine. "I'll give you a boost." He replaced his weapon in his pants and laced his fingers together. He arched a brow as she looked back at him with irritation.

"I'm really tired of climbing trees." She exhaled and put her foot into his hands. He launched her up so she could reach the lowest branch, and she swung herself up with ease.

"Do you have good visibility?" Gabe asked.

"Yeah, I see them," she said. "You'll have to draw them close enough so I'm within range."

"Try not to hit me by mistake."

Her grin was sharp as she looked down at him. "Oh, it wouldn't be a mistake."

"That's what I'm afraid of." Gabe left her there to go meet trouble head-on.

He found cover behind a tree trunk the size of a small car and waited patiently. Heavy footsteps crunched over twigs, and he stuck out his foot as two of them passed by. One of the guards tripped and went sprawling to the ground, and Gabe struck out at the other with a palm to the chest, stopping his heart instantly. He broke the neck of the one who was already down before the man could rise off his knees.

Gabe ignored the steady stream of fire that came from behind him —despite her wanting to kill him, he trusted Grace to fight at his side during battle. It was after the battle that worried him.

He went searching for his next victim.

Only a few minutes passed before he stood in the middle of a ring of twelve guards—all of them dead. None of them had fired a shot. She was even better than he remembered.

Grace was waiting for him when he caught up to where he'd left her.

"Time's ticking," he said, looking at his watch.

They picked up the pace and ran the last mile in silence and slowed as they came to a winding dirt road with deeply rutted tire tracks, making footing tricky.

"Did we miss the pickup?" Grace asked.

A forest-green Humvee coated with a thick layer of dust came out of the trees behind them and pulled to a stop. Grace had her weapon out and her finger on the trigger.

"He's mine," Gabe said, opening the back door.

Grace slid across the hot leather seat.

The driver turned and looked at Gabe. Logan Grey had worked with him on other missions. He was a quiet man, tall and sinewy with muscle. He wore his dark-blond hair long, not as a fashion statement, but to help cover the terrible scars on the back of his neck. Logan was former MI6, but an almost fatal accident had gained him retirement before he was ready. Gabe hadn't hesitated at snatching Logan up to join the team. No one knew explosives better than Logan Grey.

"You cut it close, boss," Logan said. "In thirty seconds I wouldn't be here."

"Let's roll," Gabe said. "Be on the lookout for company."

Logan glanced once at Grace and then nodded, putting his submachine gun in his lap.

Gabe closed the window that divided the front and back seat so he and Grace had complete privacy.

"Who's your friend?" Grace asked.

"Logan Grey. Don't worry. He's heard all about you and still agreed to help me find you."

"I'm sure he's a real stand-up guy."

"He'll grow on you," Gabe said, keeping his gaze on the terrain around them, looking for threats. "So what do you think? It's just like old times. We always made a great team."

"Tell me what you want, and then let me go," she said. "I've got a tight schedule to keep."

"You don't have another job lined up once you deliver the flash drive to the South Koreans. Looks like you're a free agent." Gabe watched for a reaction, but she showed no surprise that he'd been keeping up with her movements. She waited him out with her silence and a hard look, and he decided to give in to the unspoken standoff... just this once.

"I've left the CIA," he told her.

"I heard. Congratulations. Let me go."

Gabe smiled and stretched out across the seat, crowding her with the length of his legs, but she didn't budge an inch. "Did you hear I'd joined the private sector and opened my own agency?"

She laughed, low and sexy, and the smoky sound swirled around him until he was dizzy with desire. "So, good boy Gabriel Brennan has decided to become a bad boy and go rogue. I assume the agency is displeased by your decision?"

"Not at all," he said, shrugging. "They know when something is out of their control. My agency is privately funded and our reputation is above reproach. Even the CIA recognizes the benefits unknown money can buy. Governments are still hampered by rules, for the most part. Sometimes there are jobs where the rules need to be broken. That's when they call me."

"Well, bully for you," she said. "You always did manage to get what you wanted. Everything Gabe Brennan touches turns to gold."

"Nothing could be further from the truth, and you know it," he said quietly. Gabe waited patiently for her to make eye contact. It didn't take her long. She'd never been a coward.

She tilted her chin defiantly. "I don't know anything about you. I never did. Our life together was a lie. I'm not even sure you know the real you."

He kept his face impassive, even though her words pierced his heart. "How long are you going to pretend she's not sitting here between us?"

"Don't mention her!" The quiver in her voice was quickly controlled. "I'll get out of this car and disappear off the face of the planet. If you want me to stay, then the past stays in the past. It's nonnegotiable."

"Fine," Gabe said. "Whatever you say."

The SUV slowed to a stop, and Gabe pushed the door open, not waiting to see if she'd follow. It was a stupid idea to think he could fix things—to heal the wounds that had been bleeding for the last two years.

Gabe's Gulfstream sat ready for takeoff on the hard-packed dirt the small Venezuelan city called an airport. He went up the stairs and then turned to face Grace, sure she'd still be in the car. But she stood at the bottom of the steps, her face carefully blank.

"You can either come with me or you can leave. The choice is yours," Gabe said without emotion, tossing her the flash drive.

She caught it one-handed and stared at him, studying him, trying to read every angle of the situation as she'd been trained to do at the agency. She finally nodded and started up the steps. "I'll come. A deal is a deal. And my word means something."

Gabe flinched before he could control it and let the pain roll through him. He had a feeling that before this job was over, she'd have one more reason to hate him.

**AVAILABLE AT ALL RETAILERS**

# ACKNOWLEDGMENTS

Getting a book to publication takes an amazing team of people. I'm fortunate to have had these people in my corner for years.

To my editor—Imogen Howson for always making me better.

To my cover designer—Dar Albert for always blowing me away with your talent.

To my children—You're all so special. You have gifts and abilities beyond measure, and I'm excited to see what God has in store for each of you.

To Scott—thank you for answering a ridiculous amount of law enforcement questions and acting out weird scenarios with me. Any mistakes are mine alone.

# ABOUT THE AUTHOR

Liliana Hart is a *New York Times*, *USA Today*, and Publisher's Weekly bestselling author of more than eighty titles. After starting her first novel her freshman year of college, she immediately became addicted to writing and knew she'd found what she was meant to do with her life. She has no idea why she majored in music.

Since publishing in June 2011, Liliana has sold more than ten-million books. All three of her series have made multiple appearances on the *New York Times* list.

Liliana can almost always be found at her computer writing, hauling five kids to various activities, or spending time with her husband. She calls Texas home.

If you enjoyed reading this, I would appreciate it if you would help others enjoy this book, too.

**Recommend it.** Please help other readers find this book by recommending it to friends, readers' groups and discussion boards.

**Review it.** Please tell other readers why you liked this book by reviewing.

*Connect with me online:*
www.lilianahart.com

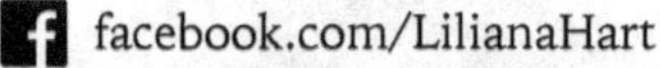 facebook.com/LilianaHart

 instagram.com/LilianaHart

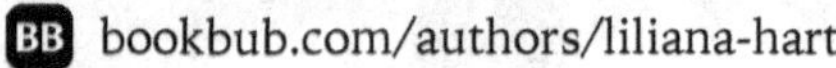 bookbub.com/authors/liliana-hart

# ALSO BY LILIANA HART

**JJ Graves Mystery Series**

Dirty Little Secrets

A Dirty Shame

Dirty Rotten Scoundrel

Down and Dirty

Dirty Deeds

Dirty Laundry

Dirty Money

A Dirty Job

Dirty Devil

Playing Dirty

Dirty Martini

Dirty Dozen

Dirty Minds

Dirty Weekend

Dirty Looks

Dirty Liars

Dirty Valentine

**Addison Holmes Mystery Series**

Whiskey Rebellion

Whiskey Sour

Whiskey For Breakfast

Whiskey, You're The Devil

Whiskey on the Rocks

Whiskey Tango Foxtrot

Whiskey and Gunpowder

Whiskey Lullaby

**The Scarlet Chronicles**

Bouncing Betty

Hand Grenade Helen

Front Line Francis

**The Harley and Davidson Mystery Series**

The Farmer's Slaughter

A Tisket a Casket

I Saw Mommy Killing Santa Claus

Get Your Murder Running

Deceased and Desist

Malice in Wonderland

Tequila Mockingbird

Gone With the Sin

Grime and Punishment

Blazing Rattles

A Salt and Battery

Curl Up and Dye

First Comes Death Then Comes Marriage

Box Set 1

Box Set 2

Box Set 3

**The Gravediggers**

The Darkest Corner

Gone to Dust

Say No More

**Laurel Valley**

Tribulation Pass

Redemption Road

Midnight Clear

Forgiveness River

Atonement Trail

www.ingramcontent.com/pod-product-compliance
Lightning Source LLC
Chambersburg PA
CBHW021042310726
48969CB00006B/1773